DEAD WRONG
AN ECOLOGICAL THRILLER

G. SPENCER MYERS
Creator of the Dr. Derk Bryan Eco-Thriller Series

Praise for Dead Wrong

"Using an EPA investigator is unique for a crime novel. I really like Derk Bryan and I really liked this book."
- Ann Bocock WXEL-TV, "Between the Sheets" Summer Reading Series.

"Dr. Derk Bryan is a hero without a Messiah complex."
- Buch 1-DM, Online Book Club

"Impressive characters headline this suspenseful tale with an ecological bent."
- Kirkus review

". . . interesting, thought-provoking, and thrilling . . . There is no doubt that audiences will be anticipating the next adventure."
- Gretchen Hansen, The US Review of Books

Other Books by G. Spencer Myers

Pest:

A man experiences a deadly premonition while fishing in the Florida Keys. A murder in Michigan causes a toxic spill. Dr. Derk Bryan, the Indiana Jones of the EPA, soon discovers that these two disparate events threaten every drop of water on the planet and every important relationship in his life. His laisse faire life on the beach is on a collision course with the maniacal chemical company magnate, Jack Von Lleuwan, and his bodyguard, Jimmy "Gloves Swingle, an ex-wrestler with anger management issues.

Von Lleuwan's newest product, *PESTfree©* , designed to replace the chemicals that are contaminating food and water worldwide, contains a deadly flaw. As a result, Kate McCardigan, Derk's college sweetheart, becomes a target when she blames Von Lleuwan for crippling her son and others. As the body count grows, Derk Bryan races against the clock to thwart disaster and save McCardigan from becoming another victim.

Praise for Pest:

"Murder leads Derk Bryan, the EPA's most creative investigator, from a chemical spill in West Michigan to Tampa Bay and back to Ohio. Pest will make you laugh and make you cry. Ultimately, you will ask, Will I be the next victim? A must-read book."

- **Ervin Harmon, Book Reviewer, and Critic**

"The engaging narrative of Pest contains much to think about regarding toxicology, environmental awareness, and the balance of nature. . . Pest leaves one wondering how closely the story resembles a true one."

- **Rachel Elaine, Author of Thoughts for Thought.**

The Girl with the Red Nails:

In The Girl with the Red Nails, Dr. Derk Bryan, the Indiana Jones of the EPA, pursues the greedy and the complicit who are fueling an approaching catastrophe.

All roads lead to the doorstep of Pendleton Danswirth III and his billionaire buddies. It looks as if he'll get away with murder and more until an ending that no one saw coming.

Greed, sex, religion and murder drive this eco-thriller. A must read!

We Are Playing Roulette With Your Future:

G. Spencer Myers issues a profound warning to Ian, his grandson, and Ian's generation that involves a threat to humanity so great that scientists have given it a name: The Anthropocene --- a human caused extinction.

Using a series of short stories Myers challenges grandsons from eight to eighty to think big and be bold in your ideas in the face of the crisis of your lifetime: Global Warming. In 1980, he became the first person in the U.S. to put 400 sq. ft. of solar panels on a multi-family residence listed on the National Register of Historic Places. Today, he drives an EV and fuels it with sunshine. Having devoted his life to reducing his own carbon footprint, he says, "There's hope. We know what to do." Read it and become inspired.

All books are available at: www.GSpencerMyers.com or your favorite online book provider.

Foreword

"Fiction is the life through which we tell the truth." Albert Camus

If you are reading this book, I hope it's because you have an interest insustaining this extraordinary place that we call Earth. I think of it as Home. It could also be that you were just looking for a quick read with some quirky characters that will make you think and sometimes laugh.

Either way, you're in luck. First, it's not too long. Even though it took me two decades to complete Dead Wrong, it will take you less than a morning to devour it. You'll be back to working on your short game, tryinga new recipe, or cleaning out the garage before lunch.

Back to "sustaining this extraordinary place." During the research for Dead Wrong, I discovered something that startled me:

"If we continue to fuel our homes, businesses, and cars with fossil fuels at the same rate we have been doing for the past 50 years, we are going to raise the temperature on Earth to a level our planet has not experienced for thirty-eight million years."

This conjured up images of Dante's Inferno, Hades, and Hell on Earth because, according to scientists, life on Earth, as we know it, cannot survive when it gets that hot.

Another sordid tidbit of ecological history emerged during my research:

"Ninety nine percent of life that has ever inhabited the Earth is gone and the average duration of a species on our planet has been 2.5 million years."

As of this writing, we (human beings) have been on the Earth for about 2.5 million years.

For the "Top 10 Ways You Can Save the Plane....Save Yourself" and a gallery of photos of our wonderful Planet, go to www.GSpencerMyers.com.

Contents

1

The humidity stuck to Derk Bryan's shoes like bubble gum, and his perspiration bounced off the pavement like water on a hot grill. The Times was reporting record highs and three hurricanes with Greek names were queued up in the Atlantic.

The professor parked the customized 1949 Harley-Davidson Panhead motorcycle in front of his favorite Passe-a-grille watering hole. The Top End, at the very end of St. Pete Beach, served average food, better beer, and the most eclectic clientele in Tampa Bay. He never knew if he'd be sitting next to a billionaire or a billiard champion.

"Damn!" he said when one leg brushed a pipe on his bike.

With one hand, he massaged the sweat into a crimson welt forming on his calf. With the other hand, he loosened the straps on his saddle bag and untied a leather case embossed with the letters Straight Shooter. He limped to the end of the bar, reached into the bottom of an ice-filled barrel, and pulled out two longnecks. Then he stuck his singed limb into the barrel, shoe and all.

The eyes of the tourists rolled while the sounds of "Yo, Derk" came from the other end of the bar. Derk nodded to familiar faces.

He commandeered his regular stool at the bar, uncapped the first brew, and threw the "usual order" glance at the barkeep. After hanging the leather case, which protected his eight-hundred-dollar Meucci pool cue, on a hook under the bar, he put his phone on the bar top and waited for the call.

"Is that your display of local color?" said Connie, glancing at the cold bottle pressed against his leg. She was pouring draughts from a tap.

"An effect of global warming," he said, grimacing.

"Looks like a third-degree burn to me, Professor," Connie said.

"Where's your motherly love?" he said.

"Sweetheart, if you need some love, I'm out of here at four."

Connie's crop of crimson curls brushed the other waitress as she sashayed behind the bar with two full mugs in hand. "There's a volleyball game at Froggy's later," she added with a wink.

Volleyball at Froggy's was played in wet tee shirts, so the prospect of seeing Connie Felton wet-wrapped in a skimpy tee was tempting, but he had a date. That was if Agnes Wiley could find a sitter for her aging mother. If so, he had invited Agnes to join him for a Grand Funk Railroad concert on the beach later that afternoon. Dating had been rare since his wife died. Agnes said she would let him know by noon, but that wasn't the call that had raised his anxiety higher than a hang glider over the Sunshine Skyway Bridge. It was the one from Ivan.

"Can you spare some ice?" he asked. He almost regretted his decision not to don long pants, but one of the reasons he lived in Florida was that the weather fit his preferred wardrobe.

He had fifteen pairs of shorts in his closet but only one suit and two other pairs of pants, casual and dress. He normally wore the suit to court when one of his cases came up for trial, but recently, he had been wearing it to funerals. It was the least fun part of his semi-retirement, actually, sabbatical. He knew he would continue to teach, and he knew he would return to his job at the EPA. He investigated crimes against the environment when someone turned up dead. His perspective on the job was simple. Those who defiled paradise threatened his life. If you poisoned the air, the water, or the soil, it was the same as a visitor in his house dumping trash on his living room floor.

"Sure. Mayo on the side?" asked Connie while writing down his order.

Derk nodded and said, "Yes," as he pulled a folded section of the newspaper from his back pocket. He opened it and motioned for someone near the cash register to toss him a pen. Then he put on his reading glasses.

"The job cutting into your party time?" Derk said when Connie returned with a plastic bag filled with crushed ice.

He laid four quarters on the bar for her and made a little gesture in the direction of Runner McCoy, who was lining up a shot. She seemed to understand that he wanted her to place them on the rail of the pool table where Melvin McCoy, his real name, once ran four tables of nine-ball in a row. It wasn't close to a record, but it was good enough to earn him the nickname. Derk didn't often play for money, but he was good enough to get an invitation to enter a doubles tournament with a big cash prize. It was a serious pool tournament, and his partner would be Leonard Stickman – best player on the beach. He had yet to commit to the $500 entry fee, partially because Ivan, the call he was expecting, had already cost him five grand. If he were to commit, playing against Runner McCoy would be an adequate test of his game.

The waitress placed his money on the pool table where Runner was playing. McCoy glanced at Derk with a nod and a smile and lip-synced, "Game on!"

Connie's valentine of a derrière was the last part of her to swerve around Derk's end of the bar on her way to the kitchen. She reminded him of a woman in a Botticelli painting. A moment of fantasy intercepted the anticipation of the call he awaited while he pondered what lay beneath her skimpy tank tee shirt. "No," he murmured. It was never going to happen. She was twenty years his junior.

"You got that right, Biker Boy," she said.

"What?" He thought she had read his mind. "Oh, no, prior commitment," he said.

"Busy social life, eh?" she said. "What's her name?"

"I'd give it all up for you, Connie," he said. "Let's get out of here now." He held out his hand and swiveled on his seat to leave.

"Goddamn!" he said when he brushed his fire-roasted calf against the stool. He dropped back onto the seat like a sack of potatoes.

"And miss your game?" she said and pointed to the table where his quarters were parked in anticipation of his match with Runner.

"It is a dilemma," he said, squinting through the pain. "My first love is you and always will be."

"If it were only true," she said, and her attention was distracted by a customer asking for a refill.

Derk exhaled deeply, then stretched out the newspaper to expose the crossword puzzle.

"Connie, I need a five-letter word for trespass." "Trump," said a voice in the room.

A chuckle came from a guy on a barstool with three empty mugs in front of him.

Derk managed only a smirk.

"Trump. It's funny," said the guy. A semi-smirk washed through a beer-fueled gaze.

"Probably," Derk said, "but I'm one of the forty percent who lives close to a coast. If Greenland keeps melting, the sea level will be up to my ceiling, and my car will be floating in my living room. That guy didn't give a damn."

"Is he always this grim?" The guy asked Rashida, the other waitress. "The next one's on me." He held up his mug and waved it at Derk.

Rashida said, "I'd listen to him. He's got six degrees." "What in?" said the guy.

Rashida looked at Derk while she listed them, "Geology, Zoology, and Andropology. Right?"

"Three," Derk whispered.

"Anthropology," Connie corrected Rashida as she passed carrying a tray of fish sandwiches and kettle chips.

The guy offering the free beer responded with a laugh that was too hard. It quieted the room.

In a low voice, Derk said to Rashida, "Botany," and several heads turned toward him.

"Botany, not Zoology. Plants, not animals," he said. "And it's one degree with three majors."

"As in PhD," Connie said to the man with the loud laugh.

"Professor Derk," said the guy. "No shit." He drained the mug in one long slug and finished with a burp he made no effort to suppress.

Derk returned to his crossword puzzle. His concentration wasn't any better today than it had been when he started working on this puzzle two Sundays ago. He took a deep breath and counted to five as he exhaled.

The call that had his neurons in a tangle was coming from a guy recommended by a friend of a friend. It was a long shot to be sure, but he was advertised to be "just the guy you need to find someone who is hard to find."

According to Derk's source, this guy's identity required the cover of darkness. That meant retired snoop, as in ex-CIA, ex-NSA, ex-KGB or something like that. Derk had been one of the EPA's best investigators, but he didn't have the clearance to check on sources of the kind this guy might have. On blind faith, he had sent five thousand dollars to a post office box in the Cayman Islands. Over a week ago, he was told to expect a call within ten days from the man who had only gone by the name of Ivan. Today was the tenth day.

"What's up, Derk?" It was Stickman entering the Top End with his pool cue and a toasty tart in tow. Stickman always had a looker by his side.

"Hey, Stick!" Runner McCoy acknowledged him.

Runner and Stickman shook hands. Their handshake was followed by a ritual that climaxed when their pool cues clicked each other like swords. Sticks' nickname was no irony. Leonard Stickman was one of the two best nine-ballers on the beach, probably good enough to turn pro. Derk had to be at his best to beat him. Stickman had been coaxing Derk to enter a two-player nine-ball pool tournament. His pitch was simple, "It's like tag team pool. First prize is ten-grand, and we're good enough to win." Derk's share would be the same amount he paid Ivan. It was appealing, but it had yet to win his favor.

Stickman directed his girlfriend to the seat next to Derk. He winced when he noticed the welt on Derk's leg. Derk turned and held up his non-beer hand to wave him off.

"I'm waiting for someone," Derk said. It wasn't true, but he wanted privacy when the call from Ivan came. "And I need to ice this thing." He laid his leg on the bar stool as Stickman and his girlfriend backed away.

"You might want to see a Doc, Professor. That's nasty," Stickman said, "Where you playing?"

Derk pointed to the table where his quarters were parked. Stickman placed four quarters next to Derk's and took a nearby table with his girlfriend. Derk nodded "hello" to the girlfriend and gave Stickman a thumbs up. Stickman was a buff forty, had a chiseled chin, stringy, dark hair, and a tattoo of a panther on his arm that ran from his wrist to his shoulder. He wore skin-tight black denim and a bowling shirt with cue sticks, and his name was embroidered on the back. His girlfriend had youthful skin, the color of Espresso, probably Jamaican, and legs so lithe they appeared to have been poured into her Liz Claiborne jeans. She was a "runway model" good-looking.

Derk motioned for Sticks to come back to his seat. "Where the hell can I get some of that stuff?"

"What stuff?" Stickman said.

"Animal magnetism," Derk said loud enough for his girlfriend to hear. She winked at Derk and blew Stickman a kiss.

"It comes with the pants," Stickman said and returned to open arms at his table.

When Connie passed Stickman with someone's order, she fanned herself. "Whew!"

"Just another pretty face," Derk said. "I need a four-letter word for insensible."

"Rude," said Connie.

"Doesn't fit," he said as she proceeded to a table where two tourists were having lunch.

His mind drifted. The Ivan contact emanated from a revelation that had shaken Derk to the core. He was standing outside his father's hospital room when his mother informed him that the man he called "Daddy" wasn't his real father. That was several years ago. He couldn't believe it. He didn't want to believe it, but that didn't stop him from searching. He needed to know the truth.

"Why are you telling me this? Why are you making up such a thing?" he kept saying to her.

His mother confessed that, while she was in high school, in a desperate attempt to make Charlie Bryan jealous, she had become pregnant by another boy. Charles Bryan married her because he thought the child was his and that it was the honorable thing to do. She had kept this secret until Charles Bryan lay in a Michigan hospital bed in a vegetative state as a result of a stroke that had left him unable to swallow. She told Derk that she was honoring two promises her husband had asked of her. "Don't keep me on life support and tell Derk the truth."

If that wasn't enough of a shock, Derk's mother wanted him to consent to taking her husband to Oregon. Through tears, she said,

"Michigan puts doctors in jail for helping already dead people die with dignity. Oregon does not."

After Charlie's death, Derk began the search for his biological father. When his mother found out, she pleaded with him, "You have only one family, the one Charlie and I created. He's gone. He died in Oregon. Promise me you'll let this go!"

He did for a while, but when his mother died a few months ago, he was left with a canyon-sized void in his heart and his heritage. After the funeral, he resumed the search for his biological father. He was getting nowhere until his introduction to the mysterious super sleuth. His friend assured him, "If anyone can find this guy, it's Ivan."

It was Derk's turn to play. He rose from his seat as Runner McCoy broke a fresh rack of balls. "Smack!"

Two of the nine balls dropped into corner pockets. The other seven came to rest thoroughly spaced out on the plush green velvet. Runner dropped in three more with easy shots, banked in two off opposite rails, and finished with a coast-to-coast shot off two rails. He held up his cue stick like a gun and blew on the tip. He winked at Derk and blew a kiss at Stickman's erotic Jamaican girlfriend. Runner had upped his game since the last time Derk played him. Derk plopped back down onto his barstool. Connie stood behind the bar, holding a grouper sandwich platter, while she stopped to watch Runner do his thing.

"Nice shooting, Cowboy," she said. She placed the hot platter, heaping with crinkle-cut fries, on the bar in front of Derk. "Whew," she said again and waved her hand in front of her face.

"Aren't we fickle?" Derk said. He took a bite of a hot French fry. "Oooh, oooh, oooh!" he cried out and took a long swig from his beer. He held up the empty bottle.

"Want another?" Connie said.

Derk shook his head frantically. With his game over and the fire in his mouth extinguished, he settled into lunch. Gazing at the large print over the mirror behind the bar, he became mesmerized. It was the famous one of the dogs playing pool. Next to it was a photograph of Michigan Stadium. The owner of the Top End was a Michigan native. The Michigan connection took him back to the attic of his mother's home in Michigan. After the auction of her furniture and her car, the only physical remnants of his attachment to Charlie and her were in a stash of dusty boxes in his mother's attic in her Michigan home.

Under a single yellow bulb that dangled from the tresses, he had sorted through the boxes. Memories whipped him like a stout willow. He flashed back to the toy soldiers given to him on his fifth birthday by Charlie Bryan. In this day of computer games and animated characters with artificial intelligence, they seemed so disparate from his life today. Yet, in the many hours of solitary play-time with those soldiers, he never suspected that Charlie was a fake.

He tossed the things into three piles. One was stuff he would keep. Another he would donate to Goodwill. Everything else would be thrown onto the scrap heap of lies. Occasionally, he would fix upon a photograph and wonder if the guy in the picture might be his father or if it was someone who knew his father. He sat in his mother's attic, immersed in the aroma of dust, mold, and cedar. Tears streaked his face as the shadows on the walls entombed him. He had never felt so alone.

"Penny for your thoughts," Connie said. She removed the empty bottles from the countertop.

He glanced at his watch and shook his head. It was twenty minutes past noon. He put four more quarters on the table.

He wasn't ready to give up on Agnes Wiley. He would call her after lunch. He took a bite of his sandwich and went back to the crossword puzzle. He still needed a four-letter word for insensible. When it didn't come to him, his thoughts returned to his mother.

After finalizing his mother's estate, he returned to his Pass-a-grille beach condo. He put some of the toy soldiers on a bookshelf and then opened his mother's senior high school yearbook to her picture. She was petite and somewhat demure, but even in the old black-and-white yearbook photo, she was a knockout. He never realized how beautiful his mother had been. He wondered why she was so fixated upon Charles Bryan.

As he leafed through the yearbook, he began to understand Charlie's appeal. He was athletic and handsome and featured over and over, usually surrounded by teammates. He had become a successful real estate salesman. Still, they were too young to marry. At that time, it's what young pregnant couples did. That didn't excuse the deceit. It was difficult to accept that his mother had lied to her husband, and then she lied to him.

As must have been the practice of the day, other students had signed their names next to her picture, along with esoteric references and philosophical quips. What riveted his attention was an inscription by Ike Dennis: "For what might have been is yours forever!" He hurried to the garage and fished his own high school yearbook from a dusty box of books, then opened to his senior picture. When he put his picture side by side with that of Ike Dennis, it was as if he was looking into a mirror.

It was his first inkling of hope. He called the high school but was told the school kept no records of its students so long after graduation. The class secretary died five years ago. All he found were dead-ends.

He shared his story with an acquaintance who said he knew a retired investigator who might be able to hook him up with someone. Along with the money, Derk had sent the yearbook pictures of Ike Dennis and his mother to the post office box in the Cayman Islands. Today, he waited for the call.

Derk had programmed his cell phone to play the William Tell Overture. It still startled him when it rang.

"Hi ho, Silver!" said Connie.

He recognized the number, but it was neither Agnes Wiley nor the man who went only by the name of Ivan.

"What is it?" Derk answered.

"Dr. Bryan, please hold for the director." Joyce, the secretary for the EPA's regional director, was unusually formal today, and she was working on a Saturday.

Derk was assigned to cases of environmental damage when the prospect of criminality was high, such as when a body ended up in a cesspool of toxicity. He took time off after his mother's death and has yet to go back.

"It's Ben. Sorry to bother you, but we've got a problem."

"I'm an elbow from a grouper sandwich, and then I've got a date," Derk said. "Besides, I'm retired."

"Somebody drove a truckful of chemicals into Lake Manatee!" Ben Waitley said. He had been the director for over twenty-five years.

"No way!" Derk whispered aloud, aware that his day was about to change.

"It's a major spill," Waitley said. "Killed the driver." "What kind of chemicals?"

"Probably pesticides. It was a farm and garden supply van." "How long's it been in the water?"

"Sometime this morning. How long will it take you to get there?"

"Less than an hour," Derk said and flipped the phone shut. He took another mouthful of his sandwich, washed it down with the rest of his beer, and threw some money on the counter.

"Gotta go," he said to Connie. "Someone drove a truckful of pesticides into Lake Manatee!" He threw disappointed looks at Runner McCoy and Leonard Stickman.

The news sobered the tourists. The faces of the locals sank like heavy metal. Images of the oil-soaked terns and gulls that washed ashore after a tanker's hull ruptured in Tampa Bay had been indelibly etched into their collective minds. The tar sometimes stuck between their toes when they walked on the beach. They knew the tourists would stop coming, and so would their tips at the local restaurants. The tee-shirt shops would lay off people. The charter fishing boats would shut down. Relationships would suffer, and apartments would be abandoned. This was a kick in the groin.

Tampa Bay was Derk's home and his playground. Lake Manatee flowed into the Manatee River and the river into Tampa Bay. It consisted of mangroves and grassy flats that provided the bedrock of the nautical food chain for the area. It began with the nutrient-rich grassy beds. The millions of microorganisms living there were fed to the shrimp and the crabs. A myriad of fish depended upon the shrimp for their survival. Game fish, like snook, bonefish, and redfish, depend on smaller fish and so on up the food chain. It was a sure bet that none of them depended upon the organophosphates or chlorinated solvents or any of the five hundred other possible poisons that might have been in that farm and garden supply truck.

The Harley started on the first kick. As Derk roared across the bridge from St. Pete Beach to St. Petersburg, between rows of stately palms and colorful hibiscus that bordered the causeway, he couldn't help but contrast the paradox between a paradise and a paradise lost.

Today, there was no breeze to mitigate the brutality of the summer sun. The familiar roar of the V-Twin and the vibration of the Panhead against the road provided little solace. Any day on his Harley was normally a good day, but this day's gleaming promises were now in jeopardy.

He wound through the gnarly weekend traffic on Route 19 and connected with I-275 South, then opened the Panhead up as he ascended the Sunshine Skyway Bridge. It was a magnificent piece of architecture, erected to replace the forerunner that had been made obsolete by a collision with a freighter attempting to negotiate Tampa Bay in the early morning fog during the 1970s. At the peak of his climb, cigarette boats and yachts from Apollo Beach to Anna Maria resembled foam bubbles on a placid turquoise plain. Ninety miles per hour on a motorcycle in the wind at this height was normally a thrill that paralleled hang-gliding, but his mood had turned solemn. He had forgotten about Agnes Wiley, five-letter word clues, and the man who went only by the name of Ivan.

2

The traffic at the entrance to S.R. 64 was being rerouted by a couple of blacks and whites. Derk presented his credentials to one of the officers.

Fifteen minutes later, he was at the bridge that traversed Lake Manatee.

A van was being pulled from the water as he approached. From looking at the damage to both the van and the guardrail, it was apparent the van had gone through the concrete banister just beyond the S-curve. He saw mullets, crabs, and turtles floating in what had become a greenish-black mortuary. The offal in this heat would become unbearable in a few hours. State police, Sheriff's officers, and rescue squads were donned with gas masks and Hazmat suits. Their cautiousness was confirmed when Derk was able to read the name on the van: Gorton Farm and Garden Supply.

He tied a bandana around his head to cover his nose and mouth.

"Derk Bryan, EPA," he introduced himself to one of the Sheriff's deputies who was watching water pour from the van as it was being loaded onto a wrecker.

"Deputy Randal," was the response as he extended one hand.

"They can't do that," Derk said.

"Do what?" said the officer. "They just got him out of the water."

"Who's in charge?" Derk said. He looked around for a familiar face.

When he spotted Doc Morton, he said, "Never mind."

He walked to the gap in the bridge and looked down at the water, a dark, deadly stew that only hours ago had been an aquatic paradise for Tampa Bay marine life. A lot of things in a farm and garden supply van could have done this damage, but he needed to know exactly what was in that van. At the water's edge, Dr. Wesley Morton, chief medical officer for the county, and a woman he didn't recognize were taking water samples. He approached as they climbed the bank to the road.

"They can't do that?" Derk asked, pointing to the van on the wrecker.

"Hello, Professor," the doctor responded. "Nasty stuff, huh?"

"They've got to put that van in a semi or something enclosed," Derk insisted.

"It's a wreck, Derk, so they called a wrecker," Doc Morton said.

"It'll drip that stuff all over," Derk said. "It's toxic. Look what it did to the lake."

"They know what they're doing," Morton said. "This isn't their first rodeo."

They were wearing heavy-duty orange rain suits with rubber boots and masks.

Derk shook his head in disbelief. Something in that van was lethal, but he let it go. His job was to find out what or who killed the fish and what was contaminating the water. He reached out a hand as Doctor Morton strained to climb the embankment.

"What do you know for sure, Doc?" Derk said.

The rotund doctor was gasping for air as he spoke, "My handicap's up, my daughter's dating a guy with six tattoos, and my wife says she's unfulfilled."

Derk couldn't hold back a chuckle. "I can't help you with your daughter, but I'd try a new position," Derk said.

Doctor Morton stood upright and stretched as he inhaled. "I changed my grip and my stance," the doctor said.

Derk laughed again. Morton's wife was a former finalist in a swimsuit contest, but the doctor had more belts than a Michelin tire. He needed a mirror to see his toes.

"I was talking about your wife," Derk said. "And I'd help you out, but I've got a policy against dating married women." The only time they had been at the same event was when the doctor's wife spent more time talking to Derk than she did with her husband.

The doctor's cheerful disposition turned sour. He frowned as his eyes narrowed.

"Somebody spotted the van in the water about seven-thirty. We figure it's been in there, at least five to six hours." He fumbled some of the water samples.

"My God, Doc!" Derk said. He reached for one of the glass containers but stopped short.

Dr. Morton waved him off. His assistant hurried to recover the dropped vials.

Dr. Morton took another deep breath. "You're not dressed to be around here."

Derk was wearing the same shorts, tee shirt, and boots he had on at the Top End.

"I gave up a grouper sandwich and a hot date for this," Derk said. "Got a suit for me?"

"In my car." The doctor pointed toward his county-issued SUV.

Derk put the mask over his face and slipped a pair of waterproof coveralls over his street clothes. Doctor Morton walked over to an ambulance where the body of Sandover "Wink" Gorton lay on a gurney. Deputy Randall joined him.

Gorton's face looked like bloated pulp.

"Must have gone through the windshield," said Deputy Randall. The doctor shrugged but said nothing. He ordered the body bagged.

An autopsy would be performed at the morgue, and a report would follow. "Anything you can tell me?" Derk asked.

Doc Morton lit a cigarette. He closed his eyes and took a deep drag through his stained fingers. Then he strained to stretch his back. "Yea, he's dead," he said and walked away.

Personnel from the special rescue unit were sorting through the soaked containers scattered throughout the van. Derk stood nearby as they searched for legible labels. The van was a long way from his Tampa store, the address of which had been stenciled on the side of the van. He wondered where Gorton had been and where he was going. If he was making deliveries, he could find out what was in the van. He made a mental note of the telephone number on the van.

Circumscribing the van, he noticed that the tires were still inflated. That eliminated a blowout. Given the extent of the damage, any number of mechanical failures could have been at fault. Most of the time, the answers to his questions turned out to be mundane human or mechanical failures, absent of malice. Sometimes, otherwise nice folks took really big chances, which ended lives and destroyed pieces of his paradise. That's when he got the call. Cynicism wasn't his nature, but he had an almost unhealthy suspicion when things like this happened. It was one of the reasons he was so damn good at his job. That is why Ben Waitley took him away from a relaxing day and why he gave up a grouper sandwich and a hot date. At this point, he assumed the worst and hoped for the best. Maybe Gorton just fell asleep at the wheel.

As he retreated to the broken balustrade where the van left the road, The Lone Ranger played on his hip. He started to unzip his protective suit to take out his cell phone. As he did, he scanned the death in the lake. Something in that van had to be very toxic to do so much damage. He zipped up the suit and kicked a piece of broken concrete into the water. His date with Agnes Wiley would have to wait.

3

Sergeant Wilson Perkins was in charge of a team whose job was to put away illegal drug pushers. A couple of months ago, he led a team of narcotics agents to a small cabin in the scrub outside Ruskin. The site was adjacent to a tomato farm twenty-five minutes north of Lake Manatee, where Wink Gorton would go through the concrete bannister. The Sergeant led them there to eradicate a patch of marijuana that had been brought to his attention by a nineteen-year-old illegal Cuban immigrant named Juan Rodriguez.

Three months prior to that, Juan and his pregnant wife, Juanita, had risked their lives to have their baby born in the United States. They left Cuba in a makeshift boat with six others. A few days later, their boat capsized off the Florida Keys, forcing them to swim to shore. Authorities were waiting for them, but Juan had escaped capture. His wife survived but was incarcerated with her unborn child in an immigrant detention facility. Federal authorities had rushed to have her deported before her child was born in the United States. The stress of her situation sent her into early labor, and she died during childbirth. Her son, Antonio, was born an American citizen.

Juan spoke little English. He worked in migrant labor camps near Ruskin, while trying to avoid capture, on his way to Tampa to see his great uncle. He was relying upon him to help reconnect with his wife and child. That was where he met Sergeant Perkins.

Juan was stopped with a cache of marijuana plants in the bed of a pickup truck that had been reported as stolen. Facing a felony charge and deportation, he learned about the death of his wife. His son instantly became another Elian Gonzalez episode for South Florida.

Bay Magazine was in the middle of a series on the human costs of illegal immigration when the Juan Rodriguez story broke.

Emotions ran high, and the story was set in primetime theater. Rodriguez wanted to retain custody of his son, but so did Juan's uncle, Eduardo Garcia. Garcia claimed that because the child was born on U.S. soil and was an American citizen, he should stay in the States. Garcia, owner of a large chain of Spanish restaurants, had the money and influence to prosecute his claim. In fairness, he retained one attorney to represent the child and another to represent Juan Rodriguez. The Cuban community was conflicted, but the general consensus was that the case against Rodriguez was contrived solely so he could be deported. Samantha Card, owner and publisher of Bay Magazine, was part of a crowd that had gathered in Eduardo Garcia's depot-sized kitchen to hear the Sheriff's attempt to appease the Hispanic community. The Sheriff was running for re-election and craved Garcia's support. He dispatched Sergeant Perkins to handle the growing criticism. Judging by the Sergeant's flailing gestures and staccato Spanish, audible from the other side of the room, Samantha assumed things were not going the Sheriff's way.

"I'm not against immigration. Hell, my family's sixth-generation German. Came through Five Points in New York," the Sergeant said.

Will Perkins, a career cop, was lean and weathered. At six-five, he peered down at the group of impatient, old-guard Cuban men. They gathered around him as he peered through dark-tinted, wire-rimmed glasses that made him look more intimidating than an ex-marine turned high-school principal.

"Any person would want to come to America," someone shouted. "He needs our help. He is Cuban, and his baby is American. They should be able to stay."

"Why do the Dutch, the Chinese, the Jamaicans—hell, everyone else—have to apply for entry visas and wait their turn while the Cubans can drift in on anything that floats and go to the head of the line?" the Sergeant countered.

"Is the law. We were kicked off our land, lost our homes and our businesses. This young man, Rodriguez, he was doing the same thing any of us would do, trying to help his family," insisted a well-dressed fifty-something Latin man with an ivory-tipped cane at his side.

It was oven-hot and noisy because everyone had congregated in the kitchen where the sounds of salsa drifted overhead, and the mojitos and Coronas flowed freely to waiting patrons. Through the double doors that opened onto a tennis-court-sized pool and patio, Samantha noticed the Sable palms strain against the Gulf breeze. Storms were brewing inside and out. She finished the empanada on which she was munching and moved close enough to hear her brother-in-law's response. Sergeant Wilson Perkins was the brother of her deceased husband.

"I know that the Cubans, and no one else, can immigrate if they make shore, but this kid didn't make it. Four immigration officers had him in their grasp. He was under arrest," the Sergeant said.

Murmurs, like hostel jungle drums, filled the room.

"He made it to shore. He should be free," shouted a distinguished Cuban man with a lit Robusto in one hand. Samantha recognized Maurico Hernandez. His father had brought his family from Cuba during the revolution and cultivated a single cigar outlet into a chain of smoke shops throughout South Florida that provided jobs for many immigrants. Maurico, the young, brash symbol of successful second-generation Cubans, had appeared on the cover of Bay Magazine at the height of cigar popularity. The Sergeant dismissed him with a backhand and then mimicked what she assumed must have been Juan Rodriguez's broken English, "One day me and Martinez see a truck drive into tall grass next to Senior Curran's farm. Later, we follow the road, but there is no farm, just weeds and marijuana. Mucho plants, but we take only a few. That's what he told us."

"It's not fair," someone said, supported by a raucous chorus of "No justo."

"The kid was caught with marijuana. He should have called us right then," Perkins said.

Samantha had only a conversational grasp of Spanish but she recognized the objections. They were louder and cruder this time.

"Malditos policias, he steal nothing." "He stole a truck!"

Mauricio Hernandez tried to lower the tone. "He drove that truck for his boss many times. He planned on returning it after using it, and you know that."

"He didn't have a driver's license," the Sergeant retorted.

"His baby is American. You cannot separate them," a middle-aged Cuban woman said.

The Sergeant shrugged. "I'm sorry, but I can't get involved in the kid's hard luck story."

Samantha knew that Will Perkins didn't really care that these Latin business owners and prominent community members identified with this kid. This kid had spent six days in an old wooden boat powered only by an old twenty-horse Johnson and four paddles on their way to the middle Keys from western Cuba. Four nights out, the Johnson died. A couple of nights later, the boat struck coral during a storm that forced everyone to swim for shore. Four people drowned before reaching Pigeon Key. Rodriguez made it to shore, lost track of his wife, and worked his way north. He took a job as a migrant worker to escape detection while he sought his uncle and information about his wife. His search for his wife and child and his struggle to remain free may have seemed completely American to these folks, but her brother-in-law once told her that he resented giving up a year of his free time to learn Spanish just to be able to talk to people in his own country. His attitude had been, "They're taking our jobs and using our resources, and what do we get in return?" She knew it was an opinion shared by many. But there was another side to the story and that is why her magazine was giving it so much attention.

"He made it to shore. He has rights," shouted the well-dressed Latin man. He waved the shiny oak cane in the air.

Her brother-in-law wouldn't discuss it with her, but thus far, she had learned that a border patrol officer said he had Juan in his grasp and was attempting to cuff him. It was dark, and in the high winds, the helicopter couldn't keep its light on them. The waves knocked them over, and Juan Rodriguez made it to shore.

Legally, Juan's son was an American citizen, but Juan's freedom was at risk. The child's grandparents wanted the child to return to Cuba. The Cuban exiles, led by Eduardo Garcia, wanted him to stay in America. It had become an immigration battle complicated by an international custody dispute.

"My mission is larger than one unfortunate young man," Sergeant Perkins retorted, loud enough to be heard above the din of clanging glasses and salsa music. "Marijuana," he continued as most of the crowd gathered in the kitchen fell silent. He lowered his voice, "is a dangerous substance, and Juan Rodriguez," and he paused briefly, "is an illegal alien who committed a felony."

"Permiso, excuse me," Samantha said as she knifed through the crowd. Her features were copyrightable. She had polished ebony skin and sparkling green eyes that seemed darker from too much eyeliner applied in haste. Her coal-tar hair hugged her head like a swim cap. Every issue of Bay Magazine contained her photograph and her editorial. She barely reached five feet in wool stockings, but she was so recognizable that several people let her slide through until she was only a few feet away from her brother-in-law. "Blacks and Hispanics make up a percentage of those in prison that far exceeds their proportion of the population," Samantha Card said, "and they're in there mostly for minor drug offenses, grounds for deportation. Care to comment on that, Sergeant?"

Will Perkins turned toward her. "Our policy," he said and removed his sunglasses to expose eyes to the depth of Black Holes, "is zero tolerance." In a lower voice, he added, "As far as I'm concerned, the only contribution the Cubans have made to American culture is salsa, and this kid sure as hell isn't going to add to that. You going to print that?" He scoffed at her and walked away.

Samantha hadn't intended to embarrass her brother-in-law, but he had become spiteful since his brother's death. As her eyes followed him across the room, they landed upon a weather map of the Atlantic Ocean beamed across a wall-mounted flat-screen television. All three hurricanes had attained category-three status. She rarely made storm preparations. She told herself it was because hurricanes rarely struck Tampa Bay. She knew, however, that her lack of urgency was due more to the stress in her life. She was a single mother, worked too much, and was obsessed with middle-aged sagging. To counter the challenge, she took up jazzercise six days a week for the past year. She took Sundays off only because the studio's owner was a born-again Christian. Fit for any age, at forty-eight, she was in the ninety-nine percentile. Unfortunately, she now had an obsession that hadn't quelled her stress. She left her exercise class in such a hurry she backed into a signpost coming out of the parking lot.

She rotated her head and massaged the nape of her neck as she slipped away from the crowd. She dialed her daughter on her cell phone to remind her to take an inventory of their hurricane supplies but stopped after the second ring. Samantha didn't want to freak her out. Jamie was an honor student, but she was also a bipolar fifteen-year-old with mood swings that ranged from her arches to her one hundred forty IQ. Since her father's death, her condition has worsened. Like a cloud on a sunny day, a twinge of guilt overcame Samantha. She wanted to kick herself for not having one of her staff cover tonight's event. She flipped the cell phone shut and went in search of the party's host.

When the magazine received the press release about the meeting, Samantha knew the Sheriff would send someone. It was an election year. She also knew that if it was Garcia's goal to embarrass the cops and to show the community's support for Rodriguez and his son, he was probably now grinning with delight.

In Samantha's opinion, her brother-in-law had become the victim of his own hypocrisy. She knew that, in spite of his zero-tolerance policy, he had plea-bargained leniency in return for information from Juan Rodriguez. He used that information to raid the Ruskin growing site and test a herbicide used in another State to eradicate marijuana plants. He once quipped, "Cops there told me, spray it on the weed and, before long, all you have is dead weed."

During the fly-over a week later, the sergeant spotted a car along the road leading to the eradicated field. In it was a trunk full of twenties, a couple of pounds of pot, and two dead Latinos.

When Eduardo Garcia found out, he called the local farm workers' union. The union's workers picked most of the tomatoes used in his restaurants. This prompted the union to file a suit against the Sheriff to stop the spraying, and they were joined by a group of Ruskin tomato farmers. In a statement released to the press, the head of the growers' cooperative stated,

"The indiscriminate spraying of marijuana plants next to tomato farms presents a serious danger to the farms, the migrant workers and the consumers. It must be stopped."

The Juan Rodriguez incident had grown from a snowball to an avalanche that was headed directly toward the Sheriff.

The Bay Magazine had reported in a previous story that *"Many Floridians have opposed the government's blanket spraying for citrus canker and Med flies."* According to the farmers and several environmental groups in Tampa Bay, this is far worse. The owner of Sunny Acres Produce was quoted, *"This kind of toxin in the middle of one of the richest growing areas in Florida could contaminate all of our food and water. What are these people thinking?"*

The farm workers' union petitioned the EPA to intervene if the police wouldn't stop the spraying. Then Garcia entreated the families of the two deceased Latinos to file a wrongful death suit.

To deflect blame, the Sheriff apparently thought it wise to have the man in charge of the whole mess, Sergeant Wilson Perkins, assuage their fears. From what Samantha witnessed, it didn't go as planned.

Her brother-in-law was none too happy when he showed up at her house an hour after her stinging confrontation at Garcia's restaurant.

"What was that about?" he said.

Samantha was filling the dishwasher while he stood, hands on hips, staring at her from behind his wire-rimmed shades. Still in uniform, he towered over her.

"I gather we've had a bad day," Samantha said.

"I've been at the firing range. Used your magazine for target practice." "I take it you blame me for your problems. I'm just doing my job," she said.

"Supporting dope pushers and illegal immigrants," he said.

"You're out of step, Will and people are questioning your methods. This isn't my problem, and I don't want you to make it mine," Samantha said.

His fist clenched, he stepped toward her. His face was contorted with contempt.

He was a huge white man with a badge, and she could have been intimidated, but she wasn't. "I don't make the news. I just report it. If you want to see me and your niece, then fine, but don't bring that attitude in here."

Her deceased husband was a cop, so she understood them, but she had never seen Will like this.

"Want a cup of coffee?" She tried to diffuse the tension.

She put two cups of water into the microwave and a can of instant coffee on the table. He was as hard as bauxite when he sat down and scoffed at the can of instant.

"I'm busy. Bring your own if it's that important to you."

"You said we were hiding something, and the Sheriff's all over me," he said.

"No!" she said, motioning toward the door. He pursed his lips and held his breath. "Sorry," he said.

"I'm sorry, too."

"You?" he said and laughed, a laugh that was tinted with acrimony. "How so?"

"I'm out of sugar," she said, grinning. She knew he always put sugar in his coffee.

"You're incorrigible," he said, pushed his chair away from the table and got up.

"You need to relax, Will."

He stared at her for a moment and then pulled his chair back to the table. "Do you know what he said?"

"Can't you keep that woman in line?" she said. "For Chris-sakes, Sammy!"

He called her Sammy when he wanted to mess with her head. It was meant to stir up feelings of inferiority. She had confided to her husband, who had apparently shared it with his brother, that due to her tiny stature, some of the boys in grade school referred to her as the runt of the litter, like a mouse. So, they shortened her name to Sammy and called her Sammy the Mouse. If only Sammy had stuck with her, it would have been tolerable, but she never shook the images from school. Kids were just damn cruel at times, but he was her brother-in-law, and he knew better.

"After feeding you to the lions, what's he going to do next?" she said.

The bell rang on the microwave. She placed the steaming cups on the table. He spooned a large scoop of instant into his cup.

"It might blow over, but if the shit hits the fan, you'll take the fall," she said. "You know what he's like."

"I doubt it," he said.

"So, what the hell did you spray on those plants?" she asked.

"A weed killer, similar to Roundup, but it's safe, and it kills pot!" "Will, I know what you're trying to do, but goddamn!" She mimicked the Sheriff's pine tar Mississippi accent. "They're supposed to be prosecuting the bad guys, not us." She did her best to coax a chuckle from him.

"He's not happy with the publicity. That's for sure," Will said. "Is Jamie here?"

"I sent her out for hurricane supplies. Heard anything?" Samantha said.

"It's still early, but if you need to, you and Jamie can go to E-comm," he said. There was a secure place in the basement of the police emergency communications building that accommodated first responders and their families. Samantha's townhouse overlooked Tampa Bay. The sunsets were spectacular, but her condo was vulnerable to an eight-foot storm surge.

"Let's hope it doesn't come to that," she said.

There may have been more that needed to be said, but conversation had been strained between them since her husband's death. With Samantha's daughter out of the house and his acrimony curtailed, she offered him no other reason to hang around. He took a couple of sips of his coffee and left. One week later, Samantha assigned a Bay Magazine reporter to attend a news conference at which the Medical Examiner and the county prosecutor announced.

"What was sprayed on the marijuana plants had been used safely in other jurisdictions. It's not harmful to humans when used properly. What happened to the deceased occurred during or as the result of the commission of a crime. Illegal marijuana was found in their car. Since the officers in question used all of the proper procedures, there is no reason to hold the Sheriff, or any of his officers, in dereliction in their duties."

Juan Rodriguez's sentence was reduced to three years, commuted to probation, and he was shipped back to Cuba with his son. The Sheriff agreed not to spray without warning; the suits had been dropped, and Sergeant Will Perkins went back on the weed warpath. By September, the incident had become nothing but flaxseed in the wind.

4

By late afternoon, the incoming tide and the cleanup effort had mitigated the damage. The police had departed after completing their search for clues to the cause of the accident. Sandy Gorton's remains had been sent to the morgue.

Derk stayed to watch the men in biohazard suits inventory the chemicals that still had labels. After each substance was tagged and recorded, the van was secured on the wrecker for transport to the crime lab. Derk followed in the hope of getting a chemical analysis before nightfall. At ten o'clock, the coroner said he needed more time. Tired as a moth in a cyclone, Derk guided his Harley back to his home on the beach.

It was close to eleven when he parked the bike in his garage. On his way up the stairs to his condo he grabbed a hard lemonade from the stock of craft beers he kept in a cooler.

The moonlight filtering through the half-open blinds formed dark blades on the living room floor. In the refrigerator, he found a half-chewed pickle and the remains of an eggplant parmesan sub. He took a bite of the cold sandwich and downed two Advil with the spiked lemonade. The arthritis in his right knee hurt like hell.

He stripped in the bathroom and plopped down on the lid of the toilet. He wished he had been able to tell Ben Waitley that he wasn't ready to take this case. The timing couldn't have been worse. His mother was gone. His father was unknown. He canceled a date and missed a Grateful Dead concert. He still hadn't heard from Ivan. Now, someone had dumped a cocktail of poisons in his front yard. He had to take this case.

He showered and, before crashing, left a message on Agnes Wiley's phone, "I'm really sorry. Something came up at work, and I couldn't say no. Call me."

***

Derk rose early when he was working on a case. His cases always involved crimes against nature, but lately, the schemes have become more creative and super sinister. He didn't know if the perpetrators had suffered a life-altering insult at the hands of Mother Earth or if they hadn't been breastfed, but this new batch of Earthstainers just didn't give a damn. They put everyone at risk. So, before he showered or read the morning paper, he popped two more Advil and called the crime lab. He was going to find out what happened to Sandy Gorton.

"The report will be available later," was the response.

"How much later?" Derk asked. "Let me talk with Doc Morton." "Sorry, he's busy. I'll have him call you."

"I'm investigating the Gorton accident, and I need that report," Derk said.

"I'm sure you do, but we're inundated."

"More inundated than a truckload of poison in Tampa Bay?" "A mass shooting at the "Y" was the response.

"No shit! Sorry," Derk said.

"Disgruntled employee. The Doc is on the scene," offered the desk sergeant.

Had Derk gotten to the second section of the morning Times, he would have learned that a YMCA employee took a gun into the natatorium, where he wounded three elderly members who were swimming laps. The story would feature a stale litany of arguments by gun control proponents and the contradictions by an array of 2nd Amendment protectors. Of course, there were racial overtones. The victims were white, and the shooter was black.

It was reported that the seriously injured men in the pool were even more seriously delinquent in their obligations to Former Med-Tech Sgt. Jackson Pomeroy, the shooter. He had become the middleman for these guys and others who had graduated to heroin from the opioids that had been scripted by their doctors. Pomeroy, a YMCA custodian, was highly trained in battlefield pain relief and small arms fire. He took a Sig Sauer MCX Rattler, billed as the world's most compact rifle, into the "Y" to get their attention.

"Gentlemen, your credit applications have been denied," he politely addressed them with the Sig Sauer visible from his unbuttoned coat. "Given your life expectancy on this shit, you're not Triple-A risks."

As he took the gun from his coat, he slipped on some poolside water and sprayed ten rounds into the seventy-five-year-old stained-glass ceiling above the natatorium. The shards rained into the pool with a staccato that was almost melodic. His three delinquent customers sustained minor cuts. One even needed a band-aid.

While this was going on a rookie at a craft brewery on the other side of town had improperly mixed the ingredients on the latest batch of Sourdough IPA. "A bit on the yeasty side" was the owner's explanation after the explosion took out two stainless tanks, the men's room and a food truck parked outside. Five people were injured.

"We've got our fucking hands full!" the desk Sarge said before Derk's line went dead.

Derk poured a glass of orange juice and went to the patio to read the newspaper. *Pet Store Bandit Strikes Again* was the headline. It was the fifth time this year someone had broken into a pet store and freed all the animals. Nothing was taken. This was the downside of living in Florida: the total fucking insanity that thrived in this otherwise sub-tropical paradise.

The news was so grim he decided to forego his morning ritual. After putting a load of clothes into the washing machine, he hopped on his bicycle for a ride he hoped would help dim the distractions. He got halfway to Reddington Beach before turning back due to the pain in his knee. Upon returning, I saw no message from Ivan. He was still entertaining the invitation to enter the nine-ball tournament, so he showered and walked to The Top End for lunch and to work on his game. The Top End's restaurant attracted investment bankers, dentists, boat owners, and others who made Pass-a-grille their first or second homes. The bar also attracted the bearded, tattooed bikers who drank long necks straight from the bottle. It attracted Derk because it had the best pool tables in the area. He put four quarters on the rail of a pool table and took a seat with his back to the bar. Connie's absence suggested she was either ill or it was her day off. He unrumpled the same crossword puzzle he had been working on for two weeks. He was about to ask the bartender for a pen when a fellow, two stools to his right offered him one he took from his pocket. He looked familiar, but Derk couldn't recall his name.

"Thanks," Derk said and held out the puzzle. "I need a four-letter word for insensible."

"Inert," the man said, and each of them shook their heads.

"I see you bring your own stick?" he said, pointing to Derk's pool case. "It's straighter than the bar-issued variety," Derk said, and seven hundred bucks more, but he kept that to himself.

"I've seen you here before. You've got a good game," said the man who loaned him the pen.

"Thanks," Derk said as he tried to get the bartender's attention.

"Name's Chad. Can I buy you a beer?" He held out his hand.

"Sure," Derk said with a meager fist bump. "Derk, Derk Bryan."

"I'll have a Paulaner," Derk said as the barkeep returned with a pen.

"German wheat beer made from a four-hundred-year-old recipe," said Chad. "Has your cue stick been chosen with the same attention to detail?" Chad seemed to be fixated on Derk's cue stick.

Derk slid the stick from its leather case and set the two black lacquered pieces on the bar top.

"May I?" Chad said. After he screwed the pieces together, he rolled the black lacquered wood in his hands and cited down the shaft. "Sweet," Chad said and returned it to Derk. "What makes it so different?"

"You can buy a pool stick for fifty bucks," Derk said. "And if you've got a fifty-dollar game, that's all you'll need. This is a Meucci Hall of Fame. Eight hundred dollars. Straighter than Pinocchio's dick and better balanced than the tires on your Beemer."

"I see. Do you have a profession beyond pool?" asked Chad.

Chad was a graying, semi-fit man in his early sixties. The faded, red cargo shorts didn't match his Ralph Lauren well starched, long sleeve shirt, but the new Sperry Topsiders and the well-chosen adjectives suggested wealth.

"Investigations," Derk said and left it at that.

"It pays well, I gather," Chad said.

"Enough for a home on the beach and a Meucci." Derk raised his glass for a toast. "That and a good weather report is almost enough, don't you agree?"

Chad volunteered as a retired commodities broker from Chicago. He had made a fortune when ethanol was mandated for use in gasoline.

"I'm in cannabis now," Chad announced with the glee of a kid who had gotten a bicycle for Christmas. Two cannabis IPOs had netted him enough to buy a four-bedroom condo in Pass-a-grille, complete with a pool, two-car garage, generator, and hurricane shutters. "The place is like a vault," he said.

"Let's hope so. There's some angry Greeks heading our way," said Derk.

With the pen, he filled in a five-letter word for lethal: *toxic*. The image of Gorton's van bobbing in the shallows of Lake Manatee popped up. He doused it with a lengthy swig of his import.

Chad had been testing a flight of mini-drafts in four-ounce glasses. "I ride, too," Chad said.

"What do you mean?" Derk said. He glanced at the pool table where he left the quarters to see if it was his turn.

"Motorcycles. I've been to all the big rallies. Daytona, Sturgis," Chad was listing them when the bartender, Hamel, asked for Derk's order.

Chad pulled a picture from his wallet. He was seated upon a classic Harley with a five-grand paint job. In the photo, Chad looked like the cover of an Edgar Winter album. His white hair almost brushed the waist of his red leather pants. The matching vest was adorned with patches from the big-name biker rallies. Up close, he resembled an aging rocker, tanned and weathered, but the tattoo on his arm looked fresh.

"No question about it. You ride," said Derk.

A couple of beers and two games later, they were debating whether it was possible to stop a Shovelhead from leaking oil. Derk was about to tell Chad about a mechanic who claimed he could do that when a forty-something dirty blonde with dimples and a broad forehead approached the bar with a cue stick.

She said in what seemed to be a Ukrainian accent, "I couldn't help but hear your conversation and my specialty implants."

Derk wasn't sure why she straightened her back as she said it, but it elicited everyone's attention. Hers were, indeed, perky.

The blonde said, "Every woman knows those old jelly models are prone to leakage."

"So, I've been told," said Derk with a smile as he settled back against the bar, the cue stick straddled between his legs.

Chad was speechless.

"I traded those in the same day the new ones came out." She did a one-eighty for them.

"Wise decision," Derk said. He tried not to stare, but she had asked for his opinion.

Chad was drooling.

"The other ones were like some men I've known," she said, looking at the broker from Chicago who was twenty years her senior. "Can't get to the john at night without dripping on the carpet."

Derk almost spit out his beer. The broker didn't laugh.

She turned to Derk and said, "And that's what those Shovelheads did. They dripped. They didn't leak. They had breathers that sweated when they became saturated."

As she inhaled, her breasts rose as if they were on a ski lift. Her wink was confident, not smug.

"And you know this how?" the commodities broker mumbled.

She faced him. "My Daddy rode nothing but Harleys, and he worked on his own bike."

"What do you ride?" the broker said.

"I'm sure you would like to know!" she answered the broker's question, but she was looking at Derk.

Derk pointed at her cue stick and said, "Do you know as much about pool as you do about bikes?"

"I know the difference between a cue ball and an oddball."

"I'll bet you do," Derk said.

The sound of a cue ball being struck dead center filled the room as if it had been orchestrated. The break of the nine balls ensued and was followed by the sound of balls being hugged by the pockets before nesting into cocoons of leather below the table. Derk liked to go to the Top End, sit at the bar, and wait for that sound. When he heard it repeated at the same table, he would get off his barstool, mosey over, and put his coins on the rail of that pool table. Then, he would wait his turn to play against the guy who created that sound. He always wanted to test his game against the best player in the room.

His attention was diverted for only a reflexive glance. The Ukrainian gal had him in her sights, and he was curious about where she wanted to take him.

The broker made his play. "May we buy you a drink?"

Her response was instant. "I never let a man buy me a drink until I've slept with him, at least twice," she said, waving away his offer with a seductive grin. She peered at Derk as if she were reading his thoughts, but she said nothing.

In response to the question mark on the broker's face, she added, "By then, I know whether his offer is purely seductive or true charity." She held his attention for an awkward moment.

Derk tried to hold back a laugh while the broker tried not to trip over his words again. "I didn't; I mean, I wasn't trying to . . ." Chad said.

"Seduce me?" she said. "Why not? I'm hot!" She put one end of the cue stick on the floor and pirouetted around it a second time.

She laid a ten on the countertop when her drink arrived and took a swig straight from the bottle.

"Baltika?" Derk said. Baltika was a Russian beer with different colored labels, each with its own number. Derk preferred four and six.

"Number four," she said.

He stepped off his barstool and took her by one arm. "We need to talk."

The broker whispered, "Good luck."

His goal was an open table at the back of the room, but she stopped him at a table where a man and a woman were wrapping up a game of Eight Ball.

"I've got the next game here," she said and pointed to four newly minted quarters on the rail of the table. They were so bright and shiny a prism of colors reflected in them from the Tiffany lamps illuminating the tables.

Her accent was Russian, as was her beer, and Derk had five grand invested in a guy with a common Russian name. He had a million questions, but he started with, "Do you know a guy named Ivan?" and immediately felt ridiculous for saying it.

That's like asking if she knew someone named Smith. It drew a not unexpected frown. *What a dimwit* she must be thinking. Was he losing his edge? He had fronted an enigma to find a phantom and now he couldn't even charm a woman who had the hots for him.

The previous players finished their game. Derk took her quarters from the rail and replaced them with four of his own. Then he put her money back onto the table. They were either bleached clean or had come straight from the mint. He stood behind the table with his head clamped between his hands.

"Eight ball?" Derk said after racking the balls.

"Okay," she said just before a kaleidoscope of color ricocheted from rail to rail. Balls disappeared into three pockets.

Backpedaling, Derk said, "Who are you?"

She said nothing until she dropped the last ball into the side pocket off the opposing rail. It was a shot that amateurs seldom attempted and rarely made. She put one end of the cue stick on the floor, held the other between her hands, and rolled it. She was giddy. Derk couldn't tell if she was a joyful savant or a gifted shark.

"Who the hell is Ivan?" she said when she looked up.

He couldn't believe the next thing he said, "I paid a guy named Ivan $5000 to find someone."

With the cue stick in one hand, she held out the other hand, palms up as if to say, "So?"

"I've never seen or met him," he said.

She shrugged, but it was a familiar gesture, not unlike something his mother used to do. Derk surprised his mother often, and sometimes he disappointed her, but she was never judgmental. Her smile would melt away any guilt he may have harbored. This bawdy bundle of paradoxes had the same smile. A soft tan line peaked from above her latest product models as she prepared for the next shot. Passing the next table, a server almost tripped over the tongues of two guys in Jos. A Bank suit is watching nearby.

Only two balls went into pockets on her next break, but she didn't miss a shot until halfway through the second game. An audience had grown, and the bar had become quiet. It was Derk's turn.

He felt like the second-string quarterback who'd been thrust into the game having to make a perfect throw on his first play. His shot kissed one of her balls and rolled into a side pocket. Instant scratch. "Spectacular," he lip-synced.

Before her turn, she rubbed her fingers together and said, "It must be somebody important."

Shine, the name he had already attached to her due to the freshly milled coins she used to stake her turn at the table, ran the table. She rammed the eight ball into the corner pocket on a full-length bank shot to declare victory.

"Who did you say you are?" He whispered again to her across the table. She responded with a sultry wink. "I've never been this lucky."

"Right!" he said, fumbling for pocket change.

Three other guys had already placed their quarters on the table before Derk placed four dingy coins onto the rail. She nodded yes to Derk's offer and no to the other guys. They shuffled away, disappointment shadowing their faces.

"For a guy with his own stick, I thought you'd be better at this," she said.

"Me, too," Derk said.

"Ever play Nine-ball?" she said. "I know the game."

"Five dollars a ball?" she said, raising her eyebrows.

He should have seen it coming. If you know your opponent is, at least, as good as you, you can't say you were hustled. But that's exactly what she had done. After five games, she was up fifty dollars, but true to her word, she bought her own beer. She was the best female player, hell, the best Nine-baller he'd seen at the Top End in a long time. Between games, they sampled a generous portion of the craft beer menu while he told her about the death of his mother, the search for his father, and the spook who went only by the name of Ivan. He stopped several times to apologize for his introduction. Later, they couldn't stop laughing when she mimicked him: "Do you know a guy named Ivan?" It sounded even funnier in her Ukraine accent. For the first time in months, he was relaxed. He had completely forgotten about Sandy Gorton.

She didn't reveal much of herself, but he found that she learned to play pool while at a girl's academy. Actually, it was at the men's school across the street from her school. She had come to the United States when her father was recruited to work as an engineer for an oil company. She tried to hide a smirk when she said it. She was leaning across the table, which exposed her assets, top and bottom.

Asked about her current line of work, she puffed up her perky bust again. "These replaced the first set my husband got me after we had dated for two weeks. A bigger is better kind of guy. He said *you can't sell Cadillacs driving a Yugo.*"

Derk searched the room for a sign of a man or a husband.

"No hubby here," she said. "I'm here on a cruise while recuperating." "Sorry to hear that," Derk said as he quickly surveyed her, top to

bottom, expecting an explanation involving major surgery.

"Nothing like that. A major fucking dump-on is what it was. All he left was a note on the kitchen table with the deed to the house and the title to the car. It said I am moving to Sweden to marry Sven."

Then she sliced the cue ball over the rail onto the next table. "Holy shit!" he said. "I gather you didn't see that coming."

She held her breath, steepled her hands, and waited for the guys on the next table to say something. Her glare muted them. One of the guys handed the rogue cue ball to Derk.

"I should have. The last time I walked into the kitchen, au-natural and freshly trimmed, he glanced up from the wok and said I think it needs a pinch of ginger."

Derk laughed, then said, "I'm sorry."

"Me too. He was a stud," she said, "until he went AC/DC on me. Men liked him as much as women."

She pulled a plastic card from her shorts. "This trip's on Benjamin.

Buy you a beer?"

"Hell, yes, if it's on Bennie!" He held up his beer glass and finished it off.

She grabbed him by the belt buckle and pulled him close to her. The cue stick, the only thing separating them, rolled between their bodies. She looked into his eyes, feigned a kiss, and flicked her head to one side. Her hair smelled like the mist of a mountain waterfall as it sashayed across him. A bonfire ignited within him.

The television weather report broke the tension. Three hurricanes were being tracked.

"Are you in harm's way?" Derk asked.

"I don't think so." She shook her head.

"If not, would you like to join me for dinner at my place? It's just up the street. It features a fine selection of craft brews, a not too shabby view and is almost impervious to cyclonic activity," Professor Bryan said.

She moved close enough that he could feel her breath. Her breasts almost brushed against him as she waved the credit card again. "Why don't you join us at the Don Caesar?"

"It's on Benjamin?" Derk said.

"Uh-huh. The main dining room at eight," she said. "Hey, Shine, what's with the new quarters?"

"A girl's got to have some secrets," she said.

"By the way, Shine, my name's Derk, Derk Bryan."

"I know," she said. "The guy behind the counter said Derk when I asked him who is the best pool player in the bar."

She was playing him like a Gibson guitar. He wrote his cell number on his card and gave it to her. She wrote her room number on the same card and gave it back to him.

"Make it seven," she said.

He kissed her on the cheek and whispered into her ear, "Thank you," and, as he backed away, he said, "Benjamin."

***

When Derk returned to his condo, listing but buoyed by the anticipation of an evening with the Ukrainian pool shark, there was a message from Emma Young on his answering machine.

Emma was a former lover and occasionally his spiritual advisor. He had known her for years, and she had been a good friend during his wife's extended illness. She had a unique ability to bring clarity and calmness to him when he was out of balance.

She was also a bevy of dichotomies, fastidious to a fault, and, until tonight, she was the least predictable woman he had ever met. Fit for any age, and remarkably so for a woman in her sixties, she was prissy. Although not classically beautiful, she exuded sensuality. She seemed centered but easily unnerved. She was passionate yet cautious, and she was one of the most sincere and gentle people he had ever known. Since the divorce from her drill sergeant husband, she had gone

41

through more changes than a New York fashion model. A call from Emma Young was sure to be accompanied by drama.

"Hi, Derk, it's Emma. I hope you haven't forgotten me. I know we haven't talked in a while, but with both jobs I seldom have time. I hope you're doing okay. You really deserve to be happy."

Her voice was as sweet as banana pudding and a deflection from what he knew was coming.

"Anyway, I called because," she paused and then continued, "Well, you won't believe what happened to me. I, well, I think I might be in trouble, and," she paused again. "I thought you might be able to help. Don't drop everything, but it's really important." She left her number along with the best times to call and then added, "It will be good to see you again."

The message left little doubt that another chapter in Emma's soap opera had begun. He knew her number, but he wrote it down on a pad next to the telephone and hit the sack for a nap before his dinner date. His head had barely dented the pillow when the telephone rang.

"Hello," Derk whispered.

"Vwee Rooskie!" A deep male voice proclaimed, accompanied by a hearty laugh.

"Wrong number, pal!" Derk said.

"Derek Bryan?" The accent was Eastern European. "Who is this?"

"You Russian, Derek Bryan," declared the drunken man, followed by an even bawdier laugh.

Derk sat up in bed. "Ivan?" "Da," he said.

"It's Derk, not Derek, and speak English," Derk said.

"Did you hear what I said?" This time in mid-western English.

"You found my father?"

"I can't talk long," Ivan said.

"Did you find my father?"

"Breath deep, comrade," Ivan said, returning to the Russian accent.

There were also Russian voices in the background. "Are you in Russia?"

"Red Square, Times Square! What does it matter?" Ivan said. "You always like this?" The dialect was Long Island this time.

"I paid you five grand for this," Derk said. "Did you find my father?"

"Maybe," the caller said. Derk heard something being announced over an intercom as if Ivan was in a bus terminal or an airport. "I need you to do something."

"I'm paying you to do this," said Derk.

"I need you to find out everything you can about Ike Dennis' father."

"His father?" Derk said. "What about Ike Dennis? Is he my father?"

"Too early to tell, but his name is Ileay Denisovich. I'll call you in a couple of days."

"Wait." Derk fumbled for pen and paper. "How do you spell Ileay Denis …?" he said and realized the caller had hung up.

<h1 style="text-align:center">5</h1>

Upon awakening, Derk had forgotten the calls from his spiritual advisor and the drunken secret agent with multiple personalities. Those calls seemed irrelevant compared with the gorgeous maven lying next to him. He put an arm around her, which summoned a twitch and a slight moan. It was followed by instant arousal and glowing confidence. Three days ago, his doctor told him the recurring scrotal tenderness was probably due to years of long-distance bicycling. The realization that it hadn't been a factor all night encouraged a full state of readiness. She rolled over and into his waiting arms.

Last night, she met him at the door with two glasses of 2006 Dom Perignon, which were followed by an Antinori Tignanello Super Tuscan Chianti. The drinks alone, he calculated, set Benny back at least five hundred dollars.

Shine held up her glass and declared, "This will speed my recovery." Then she wiggled out of the only item she was wearing, a silky tropical sarong, which fell to the carpet of her suit like soft light.

He swept her into his arms and did what a gentleman never divulges. Benjamin paid for the room, the drinks, the dinner, and everything else, including her artificially enhanced Double Ds. As a result, he hadn't slept more than four hours all night, well below the needs of someone approaching Medicare eligibility. But he was ready to go again.

After some heavy caressing, Shine slowly slid free from his embrace and went to the bathroom. He heard the sound of the shower. A few minutes later, she returned, her body damp like morning dew on a fresh papaya. She wore only a Don Cesar towel, which was wrapped around her hair.

She snuggled beneath the sheets with him. "Oooee, you are happy to see me. Good morning."

He coaxed the towel from her hair and swallowed her in his arms. As he was about to enter her, she stopped and sat up in bed.

"I've got to catch a boat. The captain said we have to leave early to avoid the hurricanes."

She was on a cruise to St. Thomas and St. Kitts, also compliments of Benny.

He winced. His grip loosened, but the rest of his body was unconvinced. "Whoa, girl, you've got to work on your timing."

"Sorry, I'll do that." "We'll do this again?"

"When everything blows over," she said.

She straddled him while getting off the bed. Her hair smelled like fresh rain as it cascaded onto his face.

She leaned down and kissed him between the legs. "Can you keep it chalked 'til then?"

***

Back at the ranch, he took a glass of orange juice and the morning newspaper to the patio. Great sex had apparently removed all signs of ageing from his oft-swollen joints. However, the super-heated Gulf breeze chased him back inside.

He had left his mother's high school yearbook on the kitchen table. He opened it to the photograph of Ike Dennis. There was no caption under his picture that revealed, "Ike Dennis: Russian father of Derk Bryan," so he held the yearbook picture next to his face again. In the wall mirror, the similarities were startling.

He threw the book onto the couch and went back to the patio. The breeze from the Southeast hit him like a blast furnace. Again, he returned to the air conditioning.

He took the newspaper to the kitchen for some juice. He stopped short when he realized he had left his glass in the living room. He did an abrupt one-eighty and then remembered that he left his cell phone in the kitchen. He stopped, stood upright with his hands behind his head, and took a deep breath. He was confused, bothered, indecisive, and six other things he hadn't felt since the first time he made love with Jenny, his deceased wife. He took a minute to inhale the afterglow. He could still feel Shine next to him.

He plopped down on the couch in the living room, where he could put his feet up. She was on his mind and in the air. He relaxed and breathed in and out with longer and longer exhalations until he dosed off. His dream focused on a single picture. In an array of family photographs displayed throughout his condo, only one drew his focus. It was the one of Charlie with his mother and him together. Each of them seemed cheerful. He didn't know he was dreaming, so he tried to detach himself from the photo to dull his emotions so he could ask himself, "Are these people really happy?" He woke with the memory of his smiling mother. His mother adored Charlie Bryan as if he were part of her body. For the most part, Charlie was there for each of them. He had to admit that Charles Bryan had been a good father, and the picture of his mother with Ike Dennis didn't mesh with his recollections. People have look-a-likes.

Why should he care so much about someone he never met and never knew? He tried to dismiss the Russian connection. It didn't mesh with his view of history. Cold War travel restrictions would have made it difficult to get to the States from Russia. And if he had made it to the States, the language and cultural barriers between them, would have been great. It made no sense that his mother would have connected with this young man unless she picked him because she could not connect with him in any other way than sex. What stirs up more jealousy than sex? With five- grand in hand, Ivan had little incentive to do squat other than make a few phone calls. Each attempt, however, to convince himself that the call from Ivan was a ruse ran smack dab up against two things he knew for sure. He trusted the friend who had referred him to Ivan, and the high school photos of Ike Dennis and him were almost interchangeable.

He stripped in the bathroom and dallied in the shower while he inhaled the remnants of Shine that lingered on his body. After dressing, he recovered the notepad on which he had scribbled the name Ileay Denisovich. He returned to the patio and rested his elbows on the wrought iron balustrade. A middle-aged couple with their cuffs rolled up strolled the beach, hand in hand, as they looked for shells. They held their hats against the wind. Did they know about the approaching hurricanes? For some reason, he imagined they knew, but they were immune from danger because they had each other. At one point, he had felt that way. He and Jenny were inseparable. Damn the cancer!

The overhead fans were on high, but it only made the air more intolerable. He slipped back into the air conditioning and dropped onto the couch again, clutching Ileay Denisovich's name in his palm. It was all he had. He opened the high school yearbook again to the picture of Ike Dennis. "Who the hell are you?"

He resisted the urge to call Shine to bade her Bon Voyage. He wanted to hear her voice. He needed to know if it conformed with the voice in his head. A tingle from last night's passion reminded him of a clue in the crossword puzzle he had been doing. He needed a six-letter word for aphrodisiac. He wrote down *desire* on the pad below the name of Ileay Denisovich. He needed to get on with his day.

It was too early to call Emma Young so he donned cycling gear for a ride up the beach. By the time he reached the bridge at Sand Key he was near lactic acid overload. To his surprise his knee barely ached. He emptied the remainder of the two large water bottles and cruised home.

After another shower, he called the coroner's office. As expected, the results of the Gorton autopsy wouldn't be available until the next day.

He then called his office to update the director, Ben Waitley, and entreat him to use his influence to speed up the reports. There was nothing else he could do on the Gorton case without them.

He "Googled" Ileay Denisovich. What came up was a multitude of references to a book that Alexander Solzhenitsyn wrote in 1962. It chronicled a dismal day in the life of a Soviet-era labor camp prisoner named Ivan Denisovich Shukhov. The book was entitled <u>One Day in the</u> <u>Life of Ivan Denisovich</u>. What the hell was Ivan trying to tell him?

A previous Internet search for Ike Dennis turned up hundreds of names. He had already spent a month trying to narrow the search for people about the age of his mother and Ike Dennis. He tracked down a guy in a Seattle nursing home and another in Port Arthur, Texas but they were not connected to his mother or his family. He logged off and called Agnes Wiley. Once again, he listened to her answering machine and wondered why he waited to leave a message. This time he said nothing.

It was almost eleven and a civil time to contact Emma Young. He arched his back, sucked in half the air in his condo, and prepared himself.

"Oh, hi, Derk," she said. "I'm just walking out the door. Can you call me later?"

"Want to have lunch?" Derk said.

"Sure," she said, and her sigh was palpable, "but I have to be at work at three."

"No problem. Your place at one?" he said.

"You're sure it's okay? Her tone was fastidious. He never got used to that.

"Of course."

"Thank you, Derk." He was about to disconnect when she said, "Did you hear what happened to me?"

"I thought you had to go," he said.

"They might take my house," she said, followed by a giggle, a trademarked habit.

"Who might take your house?" Derk asked. "I'm sorry. How are you, Derk?"

"What are you talking about? Who's going to take your house?" Derk said.

"I need to talk with you, but I really do have to go. I'll see you at one.

Okay?" she said and waited for him to concur.

What was appealing about Emma was also annoying. Her voice was soft and replete with the neediness of a damsel in distress. Clearly, men found this behavior alluring because she never lacked suitors. Prior to her divorce, her life had been insulated, although she spoke five languages acquired from living in various countries as a result of her husband's military life. Not anymore. Derk met her at his fitness center. They had been strangers until she asked him for a date while he was churning gears on an exercise bike. Their romantic fuse burned quickly, and since then, she had gotten involved with seedy businessmen, dishonest employers, and paternalistic caretakers. He knew this because the interstices between her calming philosophical counsels were filled with details of her latest risqué adventure. They had remained friends because she was a practitioner of The Course on Miracles and was willing to act as a sort of spiritual advisor to him. She did have a gift that was unique, and she was also the kind of woman that, if you were with her, caused other women to take an interest in you.

"I'll be there," he said.

***

Emma Young lived across the bay in Tampa. Derk would have stopped to pick up a bottle of wine, but Emma was a teetotaler. In fact, as long as he had known her, she was a total vegetarian. That may have led to one of her jobs as an assistant manager of a health food store. A head of lettuce and some alfalfa sprouts didn't seem appropriate, so he went bare-handed. "Hi, Derk," she said, standing in the doorway of her condo. She was wearing a vitamin complexion and a troubled smile.

"It's nice to see you, Emma," he said, and they hugged. Her implants dented his chest, but he never complained. A trophy wife, her ex-husband had demanded them shortly after she married him. He hoped to avoid her self-deprecating small talk, so he delved into the subject at hand. "What's this thing about your house?"

"Oh, Derk," she said. The air rushed from her like a flat tire. "Come in. Would you like a cup of tea?"

A cold beer is what he wanted but he accepted her offer.

"I really appreciate you coming," she said and took him by the hand into the kitchen. "I'm making us lunch."

The image of sprouts and humus didn't excite him, but he forced a smile and offered an option. "You didn't have to. I was going to take you out."

"How have you been?" she said, ignoring his offer and diverting attention away from herself.

"I was retired, but as soon as I decided to take time off, some guy drove a truck full of weed killers into Lake Manatee," he said.

"I heard about that. Somebody died?" she said. Her shoulders stiffened, and she raised one hand in front of her as if to defend herself from his confirmation.

He nodded.

She exhaled and changed the subject and the tone of her voice. "Well, I'm making kasha. You do like kasha, don't you?"

He didn't have a clue if he liked kasha. Before he answered, she turned from him and reached into the cupboard. When she turned around, with a teacup in each hand, Derk squeezed her gently against the counter and held her shoulders. She froze like a doe in a spotlight.

"Derk, what are you doing?" she said.

"Talk to me, Emma. What's going on?" he said. The teapot whistled.

"Oh no!" she said and shook loose of his grip. "The tea!"

She slid the teapot onto a trivet. Another gush of steam rose from a pan on the stove. She removed the lid and stirred in something grainy like oatmeal. Then she shifted it onto a dead burner. She put the teapot onto a silver serving tray and dropped a tea ball into it. The aroma of raspberries and mint wafted from the pot. He also sensed a hint of lemon. After adding the cups, saucers, and honey they went into her living room and sat on the couch.

"You do believe that everything happens for a reason, don't you, Derk?"

This was Emma's way of answering a troubling question. He pursed his lips and awaited further illumination.

"Well, you know, I've taken this Course on Miracles. I mean I'm still in it," she lowered her voice as she talked. "It says that we often believe what our eyes cannot see does not exist. What this means is that fear is born of the belief that darkness can hide. But it can't hide, Derk. There are no coincidences. Everything happens for a reason. I believe this, but sometimes it is difficult to see the good in things. Don't you agree?"

It was one of those times when he needed to recognize patience as the virtue it is. He pinched his chin and tilted his head to one side. She must have assumed this gesture was one of concurrence.

"So," she continued, "the police want to take my house, and I know it's just a thing, but I don't think it's fair. I mean . . ."

He interrupted her, "You didn't default on your loan, did you?"

She shook her head. "No. Nothing like that, dear."

"Then what happened?" he said.

"They found pot in my house," she whispered, which was followed by a nervous giggle.

"Marijuana! They found marijuana in *your* house?"

This time the small furrows in her forehead confiscated most of her smile.

"When? How can that be?"

"A couple of months ago. I didn't know they were there. Curt was growing them," she said.

"How are they going to take your house? How much was there?" he asked.

"They haven't actually said they're going to do that, but I guess they can. Did you know that?" she said.

"I used to live in Michigan, and there was this old, red-shingled building onto which someone had sprayed paint in large, white script letters; *Society is a carnivorous flower*. It was such a prophetic statement no one would take it down. One day, the cops raided the building, found a pot, and confiscated the property. It had been a former neighborhood grocery store converted into a residence by the people who were renting it from an elderly couple. The old folks counted upon the rent to pay for their retirement. The cops bulldozed it to the ground. So, yes, they can," Derk said. "What happened to Curt?"

"They arrested him, well, both of us. We're going to trial," she said. Her voice was gentle but affected. "They took us to jail, got our fingerprints, and took our pictures. It was kind of awful. The handcuffs hurt my wrists," she said, turning her palms up and massaging her wrists. "I've never been in jail, Derk."

"Did you get a lawyer?" he said.

The guilty smile prefaced her answer. "You know the attorney I used to date?"

"Yea, the one who drank too much and always wanted to get into your pants."

"Derk!" she scowled.

"Aaron Kelly, wasn't it?" he said.

"He still likes me and he said he would help," she said, "and you and I are not a thing anymore."

"But Aaron Kelly?" Derk winced.

"I don't even think he's going to charge me," she said in a hushed voice. Then in a normal tone, she added, "But, I can't let him do that. Can I? I've got to pay him something. I don't want him to think, well, you know what I mean."

"Exact-o-mundo!" Derk said.

"Men just seem to think I'm helpless or something, and they want to rescue me," she said, "even though most of them just want to mess around." The nervous giggle returned. "But I do need him."

Derk slid over next to her and put his arms around her. "So do I," he said.

"What? You think I'm helpless?" She tried to pry loose from his arms.

"No, Silly. I think you're beautiful," Derk said and squeezed her against him.

When he released her, she slid back, curled up on the couch, and gave him an 'I'm not sure about you, Derk' look.

"Relax, Emma. You're among friends," he said and held out his hand.

She took it gingerly.

"Aaron said some guy named Perkins, who heads up the anti-drug task force is taking peoples' homes and cars," she said, her voice tinted with fear. She squeezed his hand. "I don't know where I'd get the money to pay him." Derk clasped her hands in his as she continued. "I can't ask my folks for it. I still haven't told them. Do you think that's wrong?"

He knew she didn't really want his advice. Emma's mood changes were as frequent as the costumes in a big city musical. She seemed to enjoy creating that innocent neediness that attracted men to her as if it were sex in a bottle.

He hated clichés but went with a pat hand. "Honesty is usually the best policy."

She turned her head and squinted. The tiniest of tracks, like the tide trickling back to the sea on the beach sand, tattled her true age. "You're right. Let's eat," she said, got up, and went to the kitchen, carrying her teacup.

During lunch, she told him that her son had been growing marijuana plants on the patio. She was having a difficult time blaming him. Curt was twenty-three, had worked his way into medical school, and was mature enough to decide for himself. She didn't smoke pot, but she said she couldn't make that decision for others.

"I thought marijuana was legal in Florida," she said.

"Only for medical purposes," he said.

"Well, if kids smoke pot, it's better than drinking and driving. Isn't it?" she said. "Besides, it has all sorts of health benefits."

She started to tell the story about a customer who claimed that CBD oil calmed him during his chemotherapy treatments, but Derk interrupted her.

"How did the cops find out about the plants?" Derk asked.

"Some guy working on the neighbor's air conditioning system saw them and called the police," Emma said. "Boy was Sheila livid. She's my neighbor. She told me to file a suit against that man and his company for invasion of privacy. For being a peeking-tom. What do you think? Can I do that?"

"That's a call for Aaron," he said.

"Curt could lose his student loans, and he'd have to drop out of college.

I can't let that happen to him," she said. "What should I do?"

Derk knew that the forfeiture laws that had been enacted to fight the war on drugs, but the government didn't know what he knew. Emma Young didn't smoke anything. She was a total health fanatic. He was as empathetic as he could be.

"I don't know how a compassionate government can take someone's home over a few pot plants. You need a really good lawyer," he said.

"It's bad, isn't it?" she said. She rose slowly and began clearing the kitchen table.

"Sounds like it," he said. "You have to be at work at three?" he said glancing at his watch. It was half past two.

"I'm supposed to, but a few minutes won't make much of a difference," she said after drying the table with a dish-rag. Then she sat down across from him, lowered her voice and said, "Do you know what I do, Derk?"

"Some modeling and you work at the health food store," he said.

"The modeling got too slow and the store wouldn't give me enough hours, so I had to take another job," she said and waited for him to ask. "Okay, what do you do?"

This time the giggle in her voice was devilish. "I dub in the women's voices on the Porn sites."

"No way!"

"I got the job because I can do it in several languages. I'm good at it and it pays well," she said, trying to hide a guilty smirk.

The irony of this new chapter in Emma's life caused him to laugh out loud. He couldn't imagine this seemingly shy and innocent creature with such a soothing voice moaning and groaning on cue for taped sex scenes. "You get rated for authenticity, and I'm better than most of the girls who have been there much longer," she said with a note of pride. "So what's your secret?" he said through a laugh.

She giggled again. "I don't know. They like my voice, I guess."

He couldn't help but ask for details. "Is it live? Are you there when ….?" he couldn't finish his question.

"Oh no. I don't think I could do that," she said. I have to watch the tapes and then add the sound."

She lowered her voice. "You know, when they get off. That's the hardest part. They say I do that better than anyone."

After a moment of silence, the only thing Derk could say was, "I always thought so."

"Oh, Derk. You're bad," she said and gave him a friendly shove. She giggled again, but this time, it was with him.

"Emma, you are amazing," he said, then stood up, pulled her up by her hands and they hugged.

"You think?"

"Yes, I do," he said.

"Thanks for your help," she said. They left a few minutes after three.

"Stay in touch," he said. With a foot out the door, he turned and said, "Do you know a four-letter word for insensible?"

When she looked askance at him, he said, "Never mind," and he left.

6

The crowd gathered at the Top End. The star of the show was a buxomly blonde with a cue stick and an attitude. She floated around the table like a swan: untamed, sophisticated, and droolingly seductive. The men wanted her. The women wanted to be like her.

Puff, like mist evaporating, she disappeared.

Derk flinched. To be sure he wasn't dreaming, he slid his leg across the satin sheets. She wasn't there. Nor were the sheets. He felt only cool leather, followed by confusion and then panic! Then, the sound of music. It came from another room. He was trying to recall the tune, something from the Peer Gynt, he thought when he rolled over and "plopped." He was on the floor, inebriated by the past forty-eight hours. It had been a total rush. He felt stuck to the floor. He laid back and stared at the ceiling.

After a minute or two he noticed, for the first time, a mild discoloration in one corner.

"Roof leak!" he said and jumped to his feet. The "Morning" track from the Peer Gynt Suite was in the background.

"Whew!" he said aloud before noticing he was fully dressed. He ran his hands across his face and through his hair.

He felt like he'd been at a progressive party with free drinks. His last stop was for a beer at the Top End. He needed it after his visit with Emma Young. While there, he got into a game of nine-ball that lasted almost a six-pack. Midway through the fourth St. Pauli Girl, he said, "Fuck it, I need a night off," and well, that's why he headed straight for the bathroom. When he returned, he noticed the red light flashing on his answering machine. He hadn't erased the message from Agnes Wiley. Their conversation had been brief.

"Derk, I really like you," she began. "You're smart, you're funny, and you have more integrity than most of the guys I go out with."

He knew a *but* was coming.

"But my sister married a cop. The hours, the risk, and all that stuff." "What stuff?" he asked.

"She never knew if he was coming home and the silence, the things he couldn't talk about."

"I'm not a cop, Agnes. I work for the EPA," he said, but this wasn't a two-way conversation.

"The undercover operations, too," she continued.

"I think you've got me confused with the CIA," he said.

"So, before we get too involved or anything," she said.

"What's wrong with a little involvement?" He thought.

"I'll probably be happier in the long run with an accountant who has regular hours and doesn't mind running an escort service for aging parents."

At that point, he realized he had lost a potential girlfriend. He hadn't lost his sense of humor.

"Agnes, Agnes," he interrupted her. "I'm surprised at you. A bean-counter? Really. Think higher. You are executive material," he said.

"What do you mean?" she said.

"CEO, Agnes. Go all the way," he said, and before she could muster a retort, he added, "I wish you well, Agnes Wiley. I really do."

After a shower, he poured a glass of orange juice and fetched the morning newspaper. The headline was an attention monger: "KILLER WEED." Below the headline were photographs of two teenagers, Carrie Crimshaw and Delmont Hankins. The newspaper reported that Carrie was the daughter of a State Senator, and the young man was the son of a former local college basketball star and currently the president of the Chamber of Commerce. The teens had apparently died after smoking marijuana at a frat party near the university. This case would confiscate the headlines for days since the Crimshaw girl was white and the Hankins boy was black. The paths of the hurricanes were also on the front page, but there was no mention of the Gorton case or the contamination of Lake Manatee.

The notepad on the table reminded him that he had to call the school for information about Ike Dennis and Ileay Denisovich. He would wait until mid-morning when the kids were in their classes, and the Principal was free. Instead, he dialed the crime lab. They had yet to determine the cause of the accident that killed Sandover Gorton.

"Why not?" he said.

"The Senator's daughter was killed," said an unfamiliar voice.

"Yea, I read that," Derk said.

"How about the cause of death?"

"Bad weed, we think."

"No, I'm talking about the Gorton accident."

"Respiratory failure." Dr. Wesley Morton was now on the line.

"Good morning, Doc," Derk said. "From the pesticides?"

"Nope."

"Alcohol, drugs?" Derk said.

"Nope. And he sustained substantial facial and head injuries, but none of those was the cause of death," said the doctor.

"What was it?" Derk said.

"Water in his lungs," Dr. Morton said.

"Water in his lungs?" Derk said.

"Yes, he drowned. He drove into a lake. Anything else?" The doctor said.

Among the few things that Derk knew about Wesley Morton was that his weekends were dedicated to golf, cigars, and trying to get his over-sexed wife to throw something in his direction. With multiple high-profile cases interfering with his weekend, Derk could accept Morton's crankiness, but the medical examiner's tone was dismissive.

And people don't die from smoking marijuana. The doctor surely knew that.

"Maybe Gorton was going too fast. Maybe he swerved to avoid an armadillo. Maybe it's that simple, but it's in my job to be suspicious," Derk said. "When you find the time, please send me the report."

"As soon as the scanner gets fixed," Dr. Morton said.

"That's one high-tech operation you're running there, Doc," Derk said and put the phone down.

He was used to dealing with medical examiners. He knew their offices were notoriously underfunded. He knew the position didn't require a medical degree, although Wesley Morton had one, and he was aware that the pay was less than half of what a qualified practitioner could make in the private sector. Another thing Derk knew from an old newspaper article was that Wesley Morton lived in an upscale country club community. He assumed that the money came from his wife's side of the family.

Coverage of the cleanup at Lake Manatee was on the first page of the local section. **Spill Damage Serious But Not Lasting** was the headline. The article reported that "The van full of chemicals that Sandover 'Wink' Gorton was driving when it crashed into Lake Manatee and killed him affected more of the lake than we initially suspected, but the impact upon the lake's wildlife will not be lasting. Lake Manatee serves as an interface between fresh water and the ocean and is continually changing. This allows for the rapid dispersion and dilution of the chemicals, which will mitigate the damage," according to Stanley Wormsley, Public Information Officer for the State Department of Wildlife.

Derk despised this sort of spin, but it was a common refrain from the Florida government. The article didn't mention that most of those chemicals would find their way into the tissues of living organisms. As these creatures progressed from algae to shrimp to grouper along the food chain, someone would ultimately eat them, and the seeds of cancer would be planted. Environmental damage was so politically sensitive in Florida that some past governors hadn't allowed any references to global warming or climate change to seep into official State publications. Nothing should be said that might dissuade another thousand people from moving into Florida each day. What had once been a natural paradise had become a real estate developer's paradise. It began with Flagler, and it seemed that his trains could not be stopped.

The accident that caused the spill was in stark contrast to the **Killer Weed** story. The calls for safer packaging for pesticides, improved storage during transportation, stiffer penalties for violations, and stepped-up enforcement fell on deaf ears. Seldom a day passed, and there wasn't news of an environmental mishap where people or wildlife were killed, or their food and water were threatened. On the other hand, U.S. Representative Harv Swanson had already pledged to introduce legislation calling for the death penalty for anyone caught distributing, selling or providing marijuana to someone who dies as a result. The message seemed perpendicular to the popular consensus, given that medical marijuana was already legal in the State along with thirty-eight others. None of this deterred Derk from his job. It just made him angry.

The obituary on Gorton was just as succinct and unsettling:

"Sandover "Wink" Gorton, 53, died in an automobile accident at Lake Manatee on Saturday, a few miles west of his home in Manatee County. He had owned and operated Gorton's Farm and Garden Supply in Hillsborough County for fifteen years. He is survived by his children, Jamie Gorton and Jan "Gorton" Turley."

For a moment, he hoped that Gorton's accident and the contamination of Lake Manatee had been the result of unfortunate circumstances, but Emma Young had once convinced him, "There is no such thing as a coincidence." It was also impossible to ignore the dead bodies. He needed the autopsy report, the accident report, and an analysis of the water samples. He washed down a bran muffin with a cup of Oolong tea and went back do the crossword puzzle. He needed a six-letter word for frenetic.

Hectic, he wrote down, just like his life.

7

The storms lined up in the Atlantic were so threatening that they were given the ominous Greek names Cera, Deimos, and Eris. A strike by any of these tempests would send Samantha's already tangled life into an absolute frenzy.

The previous night, she discovered that her daughter had progressed from writing poetry, replete with suicidal meanderings, to tattooing ghoulish images on her forearms with a mat knife. Samantha spent the next three hours in the E.R. waiting room, part of it debating plastic surgery with one of the staff physicians while the nurses alternated babysitting her daughter. After surgery was ruled out, Jamie was held overnight for observation.

Samantha knew that bipolar kids can overload when faced with multiple tasks, and she regretted her response when her daughter returned from an errand to buy hurricane supplies with only two bottles of water and a large package of trail mix.

"How can a friggin' honor student find only two things on a list of ten? I can't do this all by myself, Jamie. You've got to pull yourself together!"

Dealing ineffectively with over-choice was one of Jamie's special burdens, and the most important attribute of parenting such a child is patience. Samantha had lost it. As a result, she anticipated a call from Child Protective Services, whereupon she would tell them, "If you want to raise a bi-polar child with ADHD and an IQ of 150, be my guest."

She kept reminding herself what Jamie's therapist had told her, "It's only for the rest of your life, but it tends to taper off after the teenage years."

That was only a few years away, but right now, she needed to get through the day. By sunrise, she had left messages with her daughter's therapist and her attorney requesting immediate appointments.

As a result, she entered Judge Evander Okin's courtroom at 8:35 a.m. as tired as a student who just pulled an all-nighter. Her brother-in-law, Sergeant Wilson Perkins, was standing by the witness chair, chatting glibly with the bailiff. He didn't seem at all disturbed about the scourge of events surrounding him. Along with the Sheriff and the entire county, he was being sued for one hundred million dollars in a wrongful death action.

Samantha worried about her brother-in-law because he was her daughter's only uncle and part of her dwindling family. What strained their relationship was the truth he never wanted to hear. Since her husband's death, Will had hardened. He was difficult to suffer, even in small doses, and his method of policing was leaving carnage in its wake. She had tried to tell him in a way that wouldn't separate him from Jamie or her, but it wasn't working. He was not listening to anyone. She didn't know that losing a brother could be as challenging as losing a spouse, and she was worried about losing another piece of her family.

On the way to the courthouse, she made a C-store stop for a large latte with extra caffeine. She held a second cup, acquired after three kicks of the courthouse vending machine, behind her as she put a shoulder into the door of courtroom number twelve. With only thirty seconds of REM sleep last night, it took every one of her one hundred and three pounds to open it without incurring second-degree burns on her arm. She decided right then to double up on the jazzercise classes.

She made a little "come here" gesture when Will noticed her, but he went on talking. She took a seat in the front row, put down her coffee cups and held up a copy of the Times' frontpage story about the **Killer Weed.**

"We have to talk," she mouthed.

As the Judge entered the room, an aging bailiff announced loud enough for everyone in the same zip code to hear, "All rise!"

Will took a seat in front of her at the defense attorney's table. She handed him the napkin that had been wrapped around her coffee cup onto which she had scribbled, "We've got to talk!!!" He crumpled the paper into one hand.

"The 6th District Court is now in session, the Honorable Evander Okin presiding," the bailiff bellowed.

The Judge pointed to the bailiff's ear. As the bailiff adjusted his hearing aid the judge motioned for all to be seated.

Sergeant Wilson Perkins sat upright in his regally adorned police uniform and stared straight ahead. What some may have taken for a display of confidence was arrogance to Samantha. He was a career cop with two ex-wives and teenage kids that seldom talked with him. Still, he considered himself qualified to critique Samantha's parenting skills. She was too tolerant. He was also critical of her for keeping her maiden-name after marrying his brother.

"It suggests a lack of commitment, and it's confusing for children," he once told her. And he kept no secret of his contempt for her magazine. "You glamorize the bizarre, the misfits, and the faggots."

She shivered at his coldness.

Across from her brother-in-law sat Aaron Kelly, the plaintiff's attorney. Next to Kelly was his client, Esther Hixon. Mrs. Hixon was the only member of her family physically able to make the trip to the courthouse subsequent to the police raid that left her husband paralyzed and her son dead. Mr. Kelly was about to make his opening statement.

Prior to the trial Samantha had asked Colleen Reed, her researcher, part-time reporter and full-time cynic, to look into the case against her brother-in-law. She had even interviewed Esther Hixon. It was Colleen's attempt to cheer her up that was also troubling her when she entered the courtroom.

"It doesn't matter that the police manufacture evidence all the time in these cases. It's a victimless crime. What can they do? And they always get away with it. So, you don't have to worry about your brother-in-law," Colleen said.

That was not the kind of information that Samantha found comforting. She felt even worse after Colleen told her, "On the other hand, in Willie and Esther Hixon's neighborhood, one in three black males under the age of thirty-five has been arrested or put in jail, over 50% for illegal drugs. That's far greater than their percentage of the population. It's discrimination of the worst kind, and Aaron Kelly is unlikely to let it pass." Samantha had been reporting long enough to know that any half-witted attorney could soften a jury by putting faces on these statistics.

Esther Hixon was one of those faces, and Aaron Kelly had graduated Magna Cum Laud.

Kelly began, "Willie Hixon was a proud black man. In his neighborhood many of the homes are boarded up or are in ill repair. But just as many are colorfully painted and sport well-manicured lawns. It's an inner-city neighborhood, replete with high unemployment, gangs and other problems. It's exactly the kind of neighborhood in which Willie and Esther Hixon grew up."

He turned and looked at Esther as he spoke. "Esther and Willie met in high school. During those days Willie was a big, tough guy with a rusty-nail attitude. He needed to be that way to survive in that neighborhood. But as you will hear others testify, he had a puppy dog's heart."

Tears welled in Esther's eyes as her attorney extolled her husband's life. "After high school, they got married. Willie worked as a mechanic. He could fix anything. Esther got a job as a beautician. They worked hard. On evenings and weekends, she did hair in the kitchen, and he worked on his friends' cars so they could save enough money to move to the suburbs. Willie wanted to open his own auto repair shop. Willie and Esther Hixon, two kids trying to live the American dream."

The attention of the three women on the jury was riveted upon Esther Hixon. She was in tears.

"They saved enough to move to the suburbs, but Willie thought too many blacks going to the suburbs left a big hole in the city. He convinced Esther to stay put. They fixed up their house and opened their own business. Willie even coached Pop Warner football when his son was old enough to play. Eventually, Willie and Esther Hixon sent their son, Arliss, to college."

Aaron Kelly had been standing behind Esther, but he came around to face her when he mentioned her son by name. He handed his handkerchief to her to dry her eyes.

"*Oh, this guy is good,*" thought Samantha. My brother-in-law is in deep shit.

"If he were alive today, he'd be the only one in their family to have graduated from college," Kelly declared, loud enough that the bailiff snorted and kicked a leg on the table as he awakened.

The judge's sigh was palpable, but he said nothing.

Attorney Kelly concluded, "And we are going to prove that Sergeant Wilson Perkins and his Gestapos …"

"Objection," said the county prosecutor.

"Narco-bullies," responded Aaron Kelly.

"Your honor," the prosecutor objected again.

"Buddies," Kelly said, turning to look at the prosecutor. "Do you mind? This is *my* opening statement."

It went on like this for a while. After Aaron Kelly finished, the defense attorney presented his opening statement, and the judge then asked Aaron Kelly to call his first witness. After a few character witnesses raved about the Hixons' luminescent behavior and their beneficent contributions to the community, the plaintiff's attorney got into the meat of the matter. He called Sergeant Wilson Anthony Perkins to the stand.

"Sergeant Perkins, you're in charge of the multi-jurisdictional task force on drugs?"

The sergeant nodded but said nothing.

"Was that a yes?" said Kelly.

The sergeant turned toward the judge and sneered.

Judge Okin peered at the Sergeant through wire-rimmed glasses. The silent but stern response reminded Samantha of her junior high school principal. Although corporal punishment was illegal, he kept a worn paddle next to his desk for all to view.

"Yes, sir," Sergeant Perkins answered the counselor's question with nothing short of contempt.

Kelly continued, "Sergeant Perkins, what caused you to target the Hixon's house, law-abiding citizens who run their own business?"

Perkins responded loud enough for everyone in the courtroom to hear, "You may think you know Willie Hixon, but you don't. We bust a crack house or pot dealer every month in that neighborhood. The week before our raid, a helicopter with infrared sensors picked up a high amount of heat coming from the Hixon's home, the kind of reading we get from those grow lights used by indoor pot farms."

"And you got a search warrant with *that* information?" Kelly said.

"Their kid was enrolled in a pot class," Perkins said.

Her brother-in-law probably considered his testimony just a statement of facts. Samantha viewed him as smug.

"You're referring to Arliss Hixon and the class he took at the University of Tampa?"

"Yes, sir," the Sergeant replied nicely, then smiled at the judge. Samantha cringed.

"That's Professor Weedleston's class, the *Economics of the Black Markets.*"

"He's not a teacher. He's a drug pusher," Perkins reacted.

The judge cleared his throat as he glared at the officer on the witness stand.

"Excuse me, your honor," said Sergeant Perkins.

"You're aware it's a history class?" Kelly continued.

"The Hixon kid thought pot should be legal. They teach them to grow dope there," said Perkins.

"Hemp, Sergeant," Kelly said. "What's the difference!"

"Arliss Hixon suggested that hemp, a form of cannabis with no hallucinogenic properties, and legal in every State, should be promoted as a source of fiber for all sorts of industrial applications," the attorney elucidated.

Perkins scoffed.

"Sergeant, you were able to get a search warrant and a multi-jurisdictional task force to break down Willie Hixon's door because his son was taking a class on the historical relationships of alcohol, cigarettes, and marijuana to the underground economy and," the attorney paused for emphasis, "their contributions to police corruption?"

"That's absolute bull . . ." Perkins stopped mid-sentence and turned toward the judge. "We knew the kid smoked pot. We had a witness."

"And that gave you the authority to shoot him in the back and crush in his father's chest with the stock of your shotgun?" Kelly said.

Perkins leaned forward, almost off the seat of the witness chair, and said, "I've been protecting this city for twenty years."

"Relax, Sergeant Perkins!" said Judge Okin, a crusty older man with a capricious tuft of white hair that wafted across his pointy head.

Perkins continued, "Against druggies like Arliss Hixon since you were still on your mother's teet."

"Now! Sergeant," the judge said, "and watch your mouth."

Perkins eased back into the witness chair.

"Why didn't you just wait for the kid to come out and arrest him?" The counselor asked.

Perkins exhaled through his teeth but said nothing.

"If they're black and they live in that neighborhood, they're probably selling drugs. Is that your answer, Sergeant?"

"Objection!" said Leroy Barnes, attorney for the sergeant.

"Sergeant Perkins, were you aware that Willie Hixon had gotten the mayor to form a task force to study accusations of police abuse and racial profiling in his neighborhood by you and other officers, as well the lack of police attention to a series of burglaries that had been plaguing black-owned businesses?"

"So what?" said Perkins.

"Isn't that really why you rammed in Willie Hixon's door without announcing yourself? And why you brutally attacked him and his family? You wanted to shut him up."

"Judge!" pleaded the defense attorney, but Sergeant Perkins answered the question.

"Absolutely not! There was no evidence of that." The sergeant inched toward the attorney. Just above a whisper, he said, "Watch where you're going, you little . . ."

"Sergeant!" Judge Okin raised his voice. Perkins slowly relaxed.

"Sergeant, did you ever find any marijuana in the Hixon's home?" Kelly asked.

"No," Perkins mumbled.

"What was that?" said Kelly.

"*No*," he shook his head.

"Loud enough for the jury to hear," said Kelly.

"No," said Sergeant Perkins.

Murmurs filled the courtroom. Samantha felt like a balloon that had just been popped.

Her brother-in-law's testy disposition, however, was now making sense. Reporters are not usually allowed into depositions, but Will Perkins had shared some troubling testimony with her one evening after a conference with his attorney. When he arrived at her home, he went into a tirade over the misinformation and lies that were being propagated by Aaron Kelly and his client.

He told her, "I've been a good cop for twenty years, and I'm outraged that the legal system would allow this assault on the integrity of our efforts. This threatens all the good things we've done, the drug dealers we've taken off the street, and the young lives we've saved."

He rarely shared much of himself, and she was touched by the genuine concern he expressed for the effect of this trial upon the entire police department. It also caused her to consider whether she was too close to the story to remain objective.

"Kelly, that insolent ACLU pimp, is pandering bullshit so deep," he said and his anger swelled the veins in his neck to a visible level. He didn't complete his thought.

"You've been through it before," Samantha said. "This is different."

"How?"

"Fucking bleeding hearts! They don't know the evil they're dealing with," he said. "They paint a pretty picture but it's not real. The kids, the mothers, their neighbors, they'll be the ones that'll suffer, along with a lot of good cops," he said. "I'm tired of this." His head slumped onto her kitchen table, and he ran his hands through his hair.

"I'm sorry," she said and reached across the kitchen table for his arm. He pulled it back and got up to leave.

"It makes it so damn hard for us to do our jobs. We'll just have to get tougher."

A dark foreboding lingered in the air. She folded her arms across her chest.

"Okay, tell me what happened," Samantha said.

She wanted to know what went down during the raid, but he sat down and told her about the deposition.

"He had a lunch line full of people come in and say that Willie Hixon was this gentle, loving man, never prone to violence. What a crock! Willie Hixon was goddamn intimidating. He was six-eight, played tackle in high school, and carried a cane made from tie rod ends he welded together. Never went out without it."

"Really?" she said.

"Yea. He used it for whacking people."

"How do you know that?" she said.

"He had a limp. Said it was from when a car slipped off a jack and broke his leg, but there's no hospital record. He told us a doctor at a neighborhood clinic took care of it, but the clinic closed, and the records conveniently got lost."

"What's that have to do with whacking people?"

"Hixon got his leg broken in a fight over some work he did or did not do on a guy's car. The other guy still needs a wheelchair to get around. Hixon hit him with a piece of metal. He's a goddamn burning fuse."

"You know that for sure?"

"I've got sources."

"More than hearsay?"

"You've been watching too much Law and Order," he said. "We got an anonymous call one time that some big guy with a stick or a piece of iron went to work on LeDevon Carter. Carter was a former employee that Hixon accused of stealing tools. The dicks told him they didn't have the evidence to take the guy in. We found LeDevon in the hospital with a groove across his ribs shaped like a long, round object. LeDevon claimed that he slipped on some oil in his driveway and fell against the tailgate of his pickup. Bullshit! Then Hixon dropped the charges. Said someone must have borrowed the tools without telling him, 'Cuz they just showed up one day outta the blue." Hell, everybody knew what happened. It was Willie's way of saying, "Don't fuck with me."

"What really happened out there, Will?" she asked again.

He sighed, then craned his neck back far enough that she heard the cracking of vertebrae. "Hey, I'm tired. Sorry I bothered you with all this."

"You know the magazine has to cover this," she said.

"Don't worry about it. I'll talk with you later," he said and brushed her shoulder. He opened the door partway, then turned and said, "They can't prove shit and they don't know who they're dealing with."

He never told her what happened that morning at the Hixons' home, and trials don't always lead to the truth or justice. She tried to think like the reporter she was, but it was difficult to remain objective.

Aaron Kelly asked the judge that the witness be excused but that he wanted to recall him later. "At this time, I'd like to call Esther Hixon to the stand."

Esther Hixon was a forty-something, squatty woman with prematurely graying hair. She wore a black suit over a white blouse and sported a grandmotherly demeanor that was disarming.

"Where were you when the police broke into your house?" her lawyer began.

"Objection!" said Leroy Barnes. "Draws a conclusion that's not been proven."

"Sustained," said Judge Okin.

"Mrs. Hixon, where were you when the police entered your home?" Kelly rephrased the question.

"I was in the kitchen making breakfast, and my huz . . . huz . . . huz, Willie was in the bathroom, you know, gettin' ready for, for work."

Sergeant Perkins choked on his Rolaids so loud it interrupted Mrs.

Hixon's testimony.

"Sergeant Perkins, feel free to leave the room if you need to," said Judge Okin.

Samantha Card covered her mouth to keep from laughing. Mrs. Hixon's stutter and difficulty in pronouncing certain words was almost theatrical, and her brother-in-law wasn't going to give her an inch of room if he could help it.

The stutter continued. "He u . . . u . . . usually goes in about eight o'clock on Saturdays. I heard something hit the front door. No voice, no knock, nothing, just a loud crushing noise. So loud it frightened me. I thought maybe a car had gone off the road and hit the house. It happened to Issamae's house. She lives across the street."

Aaron Kelly prodded Mrs. Hixon with an "Uh huh."

"Willie must a heard it, too, 'cuz I heard him running t'ward the door. Then he said, 'Who da-hell are you?' Excuse me, your honor," she said, "but my husband never cusses so I knew it was something bad."

She looked back at the attorney. "Then the shot, that terrible, awful shot." She paused, grief-struck, as her head dipped almost into her lap. "They killed my baby. They killed my baby." She sobbed.

"Your honor, please," pleaded Counselor Barnes while Aaron Kelly handed his handkerchief to his client.

"Would you like a recess, Mrs. Hixon?" asked the judge.

She sat upright. "Thank you, your, your honor, I'm okay," Esther said.

"Mrs. Hixon, your son was a senior honors student majoring in horticulture and economics at the University of Tampa?" Aaron Kelly said.

Mrs. Hixon nodded.

"Please answer the question yes or no," the judge said. "Yes, sir."

"Wasn't it true that your son's arguments for hemp were based upon its agricultural and economic benefits?"

As she dried her eyes, she nodded again. "Excuse me. I guess. I don't know much about that. It was just a class at the college."

"You did know that he was so committed to horticulture that he convinced you and your husband to add a greenhouse to the back of your home," Kelly said.

Esther nodded her acknowledgement. "Oh, yes. Sorry," she added.

"Complete with hydroponic beds and high wattage grow lights?"

This time she answered aloud. "Yes."

"So that he could gain first-hand knowledge in this field? Isn't that correct, Mrs. Hixon?" asked her attorney.

"At first, we were against it, but he was so committed, and he wanted to study plants from all over the world that might help people," she said.

"Did he grow marijuana?" Kelly asked.

"Never anything illegal," she said, waving her head from side to side. "Arliss always wanted to know how things worked, just like his father."

"So, instead of automobiles, Arliss chose to work with plants, just like Mendel or Carver," Kelly said.

"Your honor," Barnes protested, "counselor is leading the witness." No wonder Samantha Card's brother-in-law had been concerned.

Kelly was painting a picture of the all-American, pull yourself up by your bootstraps family that was torn apart by an over-zealous, racially-biased, out-of-control group of cops led by her brother-in-law.

Barnes questioned Mrs. Hixon and determined that she didn't actually see the police enter her home or her husband being attacked by the police. She did see her son lying on the floor in the hallway near the back door, his body nearly torn in half by the blast of a shotgun. One hand still held the garden tool that had apparently been mistaken for a weapon.

Another officer testified that they were dressed in black from head to toe with black helmets and masks, and they carried shotguns and nightsticks when they entered the Hixon's house.

"Intimidation normally mitigates any attempt by perpetrators to escape," the officer said. He also testified that Sergeant Perkins announced himself with two quick knocks on the door, and they only entered when no one responded, maybe five to ten seconds later.

"When Willie Hixon entered the living room, he defied a direct order to lie on the floor and instead, came at Sergeant Perkins, waving a steel object. The sergeant hit him in the chest with his twelve-gage pump gun. The blow knocked Willie Hixon through the doorway into the hall, and Sergeant Perkins' shotgun went off." This was the testimony of one of the sergeant's team members.

Another officer testified that he waited at the back door. Just after the shot was fired, the back door opened, and a young man, later identified as Arliss Hixon, appeared with a weapon in his hand. Officer Wentwork, who was directly behind him, fired at the subject. Officer Wentworth later testified that he thought the object in the suspect's hand might be a weapon.

Aaron Kelly had a whole line of questions for the officer whose deposition contained the words *might be a weapon,* but he recalled Sergeant Perkins to the stand.

"How many times did you knock before entering?" asked Aaron Kelly.

"A couple of times, maybe more," the sergeant said.

"Loud knocks? So that someone in another part of the house could hear? And did you wait for a response?"

"I'm not the Avon Lady. We announce ourselves, and then we go in." "So, it's possible that no one in the Hixon's home heard you until you blew down their door?" Kelly said.

"He heard us alright. He came at me yelling and screaming and waving that scrap iron cane!" Perkins said.

"There must have been five other officers in that house by then brandishing repeating weapons and one old man with a cane, and you felt you had to use brute force, Sergeant?"

Perkins did not answer.

"Did you ever find any drugs in the Hixon's house?"

"No," the sergeant muttered.

"Sergeant Perkins, did you find marijuana or drugs of any kind in the Hixon home?" Kelly repeated more loudly.

"No, we did not," answered Sergeant Perkins, and he slumped into his seat.

***

During the week of the trial, Samantha's assistant discovered that Sergeant Wilson Perkins deployed ten officers and over a million dollars worth of high-tech surveillance equipment, patrol cars, and patty wagons while posing as drug buyers and sellers in and around three county parks. Their efforts resulted in the arrest of eleven people with drugs having a street value of twelve hundred and fifty-three dollars.

That amount of firepower for such paltry results seemed like overkill to Samantha, but when her research assistant checked with the Sheriff Department's Information Officer, she was provided with a report that their officers had also confiscated two Hummers, two Lexis, a Mercedes SL, and five other automobiles worth over three hundred thousand dollars. What the Information Office did not say, and what Samantha Card discovered a few days later, was that the Sheriff had begun proceedings to seize the home of a middle-aged mother who was working two jobs to get her son through college. Samantha's brother-in-law and his team stormed the woman's home while she and her son were having dinner. This occurred after Will Perkins had received a tip from an air conditioning repairman that there were cannabis plants growing on her screened-in patio. The woman was Emma Young.

8

Tibbetts Foster practiced a tricky bank shot off two rails as he contemplated what to do with his rogue sergeant. He hated conflict but he had to do something.

In his step daddy's little berg all he would had have to do is give an order and everyone would have fallen in line. There were no unions, commissioners or TV reporters to question him.

"Can you use a little more discretion before bashing down someone's door?" the Sheriff had nicely asked Will Pekins. "If so, I can make your life a lot easier."

That message was not getting through. All Perkins wanted to do was break down doors and bust people. The Sheriff was dismayed that the sergeant had no business sense, and he was tired of seeing Perkin's face on the six o'clock news. The publicity he was generating put the Sheriff and his partner at risk.

"If you can't control your own man, I will," Dominic told him.

This was the part of his partnership with Dominic that made him uneasy. He had been bullied as a child, and he became fidgety at the thought of any physical altercation.

He wasn't sure what Dominic might do, but his partner didn't have to deal with the media shitstorm that the disappearance of the leader of a multi-jurisdictional drug task force would surely arouse. Tibbetts spent his time taking advantage of the law, just as his step-daddy had done, to churn out a comfortable living. He didn't have to whack anyone, participate in stakeouts, or make late-night arrests in dingy back rooms. Until now, he had been enjoying a copacetic life with all of the perks that a man with a badge and a gun could acquire. Until now.

After the tenth attempt to sink the two-rail bank shot, he gave up. He was waiting for Sergeant Perkins to meet with him at his club. They would be joined by Dominic Domini and some of his associates. That meant a meeting of distraught guys with guns. He was as edgy as frog in the rain crossing a downed electrical line. The perspiration had already stained his linen leisure suit.

He put down his cue stick and sank into an Italian leather chair. Sheriff Tibbetts Foster was a big man. If he had possessed any athleticism, he could have been a defensive lineman, but he hadn't exercised a day in his life. As he whined, "Help me, god dammit, help me," Dominic and a younger man extricated him from the chair, one on each arm. His breath was short as he leaned against the mantel under an abstract Picasso print and tried three times to light the remainder of a Cohiba Robusto.

"Holy fucknuts, Tibbetts, relax!" Dominic said.

The only thing Tibbetts Foster hated about being Sheriff, more than the kowtowing of campaigning at Odd Fellows halls and nursing homes, was working with cops. It was easier working with the criminals than the cops because he knew what to expect. He didn't trust the cops, at least the ones he knew, and his bias was inherited.

His step-daddy had been the sheriff in a poor Mississippi dirt crop town. After his real father died in a freak auto accident when Foster was six, his mother took a job as a waitress in a local bar. She married the Sheriff, who she met after an altercation during a game of pool, in which she was playing to make some "get out of town cash."

When his daddy passed away, his mommy made a promise to Tibbetts. "I am going to get us out of this town."

Tibbett's mother had become a small-town pool shark. She looked like Madonna in a gingham dress, attractive and saucy. Men wanted her. She toyed with them, beat them in the pool, and took their money. Then she shrugged them off. It pissed them off, and more than a couple of times, she barely made it home with her panties intact.

His mommy thought Sheriff Elroy Debouf was her ticket out. Tibbetts remembered him as a semi-educated man with a gnarly demeanor. To his mom, though, Elroy was more promising than most of the other men in town. He owned his own home and drove a new pickup every other year, the kind with the extended cab where Tibbetts could lay down in the backseat. It wasn't an ideal relationship. Elroy made Tibbetts feel like an unwanted accessory. When Tibbetts told his mommy, she reminded him, "He buys us things, and he protects us."

His mother convinced Elroy to put a pool table in their den. It was upon this table that Tibbett's mother honed her billiards skills and where, she once let slip, she one time submitted to Elroy's voracious libido. It was upon that same pool table that Tibbetts Foster learned the art of nine ball from his mother. What he remembered most about his mommy was when she wanted something, she went after it, regardless of the conniving it took. Tibbetts was like his mother.

From his step daddy he learned the myriad ways of turning the office of Sheriff into a profit center. Elroy set up speed traps throughout the county and, with the help of the County Judge, extracted travelers' checks from visitors and fines from unsuspecting townsfolk. Were it not for his mother's hustling and his stepfather's legal extortion, Tibbetts would have grown up as poor as one of those dirt farmer's offspring.

As a result, the cops that Tibbetts Foster knew when he was a teen had resumes that included high school dropout, delinquency, and intimate familiarity with the criminal justice system. One such brutish deputy, when asked about due process, cutely remarked, "It's what happens when the morning grass is warmed by the morning sun." That smart-ass was one of the kids who used to terrorize Tibbetts when he was a child. Now that Neanderthal had a badge and a gun.

His step-daddy created a fealty from these delinquents that he transformed into an enterprise. The law that Tibbetts Foster learned was determined by greedy, manipulative despots and enforced by a bunch of juvenile delinquents with badges. Sergeant Perkins' reputation for uncompromising inflexibility and zero tolerance was interpreted by the Sheriff in a way that made him malleable to the Sheriff's will. Tibbetts Foster tolerated his maniacal drive, sometimes praised him for it, and finally promoted him to Sergeant because of it. Then, he put him in command of the narcotics task force. He hoped that if Will Perkins was manageable, he could be counted upon to generate an ongoing cash flow as the local drug enforcement czar. Cash flow, the two words that made Tibbetts Foster almost cum in his holster, was the reason he had gotten into law enforcement.

His first opportunity presented itself during his mail-order, law school years. He and Dominic Domini, an older student with a still valid insurance license and flexibility in regard to interpreting insurance guidelines, convinced Tibbetts to sell life insurance to aging retirement home residents. They offered free cruises and trips to the Fountain of Youth, which was, in fact, a run-down spa, as incentives. They convinced an elderly veterinarian with glaucoma to certify the records of those with the worst medical conditions. Then, they persuaded some myopic investors to buy back the policies for a fraction of their value. The investors paid the premiums until the old folks died and then pocketed the death benefits of the policies. Dominic and Tibbetts received kickbacks. It wasn't a pot of gold, but by the time Tibbettss received his law degree in the mail, he was debt-free, driving a BMW and hundreds of miles away from Mississippi. Tibbett's mother died of ovarian cancer before he graduated, but he felt she would have been proud of him.

After passing the bar exam on his third try, the only work he was offered came from a small firm in South Florida. The partners at Scrum and Scrum told him they considered their toilet paper to be more valuable than his law degree, but they appreciated his initiative.

He agreed to join the firm on a commission basis. He camped at the county jail intake, and before long, he was representing every small-time criminal and drug offender who had the ability to cough up a retainer.

Things went well, six-figure well, until the mid-80s when the United States Congress passed a series of laws intended to counter drug trafficking. They turned out to be such failures that a score of States decided to legalize marijuana and return to the healthcare model. But, one of those Draconian laws persisted. It involved confiscation and enabled the government to seize an individual's property without a trial, leaving the accused without the means to pay for legal counsel.

Tibbetts Foster had represented a lot of slime-balls who probably deserved to spend time in a ten by ten, but as a lawyer, he couldn't believe that the government, with the support of the Supreme Court, had dismantled what every school kid in America knew were his and her basic rights: due process and innocent until proven guilty.

The law allowed the cops to seize one's assets for lighting a marijuana cigarette in his car or growing a few cannabis plants on her patio to ameliorate the pain of arthritis. Then, the defendant had to prove that "his or her property was not obtained by or used for or during an illegal act." Upon his arrest, he was deemed a seller of narcotics, and, poof, his Fourth, Fifth, and Sixth Amendment rights went up in smoke quicker than the ash from a home-rolled joint.

Tibbetts wasn't concerned that gutting the Constitution had transferred King George-like powers to the State. He was super-fucking perplexed that the forfeiture laws meant his clients would have difficulty rounding up the cash to pay his retainers. The same law that transformed the police and the prosecutors into profit-making enterprises had forced him to sell his forty-foot Trimaran. He had taken it in trade from a former client who used it to transport cocaine through the Florida Straits. Foster had been a two-time Key

West race champion with that rig. He not only lost the boat but also the company of the hard-bodied young men who volunteered to crew for him. He had to change sides.

Before long he began prosecuting the same people he used to defend. Within a year he prosecuted the local Sheriff who was caught in a sting by an over achieving deputy by the name of Wilson Perkins. No one knew that one of Tibbett's former clients had planted four ounces of powder in the Sheriff's hotel room during the National Sheriff's Convention in Tampa or that Tibbetts had paid someone to tip off Deputy Perkins.

Foster leveraged his newly inflated public image with his heritage, his daddy having been a sheriff with one of the highest conviction rates in Mississippi, to run for office. His former partner, Dominic Domini, financed his campaign against the defrocked sheriff in return for a piece of the action. Tibbetts Foster had convinced Dominic, "We're going to turn the asset forfeiture laws into a growth stock."

To build a team of insiders, Dominic drew up a time-tested game plan that relied upon dummy invoices, underage prostitutes, and drugs to extort and bribe the county's chief financial officer, the new prosecutor, and the coroner, who had a particular interest in young men. The Sheriff then promoted Will Perkins to sergeant and made him the coordinator of the multi-jurisdictional narcotics suppression unit, i.e., the county drug czar. Dom Dom, as he was known to his friends, set up a dummy corporation through which the county procured millions of dollars of hi-tech law enforcement equipment, buildings, and training. When the county paid the invoices with inflated prices, the dummy corporation skimmed a few thousand dollars off the top of every contract. It wasn't long before the Sheriff and his cronies had Cayman Islands' bank accounts that would have been the envy of Wall Street lawyers.

Their operation hummed like a drone until Sergeant Wilson Perkins morphed from a hard-ass cop to a maniac with a badge. The investigations and trials that the Sergeant had provoked were shining the kind of light upon the Sheriff that threatened to illuminate his corporate partners. Dominic Domini told him they were not happy and the Sheriff knew it was the kind of unhappiness where someone could end up buried in an old phosphate mine.

Tibbetts Foster wiped the sweat from his brow as he glanced at his watch.

"Where the hell is your guy?" said Dominic Domini.

9

Derk Bryan was aware that he needed to work on patience, but he guessed that the guy who said "patience is a virtue" had too much time on his hands. The most laggard of cases seemed to come at the least convenient times. In this instance he was in the middle of a life defining issue while anticipating a hurricane.

The delays in the Gorton case had logical explanations, and the professionals upon whom he relied were competent. In his experience, their mistakes were rare. He took a deep breath and decided to exercise some patience. He would drive to the crime lab and check out Gorton's van. Then, he would pick up hurricane supplies.

As he exited his garage FedEx was delivering a package. He stopped and prompted the driver to bring the package to his car.

"Must be the books I ordered," he said as he signed for a package.

He rolled it in his hands. The package was about the size of a shoe box, but the return address was unfamiliar. It had been sent from a company in Vermont called Hemp Products. He was about to call the driver back but curiosity prevailed. He tossed the package onto the passenger's seat and took off as his phone rang.

"Get the package?" A female voice asked.

'Shine!" he said. "How are you?"

"Finer than Caroliner," she said.

"Where are you?"

"Down the street, around the corner," she said. Her mood was festive. There was laughter and calypso music in the background.

"You sound like you're in your happy place."

"Happy is what happy does," she said.

"It's eight a.m., and you're absolutely blitzed," he said. "You still on the boat?"

"Pain-free on the high seas," she said. "Hey, Scratch, did you get my package?" Since their first encounter at the Top End, when he shot one over the rail and halfway across the room, she had called him Scratch.

"What package?"

"My new line," she said.

"Hold on a minute," he said and reached for the package on his front seat. "I got something from Hemp Products. Is that you?"

"That's me, Scratch, my new line," she said. "Check it out, but the Hemp Woody is for Chad."

"Hemp Woody?"

"You' don't need it, Scratch; I've got to go. Call you later."

"Who are you?" He said aloud, but no one was there.

He pulled into a convenience store parking lot and opened the package. Inside was an assortment of CBD creams, lotions, tinctures, gummies, mints, and a bottle of CBD oil. He rummaged through the box of goodies until he found the one entitled Hemp Woody. It was a squeeze tube of massage oil and the name left little doubt as to its intended application. And then it hit him. She's a hemp rep, too. This pool shark in the Dolly Parton body was the proverbial enigma wrapped in an illusion. What next? For a moment, he had completely forgotten about Ivan, Ileay, and Sandy Gorton.

By the time he arrived at the crime lab, Gorton's van was nowhere in sight. He knew it had been trucked to the lab because it had been there when he left on Saturday evening. He figured the techs must have pushed it inside to finish their investigation. He parked and went inside the two-story CBS structure. He identified himself and asked to see the van.

"You need to see Lt. Sprague," he was told. "Wait here."

He waited in the lobby for ten minutes, thumbed through a six-month-old issue of Forensics, and was about to ask for directions to the bathroom when a squatty, bespectacled man of fifty with a shock of red hair and a round, reddish face entered the lobby and talked with a uniformed officer. As the two men were about to enter an office, the receptionist interrupted them.

"Lt. Sprague, this man from EPED is here to see you," she said.

Derk stood as the Lieutenant approached.

"Lt. Sprague, what can I do for you?" He held out his hand.

"Derk Bryan. I'm working on the Gorton case. I'd like to see the van that went into Lake Manatee. They brought it in here on Saturday."

"Oh, the Gorton van. Yea, um, it's not here," the Lieutenant said. "They took it to the impound this morning."

"What?" Derk exclaimed.

"We finished with it and got it out of here. All the damn chemicals that were in that thing! Nobody wanted it around here. It was a damn hazard," Lt. Sprague said.

"What about the police report? A man was killed in that van!" Derk said.

"We did our report. The M.E. ruled it was an accident. Happens all the time," said the Lieutenant.

The other officer injected, "See you inside, Lieutenant," slid between them and scurried away.

"You took it to the impound!" Derk repeated, shaking his head in disbelief. "What about the report?"

"It was an automobile accident, handled the same as any other accident," the Lieutenant answered.

"Not exactly. This one killed half of the wildlife in Lake Manatee," Derk replied. "Who has the inventory of the chemicals in that van?"

Lt. Sprague turned to the receptionist, "Lois, do you have the inventory from the Gorton van?"

"It's in the file. I believe a copy was faxed to your office already," she said directly to Derk.

"Could you please make a copy for Mr. Bryan?" he asked. His request was polite but contained an overtone of annoyance.

While she was making a copy of the inventory, Derk asked, "Do you know who filed the accident report?"

"Sweeney, I think," he answered. "It was Sweeney, wasn't it, Lois?"

"No, it was Doc Morton," she replied.

"Wesley Morton, the Medical Examiner?" said Derk.

The Lieutenant nodded.

"Is that normal?'

"What do you mean?"

"In accident cases, does the Medical Examiner normally sign off on the cause of the accident?"

"He took a special interest in this case. I guess with all of the chemicals involved and the death of the driver."

Derk ran a hand through his hair as he accepted the report from the receptionist.

"Thank you, Lieutenant. You certainly are an efficient bunch," he said and shook his hand, followed by a nod to Lois.

The receptionist glanced at the Lieutenant, and Sprague rolled his eyes.

10

Derk left the Medical Examiner's office with the information he needed to drop the case. If he required more motivation to forget it, there were three nasty storms headed his way, and Ivan's questions about his real father were still unanswered.

He couldn't credit his next move to his intuition or his stubbornness, but forty-five minutes later, he was parked in the driveway of Sandy Gorton's house. He hadn't even hesitated when he passed the Chowder House restaurant on his way. The Chowder House had the best seafood chowder in the Bay Area.

He sat in his car for a few moments, unsure of what he was expecting to find or where to look for it. It was mid-afternoon, yet the skies were overcast, in fact, almost dark. The air was like canned heat and stifling with dread.

The Gorton country home consisted of five acres carved into the scrub. The view in all directions was the same: lush wetlands with pines, saw palmetto, Cabbage Palms and scattered cacti. A small stream transversed the back half of the parcel. The land was too rough and too wet to cultivate but ideal for grazing. He once worked on a case in this area that involved the death of a small herd. Central Florida was home to millions of beef cattle that were reared prior to shipping to the Midwest for fattening. A neighbor had, almost accidentally, contaminated another rancher's land with an aerial herbicide. It didn't take long for Derk to discover why the cattle died on one farm and not the adjacent ones. As far as he knew, that slimeball was still getting his room and board at Florida State, the prison, not the college. There was no sign of a herd on the Gorton property.

The lot included a one-story, three-bedroom, wood-framed house, a detached two-car garage, and a small barn. A late-model pickup was parked beside the garage. What caught his attention was an old Opal under a lean-to adjacent to the barn. The two-seater sports car, manufactured by Buick in the late 1960s, was rare.

In addition to his customized Harley, he kept his 1986 Mustang in working order. He enjoyed tinkering with these soon-to-be-relics of internal combustion, but Sandover "Wink" Gorton had taken on a serious restoration project.

He got out of the car and went to inspect the Opal. The seats, dash, and control panel were in good condition, but the body needed some work. What once had been a deep forest green was now a patchwork of faded colors and Bondo.

The large wooden doors of the barn were padlocked, so he walked back toward the house. The landscaping was more natural than groomed, replete with rogue weeds and unruly scrub. It was not what he expected from someone who had access to every seed catalog, fertilizer, and pesticide on the planet.

The house was built on a platform three feet off the ground and surrounded by a wrap-around porch with an old-fashioned spindle wood banister. Nice touch, he thought. Derk tried to envision Gorton sitting on the porch in a rocking chair and reading the newspaper.

He knocked on the door. No one answered, and the front door was locked. The windows had neither blinds nor curtains. The furniture ranged from Early American to traditional. The place seemed sturdy and functional, absent of female influences, suggesting he lived alone.

He strained against a gust of wind as he walked toward the two-car garage. At the side entrance he was able to see through the window in the door. It was dark, but what he could make out suggested it was a sports car, probably British and possibly from the fifties, given the laced wheels that were visible beneath the cream-covered tarpaulin.

The garage was locked, so he headed toward the barn. The latch to a side door lifted, but the door would not open. It was either swollen shut or locked from the inside. He took a chance on the former. With a shoulder against the door, he heaved. It opened a foot or two. It was completely dark as he slid inside the barn. He reached for a light switch but found none. His thigh hit a large object, and he lost his balance. He reached out to break his fall and was stopped by the feel of polished sheet metal. He went back to his car to fetch a flashlight. Once inside, he shined the light upon a fully restored 1956 Thunderbird and an Austin Healy that was in immaculate condition. If hearts could shine, Derk's was aglow. Sandy Gorton was a serious collector of vintage sportscars.

When he left the Gorton homestead, it was not yet four o'clock, and the skies were the color of coal tar. The wind was sturdy, and the aroma of approaching rain was in the air. He was a mile down the road to Bradenton, accepting that Gorton's death had been an accident when it hit him. He made an abrupt U-turn.

He came to a screeching halt in front of the Gorton home and positioned the headlamps directly onto two large green trash bins near the end of the driveway. As he approached the containers, a gust of wind from the southeast misted his face. A light rain began to fall.

He removed a handkerchief from his back pocket, wrapped it around his fingers, and tried to pry open the top of one of the trash bins. It slipped from his grasp. The bin fell over and out toppled its contents. Among the melon rinds, egg shells, and coffee grounds were envelopes, newspapers, an old coffee maker, two unlabeled, two-and-one-half gallon plastic jugs without caps, and what alarmed him: No flies! A stone, cold fear rushed through him as if it had been injected intravenously.

He ran to his car. The rain, now coming hard, stung his face like the sharp ends of loose straw and blew onto the front seat when he opened the door. He pushed Contacts on his cellphone and made the call.

"EPED," Joyce answered.

"Find out the regular day for the trash pickup at the Gorton residence and call me back right away."

"Got it," she said. "Anything else?"

"Find out if any of the Gorton kids have come to his house yet? If so, what day and ask them if any of them touched the trash cans?"

In spite of the sportscars, Derk's impression of Sandy Gorton was now foreboding. He had only two contacts with him, and each time, the stench of death was in the air. While he waited for the call from Joyce, the wind howled, and liquid pebbles bounced off his roof with the cadence of popping corn. He was not looking forward to the drive home. Five minutes later came the sound of the William Teller Overture on his cellphone.

"Once a week service, and tomorrow's the day," Joyce said.

"And his kids?"

"They're flying in tomorrow."

He was about to ask a question when Joyce asked, "What's up? You know Ben closed the Gorton case."

"Tell him to get a hazmat crew out here and check out the contents of the trash bins scattered on the front lawn," Derk said.

As she was saying, "Derk, there's a hurricane coming," he hit off on his cell phone.

What had caused him to turn around was a simple question: "Who puts the trash cans out three days before their scheduled pick up?"

It wasn't Sandy Gorton. Three days ago, he was floating face-up in Lake Manatee.

There was another thing. Most containers have recognizable sizes, shapes, and labels for marketing purposes. The ones in those trash cans were jet black, which often signified hazardous contents. And the most disturbing thing: After three days, every kind of bug imaginable is feasting upon food waste. In that trash bin there were no flies. None!

He donned a slicker he kept behind the seat on the outside chance he had been mistaken. In the trunk, he found a tire iron. He put a handkerchief over his nose and got as close to the debris as he dared. Tampa Bay was subject to torrential rains, but nothing like this. It came at him sideways and carried with it an acerbic aroma from the garbage. As he kneeled to uncover some food waste, the slick steel tool slipped from his hand, and he stumbled backward onto some rotting melon rinds. His pants were now drenched.

"That's it. I'm out of here," he said aloud.

He ran to the car. He hadn't felt this kind of anxiety since his last prostrate exam.

Through the pendulum of the automatic wiper blades, he gazed at the outline of the buildings on Gorton's property. The poles of the lean-to struggled against the wind, and the fraying canvas top made a hard flapping sound. A few Ibis had taken shelter behind the pickup next to the garage. He took a couple of deep breaths to slow his pulse. As he backed down the driveway, the rear cameras illuminated the downpour coming in sheets. He dreaded being on the road under these conditions, but half a mile down the road, he dialed the number of the Bay Magazine.

"May I speak with Samantha Card?" Derk said.

11

To Sergeant Perkins, the Bay Island Country Club was just another cookie-cutter development in South Florida, with one exception. It had the reputation as a refuge for high rollers, both legit and otherwise. He wondered why the Sheriff had summoned him there to meet.

In particular, the Sheriff had asked to meet him in the billiards room of the ritzy clubhouse north of Tampa. Like so many similar spreads the developers had given it an embellished and completely misleading name. Bay Island was nowhere near Tampa Bay, and it was surrounded by land, not water. The Sergeant had no beef with these developers nor did he give any attention to the fact that twenty million people had been crowded into Florida, most of them in the past fifty years, by the lure of the good life in a sub-tropical paradise. In fact, it didn't bother him that it was no longer paradise, at least not like the one that Ponce de Leon discovered in the fourteen-hundreds. In his mind, the Sheriff had uncovered a clandestine crack operation or wanted to alert him to some suspected drug pins living on the property. But why the billiards room?

It was his first time inside the Bay Island gate, and though he was still in uniform and flashed his badge, he was only allowed entry because Tibbetts Foster had notified the guard to expect him.

Inside the clubhouse, he sought out the Men's Room. He hadn't taken a leak since lunch due to a backlog of paperwork and a lengthy meeting with his attorney and the county administrator. It was the administrator's job to pay the Sergeant's escalating legal bills, and he was eager to find out what Perkins' attorney was planning. A continuation of the Sergeant's roughshod tactics would eventually threaten the county executive's job security. Will Perkins had left the meeting abruptly when the administrator began questioning his tactics. Both the Sheriff and the county administrator were on his case. He was not in a good mood.

He stopped abruptly outside the door to the bathroom. Into the glass had been etched a replica of Jackie Gleason in golf attire with a club in one hand and a Hoyo de Monterey in the other. He laughed. He hated golf, but Gleason always made him laugh.

As he backed away to see what had been engraved on the door to the Women's Room, he noticed the Sheriff through the opening in the door to the Billiards Room. His attempt to enter was stymied by a cut-off guy with gorilla biceps clad in a Tommy Bahama ensemble. His breath smelled like a Pina Colada.

The Sergeant looked askance at the Sheriff, who was lining up a shot. A man with a George Hamilton tan and a linebacker physique tugged on his straw hat and braced himself with a pool cue at the other end of the pool table. The Sheriff lifted his martini glass toward George Hamilton's double and nodded his approval to allow the sergeant to enter. The man with the tan motioned to the door guard with his pool stick.

"Relax, College," he said.

"What the hell's going on here, and who is this guy?" Sergeant Perkins said as he pushed a finger into the arm of the muscular troll as he entered.

"That's not a good idea, Sergeant," the Sheriff said. He held a cocktail in one hand and his cue stick in the other. His smile diminished when he spoke.

"Excuse me for one moment," the Sheriff said, put his drink on the rail of the pool table, and completed his shot.

He banked the ball into a side pocket and then hit a slow roller the length of the table to kiss in the eight ball, after which he turned to the guy with the tan and said, "That's five grand you owe me."

The Sheriff took the Sergeant by one arm and led him down the hall.

"Who the fuck are those guys?" Perkins said and, while trying to wrestle his arm free of the Sheriff's grip, realized that the Sheriff was dressed in white gauze from head to toe. He had on Birkenstock sandals. "And who are you?"

The Sheriff forced a smile but kept a firm grasp on his Sergeant's arm.

"They're just friends. Follow me," Tibbetts Foster said and led the Sergeant through the door past Jackie Gleason." His black Chow had followed him. "Stay. Stay, Buffie."

It didn't matter. The dog was coming with him.

What the Sergeant would later discover was that the man with the tan was Dominic Domini. In college he had teamed with Tibbetts Foster to run an insurance scam. After a few minor cons, he scored big by hosting legitimate gay porn sites. He parlayed those investments into marijuana with both legal and black-market activities. He became notorious for running gay sex trysts that paired wealthy older men with college-age hunks. He was certainly gay, probably bi-sexual, and positively in love with himself. He never passed a mirror without stopping. He had nicknamed his bodyguard and current boy toy "College" because he liked fucking college boys. It didn't matter that Dex McMullen had been dismissed from college after only one semester due to an incident involving steroids. At least, that was the story released by the school to the public. He had been caught by the trainer boning a male student in the equipment room. Dom Dom scoured college campuses in search of new talent. The kid needed a job, and he had the body of a Greek Warrior, so Dom Dom promoted him from boy toy to bodyguard to keep him close.

Dom Dom stepped into the hallway, holding College back with one hand. "Are you coming back?" he asked the Sheriff.

"Damn right," the Sheriff said. He walked back to hand Dominic his seven-hundred dollar Meucci Hall of Fame cue stick along with the cocktail glass he had been holding. "I'll take care of this," he whispered.

In the Men's Room, the Sheriff took so long to use the urinal and wash his hands, the Sergeant's patience broke.

"Sheriff Foster, what's going on, sir?"

Foster retorted, "I thought I told you not to wear a uniform in here."

"I'm a cop, and I'm on duty. What's this about?" said Sergeant Perkins.

"And who are those guys?"

"Friends. Come with me. There's something I want to show you," the Sheriff said and headed for the exit.

"What is it, Sheriff?" Perkins stopped.

"That's an order, Sergeant," said the Sheriff. He pointed to the door.

They walked down the hallway toward the Pro Shop.

"Come, Buffie," the Sheriff called to his dog. She was already on his heels.

The walls were covered with photos of Woods, Palmer, Niklaus and a young man with wavy blonde hair he didn't recognize. He stopped to read the caption: 2nd Place U. S. Open. The name under the photo was George Burns. Next to it in a glass case were silver trophies, antique clubs and esoteric golf memorabilia. They passed the open door to the bar and grille. It was dripping with haughty privilege.

Above the bar, wine glasses hung like tinsel over rich mahogany countertops that had been waxed to a glossy finish. Beyond the bar, through large sliding glass doors, was a view of the eighteenth green and the fairway leading up to it. Large screen televisions, that took up one half of the wall, were showing highlights from some recent golf events. A few men in garish attire had gathered to share drinks at one end of the bar.

Sheriff Foster passed the bar and hustled Sergeant Perkins through the empty Pro Shop to a waiting golf cart. The cart was painted green and had the Sheriff's name stenciled on it in white letters. It sported an antenna and carried a large cooler but no golf bag. Buffie waited for the Sheriff to take his seat and then jumped into his lap.

The Sheriff spun the cart around and headed down the cart path. After passing the driving range, he drove through a wooded trail into an opening that overlooked one of the fairways. On the other side of the fairway was a two-story home with a large outdoor patio. He could see the heads of three very buff young men bob up and down in what must have been the swimming pool. Buffie stood with its front paws on the steering wheel and barked.

The Sheriff parked the cart in a cart stall next to the garage. Sergeant Perkins followed him into the kitchen. Buffie went straight to the patio door and barked at the naked guys splashing about the pool. Then she came back to her bowl, slurped some water, and laid down on a cushion.

The kitchen opened to the great room, which led to the patio. The pool was just outside the sliding glass doors. A heavyset, white male in business attire sat at the table. He was sipping a gin and tonic, drooling over the hard bodies in the pool, and occasionally sucking on a Rubusto when they entered the room.

The Sheriff said, "You know Doc Morton. Have a seat."

They acknowledged each other but said nothing. Sergeant Perkins remained standing with hands on hips. The Sheriff tossed the ingredients for a daiquiri into a blender.

"Can I pour you a drink, Sergeant?" said the Sheriff. "Oh, I'm sorry. You're still on duty."

"Why am I here?" Perkins said, his view alternated between the boys in the pool, the medical examiner and the Sheriff.

The doctor took a long drag on his cigar while lightly tapping the fingers of one hand on a manilla folder in front of him.

"You know those guys you found a few months ago on that pot bust in Ruskin?" Sheriff Foster said. He poured the contents of the blender into three crystalline Martini glasses and slid a strawberry onto the rim of each.

"The guys with twenty pounds of weed in their trunk?" the Sergeant said. "That case is closed."

"It was but four days ago their heirs filed a wrongful death suit against us claiming the chemicals used weren't Kosher," the Sheriff said. "Do you anything about that?"

"What do you mean? We did everything by the book," Perkins reacted.

"Maybe," he said, and he pointed to Doctor Morton, who had yet to say a word.

The Doctor glanced at the Sergeant while he slowed his finger-tapping.

"Maybe! What are you talking about?" Sergeant Perkins said. Looking at Doc Morton, he said, "You signed off on that."

"The Doc says they exhumed the body and found traces of something else. It's right here," said the Sheriff and nodded at the folder under the ME's hand.

Doctor Morton took another drink of his Daiquiri but kept a hand on the manilla folder.

"No fucking way. You're not putting this on me," Perkins said. He pulled out his cell phone and started taking pictures of the Doctor, the Sheriff, and the naked boys having sex on the patio. They couldn't have been more than eighteen if that.

"Slow down, Sergeant," said the Sheriff. "We're just saying you need to relax."

The Sheriff walked over to Will Perkins with his drink in one hand.

He put the other arm around him and turned him away from the sideshow in the pool.

"Are you familiar with Keynesian economics?" the Sheriff said.

Sergeant Perkins freed himself of the Sheriff's fatherly grip.

"What are you talking about?" said the Sergeant, twisting to get another shot of the two guys in a sixty-nine formation on a Chaise Lounge. "Are they minors?"

"I'm talking about supply and demand, son. Everything is about supply and demand," said the Sheriff. And in his best southern drawl, he added, "And you, Sergeant Perkins, are fucking with the natural order of things."

12

Samantha Card dropped a copy of the Times story about the Killer Weed onto the desk of Colleen Reid, her research assistant. Mrs. Reid was wedged between two stacks of files on opposite sides of her desk.

"What do you make of this? Samantha said.

"You couldn't burn enough rope on a year-long binge in a hemp factory to do yourself in," said Colleen Reed. In addition to being the best researcher Samantha had ever known, Colleen was the mother of two "post-graduate" students and the wife of a doctor who volunteered at the *Free Clinic.* "In fact, there's never been a single study or government report that says marijuana kills people."

"So, the cops are lying?" Samantha said.

"I don't know about that," said Colleen.

Samantha shook her head in disgust and then laughed.

"What?" said Colleen.

"My father attended the first Ann Arbor *Hash Bash.*" She paused as if she were bathing in her thoughts. "I don't know if I ever told you this. He took pictures of the Narcs and published them in an underground newspaper when he was in college. The newspaper was sued, but it won."

"Makes sense. Free speech, free press," Colleen said.

"As you know, he started this magazine. He guided Bay Magazine from a small *Back to the Earth* monthly to a weekly newspaper with a grip on the local scene that is the envy of some big city dailies."

"I thought we were an entertainment rag," Colleen said, barely holding back a smirk.

It was a sensitive subject with Samantha. She published a magazine. That was true. It wasn't a newspaper. That was true. But she prided herself in news and made sure that any event that affected her readers would get coverage, in depth coverage. If the cops were misleading the public on marijuana use, now legal in some form in almost forty States, people should know about that.

"Moviegoers and jazz aficionados have as much right to know what their government is doing as anyone else," Samantha said emphatically.

"Of course," said Colleen, the grin had evaporated. "What are we going to do?"

"Find the truth and print it," said Samantha.

13

It would take an hour and a half to drive from Tampa to Myakka. Amos Grimes knew it was going to be an intense trip. The Reverend Peter Wirth hadn't stopped ranting since he heard about Emma Young's arrest. He had been a regular facilitator at the "Course on Miracles," and she had become a frequent attendant. He liked Emma Young.

Peter Wirth, an ordained minister, was a gifted orator with dreamy eyes that disarmed men and disrobed women. He had an energy level that defied his age and Amos had known him for thirty-five years. During that time Amos hadn't seen him this animated. Except for the time the Reverend testified in a Senate subcommittee against a proposed law to reduce home rule.

The co-op the Reverend Wirth founded, legally a glorified condominium association, required solar installations on all homes and businesses in its community. The community used its collective buying power to provide discounted prices for energy savings improvements while helping the owners reduce their carbon footprints as well as their utility bills. The costs of the installations were added to the owners' HOA fees.

The Reverend waved his hands and squirmed on the aging leather seat of their Jeep Wagoneer as he raved. Amos Grimes had seen him this way only a few times in his life, and each time, when the dust settled, something he hadn't seen coming showed up.

"My God!" the Reverend said and looked skyward, "This has to change!"

"Yes, brother," Amos said.

"This is beyond unfair. It's absurd," Peter exhorted. "Laws this bad need to be stopped. Emma Young never harmed a soul in her life."

"That's right," Amos said.

"She's the most sensitive, caring, and spiritually bound woman I've ever known."

"That she is," Amos said. He had learned it was best to allow his friend to fizzle out.

"What happened to her is outrageous! It's way beyond the bounds of what the average person in this country expects from its government."

"Amos, your forebearers came to this country from Jamaica and there from West Africa against their wishes. They had to fight greed, ignorance, and cruelty for centuries before becoming free men again. First, the Spanish dominated you, then the English, and now the Americans. The persecution emanating from this war on dope is just as evil as slavery was."

He slammed his fist against the dash on the passenger's side. "Sons-a-bitches! They've gone too far!"

"You got that right," said Amos. He tried to keep his attention on the road but the Reverend was grabbing his arm.

Following in his father's tracks, Peter Wirth had become a minister, and for the past twenty years his ministry had been "The Oasis," a spiritually based economic and agricultural cooperative community of homes and small businesses. The co-op paid its overhead by selling religious publications on the Internet that focused on self-sufficiency. Reverend Wirth was also a veteran of protests against racial and environmental injustice, survived anti-war rallies, and participated in women's rights marches. He had spent sixteen months in Club Fed for the non-violent exercise of his belief, which included Rastafarian rituals involving cannabis. He was a regular at the Cannabis Cup in Amsterdam and had penned some editorials for High Times during its hay days.

Amos remained silent until the Reverend withdrew into thought. Nothing more was said until they turned off the main road onto the long approach to their homes in The Oasis.

The Reverend turned to Amos and said, "How many friends do you think we have?"

"I don't know. What do you mean by friends?"

"How many people know about us?"

"A lot, I suppose," Amos replied with an inquisitive look on his face.

"I think it's time we have a meeting of our friends," Peter said, crossed his hands and sat still until the car parked in front of his house.

At that moment, Amos Grimes knew that change was afoot and life was about to get interesting again.

14

The gusts of wind had subsided. The rain was now only a steady downpour, and the window washers crossed in front of him like fan blades.

From his car, Derk called Gorton's Farm and Garden Supply and asked for the manager. He was referred to an older woman named Crystal, who spoke with a wounded voice. He introduced himself and offered condolences. In the middle of answering questions about Gorton and his business, Crystal began crying.

"He was such a nice man and we don't know what to do," she said through the tears.

"So, I've heard," Derk acquiesced.

"Except for Ina and I, there's nobody here to handle the business other than the guys in the warehouse," she said.

"I know how difficult it is to lose somebody close." He wasn't making that up.

"We don't know what to do," she said.

"Who's Ina?" Derk said.

Crystal cleared her throat. "Oh, the bookkeeper. I handle the front end, and she handles the back. She's been here for over fifteen years. Two more than me."

"Who will take over the business?" Derk said.

"Oh," her sigh was palpable, "probably his kids, but they don't know anything about this business."

"Have they been contacted?"

"Ina called them," she said. "By the way, do you know when we can get our van back? We're getting behind with the orders, and our old van is broken down more often than a one-humped camel." She giggled.

Derk guessed it was her attempt to ease the tension, but he felt something heavy fall on him. It was like the stress of losing a home or a job, or even a child. Gorton's death threatened Crystal and the others at their small company. They needed that truck back and he had told the impound to hold the vehicle until he had completed his inspection.

"I suggest you call your insurance company. I doubt anyone is driving that van again," he said. His brute-force honesty caused Crystal's voice to crack again.

"What are we going to do, Mr. Bryan?" she said.

"Do you mind if I talk with Ina?" he said.

"Ina, it's Mr. Bryan. From the EPA," Derk heard her say in segments.

"Who?" came a voice.

"The man about the van," he heard Crystal say louder.

He could tell that someone was approaching the phone because her voice became clearer. "Did he say when we're going to get the van back?"

"Talk to him," Crystal said.

"This is Ina." The voice was female and rather dainty or maybe just old.

He asked her about the books and financial records. She said she handled payroll and paid the bills as Mr. Gorton authorized her to do.

"We use QuickyBooks," she said. "It's pretty easy, so I can work part-time."

"So, you have access to the financial records if I need something?"

"He works from home sometimes, and sometimes he forgets to tell me what he's done. It would depend on what you're looking for. What's this about? Mr. Gorton died in an accident, didn't he?"

"What about bank accounts?"

"Of course. He brings me the bills to be paid, and I take care of them. We have orders to fill. When can we get the van back?" Ina said.

"As I told your manager, you should call your insurance company," he said.

"He said call the insurance company," he heard Crystal's voice in the background.

"It's part of an investigation," he was saying as Crystal came back on the line.

"Mr. Gorton's daughter will be here tomorrow or the next day. If you have any more questions about the business, you should talk with Eileen," Crystal said and hung up before Derk could leave his number.

He hit re-dial on his cellphone. He wanted to know the exact time that Eileen Post would arrive at her deceased father's store, but he canceled the call. He would call Eileen Post tomorrow. Then he called Ben Waitley at EPED.

Joyce answered on the third ring, "EPED."

"That's it. EPED! No good morning, may I help you, or this is the Environmental Protection Agency; what can I do for you?" Derk said.

"I'm leaving, Derk. There's a hurricane coming, and Ben wants to talk with you," she said, ignoring his jest. This wasn't normal Joyce.

"What's up, sweetheart?"

"I'm trying to get a report out for Ben and there's a hurricane coming.

He has something for you, though," she replied.

"Are you riding this out?" He said as he checked his messages. "Damn!" he said aloud. He had received two text messages from Ben Waitley marked urgent.

"What?"

"Nothing, sorry. What's he want?"

"I think he has another assignment for you, and they're shutting down the office tonight."

"I'm still working on this case," Derk said.

"I thought you said you weren't getting anywhere," Joyce said and added, "We're going north."

"I'm not done with this. You should see the sportscars at Gorton's place. He had an old T-Bird that was immaculate. How does a guy who drives sports cars end up in Lake Manatee for no apparent reason?" Derk said.

"I don't know, but the spill is under control, and the death was ruled an accident," Joyce said. "Derk, you should take cover or get out of town."

"Probably."

"I'm serious. Anyway, he needs your help on something else."

"What?"

"You'll find out. Hold on. Oh, by the way. How did it go with…uh… Alice?"

Derk sighed, "You mean Agnes. Do I look like I could be CIA?"

"Anyone you want to be, sweetheart. You should meet my niece."

"Turns out she prefers CPAs to NSAs, but so do I. They don't carry guns," Derk said.

"She's cute as a button," Joyce reiterated. She had been trying to hook him up with her step-daughter for quite a while.

"The one with the cats, kids, and the jealous ex who raises pit bulls? Sure."

Her picture was adorable, and animals loved him, but he once knew a woman who had two cats. One was friendly and found comfort in his lap. The other, raised from birth, was clinically psychotic. It hissed, clawed, and attacked at will, even its master, who was a meek and caring guardian. It got so bad he began wearing goggles when he entered her house. This tainted him, he knew, but he preferred dogs. If one caught a dog with its foot in the cookie jar and disciplined it with a stern word or two, it would walk around the woodwork for an entire week out of respect. If one caught a cat up to its whiskers in mischief, it would glare at you as if to say, "What the fuck do you want?" The cats made Joyce's niece a no-go.

"She's adventurous like you. She just married the wrong guy," Joyce said, "and in spite of everything I've told her about you, she still wants to meet you."

"I'd be afraid of stepping on a cat," he said. "Hold on. He's off the phone," Joyce said.

"Derk?" said Ben Waitley, the director.

"Yea. Hey, the Gorton case is not over," Derk replied.

"I need you to go to Clermont and talk with a man about his birds," the Director said.

"You want me to do what?" Derk said.

"His name is Garth O'Bannon. He's Irish or British or something like that from what I could understand," the Director said. "Heavy accent."

"I'm still working on the Lake Manatee spill," Derk said.

"That was ruled an accident. I don't have," he said but was interrupted by Derk.

"Not by me, it wasn't!" Derk said. "They think it was faulty brakes. I didn't get that report."

"Accident is the ruling. The lake will survive. Case closed," the Director said.

"Because there weren't any skid marks?" Derk said.

Waitley continued, "I don't have anyone to send up there, and this guy, Garth O'Bannon, is off the wall. He's making threats and accusing everybody but his mother of destroying his birds. He said something about the pelicans. You know the ones they found near Lake Apopka?"

"That was years ago. They were American white pelicans that dropped from the sky like fodder due to the pesticides used on the orange groves," Derk said. "The stuff washed into the Lake and contaminated the fish."

"Apparently, it's not old news to him. He says it's killing his birds, and unless we do something about it…" Ben didn't finish the sentence. "Look, this guy's probably a wacko, but if there's something to it, we need to know."

"To cover our asses," Derk said. "Sorry."

"I told him you'd be there as soon as the weather permits. Joyce will give you the address. Did she tell you we are closing the office?"

"Ben, this is a shit case. It's police business." Derk said. "I wouldn't give it to you if we had anyone else."

Derk knew that was an excuse. There had been fewer and fewer cases assigned to him over the past year. He wanted it that way, but he knew there was more to it. He thought the department wanted someone younger and more malleable. There was too much politics interfering with environmental policy these days, and he didn't like playing those games. He was probably fortunate he had been given the Gorton case. It affected a number of interests and jurisdictions with potential political ramifications. Derk's habit of tracing problems back to their roots frequently ruffled feathers higher up the food chain. What trouble could a redneck with some ailing fowl cause the agency? Probably not much, so the case was assigned to him.

"Ben, tell me again, why did you hire me instead of someone with a police background?"

"We wouldn't hire a bouncer to investigate computer crimes, so why would we hire a traffic cop to investigate environmental crimes?" There was a brief pause, then, "Dr. Bryan, you can be a pain in the ass, but you're a damn good investigator. Keep me informed." The receiver went dead.

For a moment, he traded the feeling of unfinished business, specifically the Gorton case, for the gut-level anxiety brought on by someone named Garth O'Bannon. Derk Bryan had exposed polluters, criminals, and murderers, but he couldn't arrest people. Nor did he carry a gun. He didn't even own one. His investigative toolbox was filled with intuition and experience backed by science. When it came to investigations, guns were not only unnecessary, they were unimaginative. Therefore, the days were rare that he preferred to have a weapon other than just his wits. For a reason he could not explain, he wondered if this would be one of those times.

15

Derk hadn't met Samantha Card, but he knew about her magazine. He thumbed through Bay Mag each month. It was how he became aware of upcoming performances by the Capitol Steps, Pat Matheny, Muddy Waters, the Cleveland Orchestra, and, most recently, the Grand Funk Railroad. He had seen all of them but the latter, and were it not for the death of Sandy Gorton, he would have taken Agnes Wiley to hear them. He regretted that. It may have been his last chance. His favorite bands were aging just like him.

Bay Mag published the lists of the best beach bars and waxing salons every year. One year, it published a list of the best defense attorneys working on drug cases. Emma Young needed one.

By the time he arrived at the magazine's office, the afternoon rain had subsided. That may have been due to the normal summer weather pattern in Tampa Bay or, more likely, the passing of a feeder band from the approaching hurricane. His only consolation in regard to the nasty weather was that his place was well protected, at least, for beach property. Bay Mag took up the fourth floor of an office building on Westshore Boulevard near the intersection with State Route Sixty. It was an ideal location for the magazine due to its access to the beaches in all directions.

From there, one could be in Clearwater or St. Petersburg within twenty minutes.

Except for a couple of people in the lobby, the place was deserted. The walls were covered with framed, front-page stories that the magazine had covered over the years. Piles of recent editions were stacked in racks across from the reception's vacant desk. The headline of the current edition read: *Dead Wrong.* Below it was a photo of Sheriff Tibbetts Foster followed by a story accusing the cops of jumping to conclusions about the deaths of Senator Crimshaw's daughter and Duke Hankins' son. In the middle of the article was a

114

quote from Professor Thurston Weedleston, printed in bold Helvetica, **"No One Has Ever Died From Smoking Marijuana."**

Derk perused a few more pages in search of the story about the accident at Lake Manatee. There was a two-paragraph summary at the bottom of page six.

He interrupted someone on the way out to ask for directions to Samantha Card's office. "Down the hall. Third office on the right" was the response.

The door was more than half open, but he still knocked before entering. He recognized Samantha Card from her headshot in the magazine. She was tapping keys on a word processor faster than a court stenographer.

Without looking up, she said, "What can I do for you?"

"Derk Bryan," he said. He was stunned by her appearance. The contrast between her picture and the real, in the flesh, publisher of Bay Magazine was a perpendicular one. She was older than he imagined but more distinctive and more commanding than portrayed by the black and white in the publication.

"Beg your pardon?" she said, looking up at him.

"Derk Bryan, EPA." He put his business card on her desk.

"EPA," she said, barely glancing at him. "Didn't we spin that Lake Manatee story to your liking?"

"From what I've seen, the more appropriate description would be ignored, not spin, but then bad news about the beaches is not good news for those who advertise with Bay Mag," he said.

That was enough to get her attention.

"Mr. Bryan," she said, and he interrupted her.

"It's Doctor Bryan," he said.

She took a moment to glance at his card before continuing, "Doctor Bryan, we're not in the habit of drawing conclusions without the facts," she said, but her tone was not defensive, "and I believe that was ruled an accident."

He held up the front page of her magazine. "Some might disagree with that."

She stood up, fingered through a stack of folders on her desk, picked two out, and offered them to him.

"In there are the death rates from marijuana since the government began recording them, and these are the reports from the CDC. There's no mention of anyone ever dying from smoking marijuana. Not one," she said. "Is this why you came to see me, Dr. Bryan?" She made a point to clearly enounce the doctor part.

He took them and, without opening the folders, laid them on her desk.

"What do you know about Aaron Kelly?" he said. "He's not on my speed dial," she said.

"Your magazine," he said but was interrupted. "Newspaper," she corrected him.

"Once published a list of the best defense attorneys who handle drug cases," he said. "Was he on the list?"

Samantha waved her hand for him to take a seat across from her. For the first time since he entered the room, he thought he detected a smile. Her diminutive figure and tightly cropped black hair would have reminded him of a Geisha girl if she wasn't African American. Her face was as smooth as ebony, and her eyes were wide but tired. They defied her austere demeanor. She wasn't big enough to be intimidating and not classically beautiful, but she was alluring. He had always been attracted to intelligent women and that she seemed to be.

"So, you read our newspaper," she said. She had stopped typing and leaned back into her chair.

"Yes, Ma'am, I do," Derk replied. "You list the upcoming concerts."

"Do you have a favorite?"

"It probably shows my age, but I really liked BTO and Blue Oyster Cult," he said, not expecting her to recognize the bands.

When she nodded her acknowledgment, he added, "My favorite is A Flock of Seagulls."

A hint of nostalgia was shown in her eyes. "In that era, I'm more of a Marvin Gaye or Al Stewart fan." Then, her serious tone re-emerged. "I gather you need an attorney?" She moved forward and put her hands on the arms of her chair.

"A friend of mine needs some really good legal counsel."

"You or a friend?" she said, which summoned a frown to Derk's face.

"Sorry," she said. "Thurston Weedleston would be my recommendation. He's an expert on the subject."

"You mean Professor Weed?" Derk said. "You know him?"

"Sort of. His name has come up in academic circles. I still teach some.

I forgot he was an attorney," Derk said. "Both. He teaches a class at UT."

"What do you know about Aaron Kelly?" Derk asked.

"I know Weedleston is the best. The cops hate him," Samantha said. "He's able to bring up so much data in these cases that puts law enforcement in a bad light, the kind that impacts juries."

"Is he available?"

"I'm told he only takes cases that interest him."

As he was providing her with a summary of the circumstances that led to felony charges against Emma Young, she made a call.

"Excuse me, Dr. Bryan. Colleen, find out who was the arresting officer on the Emma Young case."

Three minutes later, Colleen Reid called to tell her to check her email. "Give me a minute, if you don't mind," she said to Derk before reading Colleen's note: *"I saw this on the news but figured you knew because it involved your brother-in-law."*

Colleen had included a link to a video clip of a female reporter that confirmed everything Derk had told her about the Emma Young case.

Attached was another note from Colleen Reid. "Here's something you ought to know. A week before the Hixon's trial, Sgt. Wilson Perkins deployed over one million dollars of surveillance equipment and ten officers posing as drug buyers in and around three county parks. Their efforts resulted in the arrest of eleven people with drugs having a street value of thirty-five hundred and fifty dollars. The ratio of firepower to results seemed like overkill, so I called the Sheriff Information Officer to confirm it. She stated with great pride that the numbers were correct and that Sgt. Perkins' team had also confiscated two Hummers, two Lexis, a Mercedes SL, and six other automobiles worth over five hundred thousand dollars. All of these assets were subject to immediate forfeiture which adds to our enforcement efforts without costing the taxpayer anything. It sounded as if she was reading from a prepared script."

Derk had been waiting patiently. Samantha Card got up and extended her hand.

"Dr. Bryan, my name is Samantha Card and I publish this magazine. I'm extremely busy right now, and there's a storm approaching, but I believe we can help each other."

They exchanged contact information. Derk thanked her and left. A step from the door, he turned around. "Oh, by the way. I'm looking for a guy named Ileay Denisovich."

"Another case?"

"Not exactly."

"Send me an email," she said, "and call me Sammy. Everyone else does." As he was leaving, she managed a needful smile. "By the way, know anyone I can call to put up storm shutters?"

16

Will Perkins' meeting with the Sheriff had him fretting for the first time since becoming a cop. After his brother was gunned down by a drug dealer in a routine traffic stop, he hardened. Then he went on the offensive. Aggression, in fact, had become his armor. The casualties of this aggression hadn't chinked that armor, nor had the accusations or the lawsuits. Fifteen minutes with the Sheriff and a couple of faggots in leisure suits, however, had penetrated him.

The Sheriff knew what he had done, but he hadn't arrested or suspended him. He had doctored those weed killers, added something to them just to see what the results would be. The addition of a little Barbados Nut oil was lethal, but those kids weren't innocent. If they hadn't been in those fields trying to score some free pot, they wouldn't have died. The Sheriff knew that, too, but all he wanted to do was lecture him on Keynesian economics. "Supply and demand, supply and demand," he kept harking. Every school kid knew about that, but when the Sheriff put a fatherly arm around him and said in a deep southern drawl, "We're never going to stop this, Son, the selling and buying of drugs. Our job is to manage it. And we're entitled to make a good living while doing it. So, don't fuck this up," he felt old fashioned fear. It was the kind that made him shiver down to his marrow. The reason the Sheriff hadn't arrested him was obvious. Tibbetts Foster was somehow involved. The opulent lifestyle, the corroboration of the medical examiner, and the muscle in the leisure suits made that apparent. He had stepped over lines he wasn't aware existed. With illegal drugs comes organized crimes, and in Will Perkins' line of work, people got killed, both the good guys and the other guys, if either of them crossed the lines.

His dread came from the knowledge that most of the victims never saw it coming. This was a lonely fear, the kind he couldn't share with anyone. He felt alone because he was alone. His wife checked out several years ago. His kids didn't call, and the only person with whom he could confide, his brother, was gone. He couldn't talk with Samantha. They lived on separate planets. He kept thinking about his brother, the brainy one in the family. Each wanted to be a cop. Their dad had been one. They dressed up as cops on Halloween. They wore police uniforms around the house into their teen years. They wanted to be part of the Blue family. They relied upon that family for support. Cops had to back up each other, often because their lives depended upon it. Right now, the number one guy Will Perkins counted upon to back him up was the same guy who could have him thrown into a wood chipper with a wink or a nod.

He had to go on the offensive. He had the photos, but there was no crime against drooling over naked bodies, even if they were men, fucking in private. It was only leverage, but it was all he had. He would go to a local pharmacy first thing in the morning to make some prints. No, he couldn't do that. It was too public. He would email them, but to whom? Samantha! He would email them to Samantha. She could be discrete. No, she was a reporter, and what reporter would let a juicy lead go unused, especially when it involved the Sheriff, the Chief Medical Examiner, and a gay sex orgy.

"Brrr," he shivered as he dried himself. The hot shower hadn't alleviated his anxiety.

He slipped on a pair of shorts and a tee shirt before sending the photos from his cellphone to his computer. He had no other choice. He had to email them to Samantha, and he would attach a note for the file to be opened, like a will, only in the event of his untimely demise.

He had already hired a handyman to put up hurricane shutters over the windows, so while he waited for the pictures to upload to his computer, he made sure every door to his home was locked. He uncapped a cold beer and turned off all but one light on the desk next to his computer. He sat quietly with no radio or television on to camouflage any outside sounds. The fluttering in his stomach was not caused by butterflies. He got up and paced in the dark, sat down and got up again, and uncapped another beer. When he returned to his desk, he realized he had not finished drinking the first beer. When all of the photos had been uploaded, he collected them in a file, prepared a brief note, and hit send.

17

Derk looked forward to meeting Garth O'Bannon with the same enthusiasm he had for hemorrhoids.

He wasn't used to being told to drop a case before his report was filed, and certainly not without his opinion. It was a matter of respect, one professional to another. He knew this was due to the changes occurring beyond the control of the director. The direction and energy of the agency was more and more dependent upon political winds than application of science. He was a scientist, and it riled him that every school kid knew that climate change was an existential threat to our civilization, and yet too many people in authority opposed a concerted effort to combat it. The planet was awash in toxic chemicals that were depleting the soil and poisoning the water. It takes more nitrogen to make crops today than in 1960. It is not ironic that the invention of Fritz Haber to fix nitrogen led to the development of phosgene, a colorless and odorless chemical that became a weapon of the First World War and responsible for killing over eighty thousand people.

He had protested to the director, "Ben, we're on course to raise the level of carbon dioxide in the atmosphere, from the burning of fossil fuels to a point our planet has not experienced in thirty-eight million years. We're turning the planet into a desert, which puts us on a collision course with disaster. You know that, and you're sending me to wetnurse some nit-wit with a few sick birds. Why didn't you tell him to call a vet?"

The reason he took on these shitty cases was because it kept him in the game. Sometimes, he was tossed a larger bone, and if he could take down a bad actor, it made him feel like he was doing his part. He felt more optimistic when he was part of the solution than a part of the problem.

In spite of the prospect of a two-hour trip to Clermont, the day began with some good news. Cera, the first of the approaching hurricanes, had been sheered by an Arctic cold front and pushed out to sea. The other storms were still days away, and the sun was shining. It looked a lot like any other day in paradise. He had an urge to ride his bike from one end of the key to the other, stop for a grouper sandwich at Frenchy's, and return home for a cold Chimay in a frosty mug, but he had a job to do.

To make his visit with Garth O'Bannon more tolerable, he asked Teach McIntosh to join him. Ordinarily, he didn't invite civilians to join him on business calls, but he had an ulterior motive. He had also promised his friend he would help put up storm shutters and he needed a favor in return. Teach was a trust fund child who spent his youth smoking weed, playing music with friends, and working on his tennis game. His father wouldn't give him access to his fortune until Teach, no one called him by his given name, graduated from college. Teach parlayed six laissez-faire years into a degree while he played acoustic guitar at local cafes and perfected his groundstrokes. He had a short stint on the European tour. His long-burnished locks, chiseled chin, and cobalt eyes emanated a masculinity that was defied by his demeanor. He was kind of shy. He performed to overcome it. His forte, if one could call it that, was folk and acoustic protest music from Pete Seger. Derk never understood why rich kids took up protest music, but Teach could mimic Bob Dylan with amazing similarity. He let his hair go rogue, perfected the raspy voice, and learned the harmonica. He was talented enough to play at local coffee shops and bars on the weekends.

Teach McIntosh gained his nickname from ten years of teaching music and coaching high school students. Although it wasn't a real pull yourself up by your bootstraps kind of experience, it pleased his father. Teach once told Derk that he was never sure that his father thought he had the wits and discipline to manage the fortune that was being entrusted to him. The discipline for which his father had hoped came into his life, along with humility, when he met Nina.

Nina was a wisp of a woman with choppy brown hair, sparkling eyes, and a commanding presence. In intimate gatherings Teach could occasionally entreat her to play along with him. She loved the attention but didn't consider her talent adequate for live performances. They spent their time overseeing Teach's deceased father's estate and foundation. With his wife's insistence, they steered the foundation's work into environmentally sustainable projects. Along the way, Aloysius "Teach" McIntosh became a financial wizard.

Derk had met Teach several years ago at an outdoor concert attended by hundreds of folks on motorcycles. Teach didn't ride, nor did he possess any mechanical aptitude, but he was impressed that Derk had done most of the rebuild on his 1949 Panhead. Derk was also amused by Teach McIntosh's Bob Dylan impersonations. One night, after a performance at a charity event, he talked Derk into helping him build a custom by offering him a wad of cash. Teach was going to auction the bike off to raise money for the foundation. Derk agreed to build the custom motorcycle on two conditions. One, all of the money would go to charity, and two, he got to pick out all the parts. That was his real reward. He would get to build the bike of his dreams. On the day the first box of parts arrived, Teach McIntosh added a kicker. He replaced the old Frigidaire in Derk's garage with a walk-in cooler and stocked it with craft beers. They toasted bottles of Dunkel over a Rolling Thunder motorcycle frame and had been friends ever since.

Teach occasionally turned a wrench or provided a third hand but most of the time, he strummed his guitar and obsessed about his wife's bizarre projects. Nina ran something called The Sanctuary. It housed and nursed wounded and abused animals and birds. She had become infamous when she used donations to The Sanctuary to place large billboards along the major highways entering Florida. They read: *"You are now entering Florida. Beware of dangerous animals."* Below were the pictures of an alligator, the governor, and a former president.

Garth O'Bannon had complained about sick birds. Somehow, Derk imagined, Teach's involvement with The Sanctuary might become useful today.

They were heading north on I-75 when Teach said, "Tell me again, what are we doing, and where are we doing it?"

"An old case near Clermont," Derk said and changed the subject, "What's Nina's problem?" Derk knew that Nina didn't want her husband to leave.

"If you don't help me put up the shutters, I'm dirt," Teach said, then added, "What's there?"

"I've got to check on some birds, and I didn't want to go alone," Derk said. That was true, but he didn't tell Teach McIntosh that O'Bannon's tone suggested that it would be wise to take some backup.

Derk's destination was near Clermont, a hilly community at least two hours northeast of Tampa. In spite of his attempt to put aside the Gorton case, his doubts lingered. Two hurricanes still threatened the mainland, and he had nothing to report to Ivan. In addition, Clermont resurrected some memories.

It was the site of Sugarloaf Mountain, one of only two hills that had ever gotten the best of him. As cyclists go, he had above-average stamina, but during his climb to the peak of Sugarloaf, the lactic acid had turned his legs to wood. As he got off to walk his bike, a modestly buff woman in her late thirties passed him on the fly. He would never forget the smile on her face.

Lake Apopka, a few miles from Clermont, provoked a more sulfurous image. The lake was at the bottom of a valley. The main road through the valley ascended almost to the top of a steep grade, then made a perpendicular turn for two blocks before descending for a couple of miles. The serenity of the lake was juxtaposed against the surrounding austerity. The few homes that could be seen from the ridge were mostly abandoned. The grassy fields surrounding the lake were void of once-thriving orchards. Initially, the local newspaper reported, *"American White Pelicans drop like fodder from the sky!"* and no reason or cause for the devastation of wildlife was provided. Eventually, it was determined that these migratory birds, which gathered annually to feed on the fish in Lake Apopka, succumbed by the thousands to the pesticides that had been poured onto the orange groves surrounding the lake. Those same pesticides also exterminated ninety percent of the alligators. Derk knew that scientists had warned State officials of these consequences for years, but they did nothing.

"Why isn't the EPA taking a stronger position on these chemicals?" he kept asking Ben Waitley, who had navigated the ups and downs of the agency for years.

The director once told him after a couple of cocktails, "In the past fifty years, the number of birds on the planet has dropped by thirty percent due to the destruction of habitat, pollution, and pesticides, and these guys don't get it." He was referring to elected officials of Florida. "If thirty percent of the homes in their neighborhoods were abandoned, they'd be on that like flies on a turd."

Derk relayed this history to his friend as they drove to Clermont. "This guy we're going to meet. His name is Garth O'Bannon. He thinks the same stuff that killed those pelicans is making his birds sick."

"So, what can I do?" said Teach.

"He probably needs a vet, but you've been around a lot of birds. Maybe you can suggest something."

"I doubt it," Teach said. "Anyway, it's not the shutters. The Sanctuary is the center of her universe. She protects it like a child, the kid we never had."

After a moment of silence Teach asked, "What kind of birds?"

"I don't know," Derk said. "We've known each other for what? Three or four years. I've never heard you talk like that. You really love that woman."

Teach seemed embarrassed by the observation. "She can be on the demanding side," he said.

"Do you think she ever gets jealous?" Derk said. "Of me?"

"Well, you *are* Teach McIntosh, music man, and the lady's man," Derk said.

"Well, that's true," Teach said. "But seriously, she's fanatic about that shelter. She thinks what we're doing with animals is cruel."

"What do you mean?"

"She said the animals came before us, and for most of our existence, the time we've been on this planet, we shared the planet with the animals." He paused for Derk's response, but Derk just nodded his confirmation.

Teach continued, "Nina thinks we are no more important than the giraffes or the turtles or the manatees. What do you think about that, Professor?"

"That was essentially true until the agricultural revolution when we moved away from hunting and gathering. That's when our attitude toward animals changed. Since then, we have domesticated a number of species and subrogated them to our needs," Professor Bryan responded. Then he held up one hand to make a point, "And, then, we killed off most of the other species."

"Doesn't that seem a bit radical to you?"

"She's not the only one who feels that way."

"What do you mean?" Teach said.

"Someone has been breaking into pet stores and freeing the animals." Derk handed him the newspaper. "Check out the article on page six."

Teach tossed his head back and closed his eyes. "What!" Derk said.

"The cat burglar?" Teach said.

"Yes. Someone in a cat costume opens all the cages and lets the animals out. Then she or he spray paints a large paw on the wall with the words People Against Animal Slavery, PAAS, as in paws, or is it pause?" Derk said.

"She thinks it's a crime to keep pets. Says it's unnatural and a form of …"

"Involuntary servitude," Derk finished the sentence.

"That's exactly what they call it. They have a club. I don't know what they do, but she came home the other night with something black smeared under her eyes. She said it was just her mascara running, but she had paint on her fingers," Teach said.

"Looks as if your wife is quite the activist," Derk said.

"They'll catch her, and then what?" Teach said. Worry shadowed his face.

"They can't charge her with breaking and entering," Derk said.

"That's true. The newspaper said she hides inside and comes out when everyone leaves the store," Teach said.

"She doesn't take anything, so there's no theft." "Maybe, but one of the snakes ate a puppy," Teach said.

"What do you want me to tell you?" Derk said.

"She's obsessed, Derk. We've gone fully organic. I can't buy anything made of plastic. We can't eat red meat, and the fish are full of mercury, so I'm on a damn sprouts and tofu diet. I'm having a difficult time imagining how this will end well."

"You don't know it's her," Derk said. "Take a deep breath and enjoy the ride."

Teach looked out the window as they cruised through Lake Louisa State Park.

"These electric cars are smooth," Teach said. "It's like a Disney Land ride."

"And almost maintenance-free," Derk added.

"I don't think I told you, but I've got a new gig with new stuff."

"Not Dylan. That's your signature act."

"Bobby Zimmerman turned eighty. It's time to move on," Teach said, retrieved his guitar from the back seat, and began singing.

Derk recognized the John Prine and Iris DeMent melody from "In Spite of Ourselves" but not the lyrics:

She's not the sharpest tack in the box

She never wears nylons and she disdains lox. Got her smarts from her pedigree

Says her daddy was a PhD She's not divine

But she ain't no swine, And she's just as sweet As a carrot or a beet

Derk interrupted him, "Teach, hey, Teach. Have you listened to yourself?"

"Tacky and tasteless?" Teach said.

"Worse than that," Derk said.

"I'm hosting a Tacky and Tasteless open mike night at the Brew Pub. It'll be like the old Gong Show minus the projectiles."

Teach was beaming with pride, but Derk was shaking his head. "Stick with Dylan. He's timeless."

They passed under a flock of Ibis.

"They're smart. Getting out of Dodge," Teach said as he followed their northern flight path.

"You know I'm jealous," Derk said. "You and Nina have a good thing going, and I spend my evenings trying to find a four-letter word that means insensible."

"What happened with," Teach paused between thoughts to answer Derk's puzzle question, "Cold," he said and then continued, "Agnes, wasn't it?"

"Tried that. Doesn't fit. Neither did she." Derk said.

They slowed as they approached some congestion entering Clermont.

The traffic was bumper-to-bumper heading north.

"You know, Nina is the bird expert. Not me," Teach said.

"Yes, but you're the husband of the most knowledgeable bird person I know."

Teach rolled his eyes. "You need to get out more."

***

Garth O'Bannon lived on five sloping acres between Clermont and the lake. His plot consisted of a small, single-story CBS house with peeling paint and an equally weathered garage. Behind the garage was a barn that resembled a shed with an attached lean-to. It listed toward the downhill side of the plot. The lawn, mostly unruly saw palmetto and scrub, was littered with beer cans. A vintage VW bus, with one wheel on an aluminum ramp, was parked next to the pee-stone driveway. Between the buildings, Derk spotted a thread-bare field that had been cordoned off with barb-wire. The place had the curb appeal of a third-world country.

It was a few minutes before three when they arrived. A gangly fellow in his late forties stumbled from the house as Derk exited his car.

"Brace yourself," Derk said to Teach. "This is the fun part of the job." Teach McIntosh got out and stood by the car.

Garth O'Bannon was as red as a beet in his white tank tee shirt. Rust-colored curls cropped from beneath a ball cap that he wore backward. It had been at least five days since a razor touched his face. As he descended the porch, he tripped on a toy at the foot of the steps and spilled his beer. "Damn those ladies!" he said in a distinctly Scottish accent. He stopped to chug the remainder of his drink. "Almost lost it," he said with pride and tossed the can into the yard.

130

Derk held out his business card. "Derk Bryan from the EPA, and this is my associate, Mr. McIntosh. You are Mr. O'Bannon?"

O'Bannon's breath reached Derk before his slurred words. "Bout time you laddies got here!" he said loudly. "They're killin' my birds. Come back here and take a look." He flipped the top from another can he took from a Koozie strapped to his waste.

"Guess you don't recycle up here," Derk said.

"I just did, Laddy."

"So, Mr. O'Bannon, what kind of birds do you have?" Teach said as he joined them.

"Ostriches, Laddy. Follow me." He pointed in the direction of the barn.

Derk traded frowns with his friend.

"I guess you guys know a lot about birds," O'Bannon said.

"Mr. McIntosh is an expert," Derk said.

"Aye, Laddy, from the old country?" O'Bannon said.

"No, sir. What I know about Scotland I learned from watching Outlander," Teach said.

"Have you talked with a vet?" Teach said.

"I don't need no vet. It's the water," O'Bannon said. His posture was defensive.

Teach started to say, "The water's down there," as he pointed in the direction of the lake.

"No. No. You guys aren't going to try to shift the blame this time," O'Bannon said.

They stopped in front of an enclosed area behind the shed that was encompassed with barbed wire. There were seven or eight very large, scraggly birds lying in the yard. They didn't look well.

"These are me birdies." O'Bannon panned across the enclosed feedlot. "Ostriches, you can use everything but the gobble, gobble." O'Bannon laughed at his own remark.

When neither Derk nor Teach seemed to appreciate his humor, O'Bannon said, "I'm a taxpayer and an entre-pro-newer. You laddies work for me, right!"

"His wife's got him on a tofu diet, and it's made him a little grumpy," Derk said, attempting to lighten the mood.

O'Bannon squinted his eyes and stared at Teach for an uncomfortable moment as if he had digressed into a stupor, but he said nothing. Then he let out a loud burp.

Derk watched two of the birds bump into each other and lose their balance. One wavered after a few steps and fell like a drunken sailor. Garth finished off his beer, threw the can as far as he could beyond the fence, and belched again.

"They look drunk," Derk said and pointed to the birds trying to get up.

"What's their diet?" said Teach.

O'Bannon frowned at Teach as if he was crossing into forbidden territory. "They're not drunk. I am. They're sick," O'Bannon tried unsuccessfully not to slur his words.

"What did the vet say?" Derk rephrased the earlier question.

"I know what happened to those pel'cans. Same thing's happening to me Ostriches," O'Bannon said. The slurring was continued.

"Something has affected their balance, Mr. O'Bannon," Derk said. "In humans, that's a sign of an inner ear infection. You need to call a vet."

"You call the vet if they need one. They just cost me money and tell me what I already know," O'Bannon said. "You guys said the water was okay before, and it wasn't."

Teach had walked down the fence row to get a closer look at one of the birds whose curiosity had been aroused by the visitors. The bird stuck its head over the fence. It was over three feet tall but less than five. He knew that because his wife was five feet tall, and she came up to his armpits. Its feathers were brownish gray except on the front of its neck. The full length of its neck was imbued with various shades of blue, and its eyes were pure gold. The bird's long legs bent precariously as it stumbled. It was an oddly magnificent creature.

Teach looked into the bird's glazed eyes. He had seen that look before. "Hello, my handsome friend; what have you been eating?" He whispered.

The bird pushed toward him but looked beyond him. Teach turned to face the shed six feet behind him. A bag of bird feed had spilled open. He recalled that parrots, like most of the birds at the Sanctuary, seemed to know when there was food around. In the shed were plants on a string, hanging upside down, drying like tobacco. He took a couple of steps toward the shed before Garth noticed him.

"Hey, Laddy, don't go in there?"

Teach said, "I think he's hungry. Do you mind if I feed him?" Teach pointed at the open bag.

"Not that," Garth said. "Come over here." He hurried to close the door to the shed.

Derk waved for Teach to come back. Then he noticed the empty feeding pans in the pen.

Garth positioned himself between Teach and the entrance to the shed. "So, what are you going to do?" Garth asked again.

"Mind if I go inside?" Derk asked as he gestured toward the pen. "Go, Laddy," he said, followed by another burp.

Garth O'Bannon didn't move until Teach rejoined Derk. Once they were inside the pen, the birds became leery. Most limped to gain distance from the two intruders. Teach motioned Derk to move cautiously.

"Be careful. These big fellows can run like the wind, and they'll peck you to death if they're provoked," Teach warned.

"Teach, over here," Derk said. "What's in the barn?" Derk said. "Pot. Drying," Teach said.

"He knows you saw them?" Derk said.

"Looks like it," Teach said as they walked out of Garth's hearing range. "Smelled like some good shit, too."

"Sure made him nervous," Derk said.

"You'd be, too, if a cop showed up at your place," said Teach. "I'm not a cop, and I'm certainly not a narc," Derk whispered.

"He doesn't know that," Teach said.

While they walked toward the far end of the pen, Garth O'Bannon entered his house through the back door.

"Do I need a damn sign, NOT A NARC," Derk said.

Derk waved a hand for Teach to follow him and walked toward the fence. Before climbing through the fence, he noticed a feed pan with a greenish hue.

"Look," Derk said, bending down for a closer view. Teach joined him. "He's feeding them something."

One of the big birds stopped six feet from them. Derk kneeled to scrape the contents from the wooden bowl, sniffed his fingers, and then dipped his entire head into the pan. After a long, deep breath, he stood and licked his fingers. He held the pan up to Teach's nose. They resisted laughing aloud.

Derk slowly approached one of the birds and looked directly into its golden eyes. He saw the subtle glaze that Teach had seen. As the bird backed away, Derk noticed its feet, each with three toes. This time, he looked at Teach and burst into laughter.

Garth O'Bannon had come out of the house with a beer in one hand and a handgun in the other. Its glistening blue steel reflected in the afternoon sun.

"Come out of there," O'Bannon said and motioned with his beer for them to exit the pen. He held the gun to his side.

Garth O'Bannon closed the gate as Derk and Teach exited the pen. "You've seen enough," O'Bannon said.

"Mr. O'Bannon, do you have an invoice or any paperwork on these birds?" Derk asked in an even tone, trying to ignore the gun as he spoke.

O'Bannon threw the hand with the gun into the air. "I don't have to prove they're mine!"

The scent of beer from O'Bannon's body flooded over Derk like diesel exhaust. Teach McIntosh stiffened.

"No, you don't, but there's something you ought to know about your birds," Derk said as confidently as anyone might to a drunk man with a gun.

O'Bannon stopped waving the gun. "What's that, Laddy?"

"These birds are not Ostriches," Derk said.

"The fuck you talking 'bout?" O'Bannon said. "Have you ever seen an Ostrich?" Derk said.

"Right over there," Garth said, pointing indiscriminately into his feedlot.

"So have I, and they only have two toes," Derk said.

O'Bannon's neck snapped, like it was on a rubber band, in the direction of his collection of fowl. O'Bannon leaned forward and squinted at his livestock's feet. At the sight of three toes, the gun dropped from his hand, and he slumped against the gate. Derk didn't bother to pick up the gun.

"Emus, Mr. O'Bannon, you're raising Emus," Derk said. O'Bannon kept staring at his birds' feet.

"No fucking way!" O'Bannon said.

"Emus are smaller than Ostriches, and you wanted to fatten them up," Derk said. "Your birds aren't sick. They're stoned."

Teach had pulled up a photo of Emus on his cell phone. "Look at this," he said to the Emu farmer.

"Fuck no. He told me they were Ostriches!" O'Bannon said.

"Who did?" said Derk.

"Fuckin' Eddie!" Garth said as he rose. He twisted back and forth, contorted his face, and looked as if he wanted to lash out at someone.

"Garth," Derk said. "If you've got documentation to prove you ordered Ostriches and not Emus, you've got a legitimate grievance, and you don't need us. You need a lawyer."

O'Bannon shook his head in disbelief but held out his hand. "Sorry, can I get you lads a beer?"

Before Derk filed the report on the Garth O'Bannon case, he mulled over the scheme that resulted in a flock of emus that were supposed to be ostriches. A friend of O'Bannon had introduced him to someone named Eddie who told him how he could triple his money in six months by raising Ostriches. Eddie convinced Garth that Florida was prime breeding territory for them, just as cattle were raised here for fattening. For only fifteen thousand dollars, he would be on the ground floor of a new industry. Garth O'Bannon, proud of himself for living off the grid, didn't have a computer or access to the World Wide Web. Except for seeing one in an issue of National Geographic while waiting in his dentist's office, he didn't know the difference between an Ostrich and a turkey. When it became clear that Garth O'Bannon had given up his life savings to a guy who he knew only by one name, the irony was too much for Derk Bryan to further complicate O'Bannon's life. His report stated that Mr. O'Bannon's birds were already on the way to recovery by the time he arrived. He made no mention of the pot plants, the gun, or the stoned Emus.

18

On the way home, Derk noticed three text messages on his cell phone. The one he didn't recognize, the tenth Robo-call in the past week, confirmed that the "Do Not Call List" was as useful as a pimple on his ass. The second was from Stickman. He wanted a thumbs up or down in regard to the pool tournament in Orlando. The other message was from Samantha Card. It read, "Call me."

She answered on the first ring. "Dr. Bryan, I may have something for you."

"Shush," Derk said to Teach.

In celebration of the moment, Teach was vaping a herb he called American Dream. While strumming his guitar he was building some lyrics from their encounter with the drunken Scot and the buzzed birds.

"A name or a place?" Derk said, assuming she was referring to Ileay Denisovich.

"Are you familiar with Gorton Farm and Garden Supply?"

"You're joking," he said and waved at Teach to be still.

"And this Denisovich guy, who is he?" she said.

"The first is the case I'm working on, and the other is a longer story. What do you know?"

"There's no subtle way to ask you, but I need someone to put up my storm shutters. There's another one coming right at us," she said. "My brother-in-law usually does it, but he's not available."

"I'll be there by eight."

"Tonight?"

"Ditto," he said.

"Should I make dinner?"

"It's not really necessary, but if you insist, no dairy, please," he said.

Since he learned that the common denominator of the people who lived in Blue Zones, known for their longevity, was the absence of dairy in their diets, he had given up casein.

"I guess that leaves out pizza," she said with a laugh. Then she added, "I'm sorry to hear about Jake."

"Jake Twill?"

"I know a lot about you, Derk Bryan. Is Chinese okay?"

"There's nothing you can tell me now?" he said.

"See you at eight," she said and ended the call.

"Sounds like you've got a date," Teach said.

Derk shrugged at that notion while he immersed himself in the emotions she aroused about Jake, a former mentor and father figure. Why was he surprised that she took the time to research him and more surprised that she may know something about the Gorton case that he did not? Was she a damsel in distress or a damn good reporter? He was eager to find out. "She's researched you, Studdo. Probably knows your Jockey size," Teach said. "Who is this princess?"

After Derk provided the highlights of his meeting with the publisher of the Bay Magazine, his friend had two questions.

"Is she single, and does she have pets?"

On the way to Teach's house, Derk called Stickman to tell him he wouldn't be at The Top End that evening and that he wouldn't be disappointed if he chose someone else to be his partner in the tournament.

***

Derk didn't want to be a reason that Teach's wife divorced him, so he begged her not to blame Teach and promised her profusely that he would return in the morning to help install the shutters.

"Come hell or high water," he told each of them. "I'll be here before your birds crow."

He tried not to feel guilty for not helping his friends while he pursued a long shot in a case that had already been closed. He knew he was obsessive when he was on a case. Everyone did. But until he resolved a case to his satisfaction, it was not closed. He was also aware of the toll it took on some of those close to him. This had been explicitly explained by his deceased wife. Jenny had been his number-one fan and his biggest critic. A hundred things still reminded him of her every day. As he left his friends, he realized that he had gone from obsession to guilt to grief in less time than it took to change his pants. Maybe he had to reset his priorities, but this wasn't the time for it.

He selected a track from Boston on Pandora and turned up the volume in the hope that he wouldn't hear himself thinking. What did Samantha Card know about Sandy Gorton that she couldn't tell him over the phone? Did she really have information about Ileay Denisovich? How could the publisher of an entertainment weekly have access to resources he didn't have?

Maybe she just needed a handyman. Maybe Emma Young didn't have the corner on the damsel in distress routine. Too many maybes and he didn't think that role fit Samantha Card. She seemed to be a take-charge woman. He would soon find out.

When he reached her condo in St. Pete, a delivery man from Wang's Chinese Take-out was retreating from her doorway. A bright orange orb, nestling on the horizon, refracted brownish rays on the walls where Areca palms in planters lined the walkway. The porch light, a muted maize, would soon fill the atrium. He wasn't thrilled about installing shutters in the dark, but give a little, get a little.

A teenager's voice carried through the half-open door. "I'm not going back there!"

"Of course you are." He heard a middle-aged woman respond.

The sounds of Igor Stravinsky affected him like fingernails on a blackboard. He braced himself for torture.

"No one likes me there, and they're all so stupid." It was the teenage girl's voice again.

"You're exaggerating. And turn off that music. Thought your generation was into Rap."

The voice was more motherly than authoritative. But Rap? He'd rather have scrotal surgery than listen to it. He glanced at his watch as he rang the doorbell. The day was mostly gone but far from over.

Before he could turn around Samantha Card was opening the front door.

"Come in, Mister, I mean Dr. Bryan," she said.

Her place was a combination of contemporary and art deco, muted with pastel colors and embellished with bold abstract art. Like its owner, he had never seen any decor resembling it. Samantha was in a leotard so tight it made every curve on her body a travel destination. As she led him to the kitchen, she spoke of the egg rolls and Dim Sum from Wang's. It seemed more like jittery talk than praise of the cuisine, but it didn't matter. He hadn't eaten since breakfast, and he was more anxious than hungry.

"Mrs. Card," he said.

"It's Miss Card, but you can call me Sammy." She turned, steepled her fingers, and rubbed her hands together.

Her eyes roamed the room as if they were searching for something. When they met again with his, he held out his watch. "If I don't put up your shutters now, it'll have to wait. Do you want to talk while I'm working?"

"I'd like to, but," she didn't complete the sentence, "Let me show you what needs to be done."

She led him to each window that required shutters. In the hallway, she pointed to a door and said, "The shutters are in the garage. May I get you something to drink?"

She was gracious and polite. She was also distracted.

"Mom," came a voice from elsewhere in the house. "Can Amy come over?"

"It's my daughter. I've got to go," Samantha said.

When she turned away, he said, "About that drink, got a cold beer?"

"Sorry," she said. "How about fruit punch?"

He nodded, and she was off. As she walked away, she shouted, "No, Jamie, there's a hurricane headed this way. She can't come over."

Spinning the wing nuts to secure each shutter was tedious and little served by his rush to finish. He cursed each nut as it fell through his fingers. At the same time, he regaled in the extra investment he had made for the accordion type at his home. He could close up his entire house in ten minutes without spilling a drop of Hoegaarden.

Through the glass, he listened to the mother and daughter spar. He gathered her daughter had just returned from the hospital, and Samantha thought it was too soon for her to have visitors, not to mention the imminent storm. Her daughter protested the meds she was forced to take and that she didn't like being treated as a child.

"In this house, you are legally a child, and I'm the adult. I would gladly switch with you if I could," Samantha said.

The burden and the rewards of parenting had created ambivalence in Derk's life. He reconciled the loss by valuing the things he had, such as an IRA, hobbies, and freedom. He never worried about a babysitter, the appropriate time to go out for a beer, or meshing his schedule with soccer practice and ballet classes. He knew it wasn't that simple, but he had reconciled with the fact that Jenny couldn't have children.

Thoughts of family life brought him back to his reason for being here. Samantha's mention of Sandy Gorton affirmed the suspicion he had that this case was not closed, and he was salivating to know what she had found about Ileay Denisovich. He tried to focus on getting each wing nut onto its screw head without dropping it, but it was a challenge with his arthritic hands.

When he tightened the last wing nut, he returned to the kitchen. A gin and tonic over ice waited on the island countertop, pooled in its own condensation. A teenager, with gauze wrapped around each wrist, sat on a high stool, picking broccoli from a pizza while tapping the keys of a laptop computer.

"Oh, Jamie, you like broccoli," said Samantha, who was sitting across from her with wet hair and a change of clothes. She had slipped into black tights and a University of South Florida tee-shirt. The scent of fresh rain emanated from her hair.

Before her daughter could respond, she said to Derk, "Thought you could use something stiffer. Thanks for your help."

He nodded. He seldom ever drank liquor, but the ice-cold, piney aroma was a welcome rush.

"Never," her daughter retorted. "I hate brassicas."

"Are you sure you took your medication?" her mother said.

Jamie let out an exaggerated sigh. "Mom, it makes me feel like a zombie."

"Jamie, say hello to Dr. Bryan."

Derk smiled and held out his hand. "Nice to meet you. How do you know how a zombie feels?"

She offered her greasy pizza palm to him. "I thought you were an EPA investigator."

"He is, and he's a PhD," Samantha said.

"Can you send the oil companies execs to jail for lying about global warming?" Jamie asked.

Derk looked to Samantha for guidance.

"Well, can you?" Samantha said.

"We're working on it," he said and withdrew his hand.

He took a sip of his drink and sighed, "Oh boy, that's good!" he said.

"They funded false reports. Isn't that a crime?" Jamie said, then took a bite of pizza with the vegetables jettisoned.

He wasn't used to being tongue-tied by a teenager, but she had a point. One of the largest oil companies had funded research that produced reports denying fossil fuels' contribution to global warming. She was right to question this because she was going to live her entire life affected by the repercussions of their greed and deception.

He guessed her to be about sixteen and precocious, but the bandaged wrists and talk of medication made it clear this was a family in crisis. He wanted to engage her concerns, but it would have to wait. He was there for other reasons.

He wanted to list the nutritional deficiencies that would result from a childhood void of vegetables, but his thoughts were preempted by the television news showing the path of Deimus. It was approaching the Bahamas. Already a Cat 3, it was forecast to become more muscular as it swamped Florida. Tampa Bay was within the cone.

"You should be safe now, I think," Derk said.

"We have another option if it gets too bad," Samantha said. "At least, that's what my brother-in-law said if we can find him. What about you?"

"I can button up my place in ten minutes, but this could be a bad one, and there's another behind it," Derk said.

The reality was gripping. No one said anything as they watched a report relayed from a weather plane flying through the eye.

"Whatever you found about Ileay Denisovich can wait. If you need to get out of here, we can talk later," Derk said. He almost couldn't believe he said that.

"Where else can we go, Mom," Jamie said. Derk noticed the smart-alecky, nerdish attitude had disappeared.

"Your uncle said we could go to E-Com."

"Emergency Communications?" Derk said.

"Uncle Will's a detective," Jamie said.

"Sergeant, sweetie. Uncle Will is a sergeant," Samantha said.

"Will Perkins?" Derk said. "From the Sheriff's Office?"

"My dad was a detective, too," Jamie said, but her mother interrupted her.

"Jamie, don't you have homework?"

"Mom, you know school was canceled."

Samantha flashed a look at her daughter, which prompted her response, "Does this mean you want me to go to my room?"

"Sweetie, I need to talk with Dr. Bryan. Stay here and finish your pizza."

"Let's go into my office." Samantha pointed Derk toward another room.

She took a seat behind a chrome-framed desk with a glass top. He sank into a Mies van der Rohe leather chair. Behind Samantha was an Andy Warhol print of a can of tomato soup. Derk never understood its appeal. Photographs of people he didn't recognize, probably family members, were framed on the wall behind him. A solo Klimt hung from the ceiling opposite the entrance. Sammy Card had taken eclectic design to a new level, but the most distinctive item in the room was an end table with a glass top that had an abstract pattern of colors imposed upon it. The name Reshefsky was etched into one corner.

The furrows in her brow and the crow's feet around her eyes defied her physical fitness. Weariness prefaced her words.

"I was married to Will Perkins' brother. I kept my maiden name for the newspaper."

"That's showbiz," Derk said.

"Will and I don't always get along, but he's all Jamie has." Her words were tinted with sadness.

"And your husband?"

She took a deep breath and exhaled. "Killed while on duty."

"I'm sorry," Derk said.

"But that's not why you're here, Dr. Bryan," she said.

"Please call me Derk."

"Of course. I've been trying to reach Will for days. I thought he was avoiding me due to an article I wrote until this," she said and held out her cell phone.

On her phone were two names, Global, LLC and Gorton Farm and Garden, with the message: "Connect the dots. Then check your email."

Derk sat up in his chair. "Did you?"

"Connect the dots?" she said. "Maybe. Look at this."

She motioned for him to come to her side of the desk. She hit a couple of keys on her PC and up popped an article from a summer edition of the Bay Magazine.

"You might not recall this story, but it involved an illegal immigrant named Juan Rodriguez, who was busted for possession of marijuana and stealing a truck. He led the police, my brother-in-law, and his troops to a farm where they were growing marijuana. Will's men sprayed the fields, a couple of guys died, and it led to a suit by the farm workers' union, which was later dropped when the Sheriff said they would stop spraying close to other crops." She paused for his response.

"Vaguely. Go on," he said.

"It was probably dropped because the guys died during the commission of a crime. Clearly, it put Will and the Sheriff in a bad light. My assistant did some research and found that Gorton was named in the suit as the supplier of the chemical used by the Sheriff."

"I.E., your brother-in-law," Derk said.

She nodded and continued, "Gorton said the product was legal when used according to the label."

Derk interjected, "They're all lethal in some form, whether used correctly or not."

"Right, and Gorton referred them to the distributor," she said.

The sounds of voices, probably from a television, wandered down the hallway. Outside, darkness made the lone window in the room opaque. He leaned in to focus upon the connections she was making, so close her pheromones bordered on intoxicating. Her hair, skin, and taut physique were enhanced by the command of her voice. One's first impression of Samantha Card wouldn't be arousing, but she was an intelligent and intriguing woman.

"A common refrain," Derk said. "And the distributor backed him up?"

"More or less," Sammy said.

"That doesn't surprise me," Derk said.

"The company is registered in the Cayman Islands. They've got their hands in a lot of things like chemicals, industrial supplies, and real estate."

"But they're not made there. Just a corporate HQ," Derk said. He returned to his chair, hopeful her story was leading to a payoff.

"I'm sure. So, my assistant, Colleen, looked it up. Turns out Global owns a home at Bay Island Country Club. Guess who's listed as a partner?"

He didn't have a clue, but she must be getting to the punch line. "Tibbetts Foster," she said.

"The Sheriff?" Derk popped to attention.

"Here's the kicker," she said and invited him to look at her computer screen again.

She clicked a few keys and up popped some photos of a couple of young guys with erections doing the naked pretzel, a gentleman sucking on a fat cigar, and Sheriff Tibbetts Foster in a gauze leisure suit holding a daiquiri.

"Holy moly!" Derk said.

"Excuse my French, but what the fuck is going on?" Samantha said.

Derk resisted the urge to go directly to Will Perkins' home only because Samantha wanted to accompany him, and she didn't want to leave her daughter alone. He decided it was better to approach the sergeant during daylight hours.

On his way home, he pondered the possible connections between Sandy Gorton, the Sheriff, and some offshore company. It had to be financial, but the image of Doc Morton rubbing rumps with the boys at the pool provided other options. His cell phone rang.

"Scratch, how they hanging?"

"Shine, where are you?"

"Still riding the waves, lover."

"How's your game?" Derk asked.

"Scratch, sweetheart, you know I'm always on top, but I'm flexible," she said.

"That you are."

"And you?"

"We're talking about my game?" Derk said.

"Yes, lover. Are you going to enter the doubles tournament?" she said.

"The one in Orlando? I'm just a hacker."

"One of the best," she said. "My company will put up the entry fees for you and your partner."

"I already turned down an invite," Derk said.

"They think it's a chance to push some product."

"What do bigger boobs have to do with pool?" Derk said.

"No, silly. Surer strokes without the tokes." She made him laugh. "It begins next week. If I bring whipping cream, will you let me be your partner?

"Do you close all your sales with that line?"

"A girl's got to make a living," she said.

He heard a phone ring and then some voices in the background.

"Gotta go, Scratch. I'll call you with the details," she said, followed by a kissing sound.

Even though he was a competent pool player, he was apprehensive about competing in a major tournament. He also felt a modicum of guilt because Stickman had been pursuing him for weeks. And, there were his arthritic hands. There were days it took until noon for the stiffness to subside. But hey, someone else was paying the bill, and a night with Shine, including champagne and meringue, left him tingly with anticipation. He wasn't sure how to tell Stickman he had a different partner.

He sent a text message to Teach, reminding him he would be there in the morning to finish the hurricane preparations, and thanked him for the advice. Whenever Derk was stuck on a case, Teach would remind him, "Follow the money, my friend."

***

Without moonlight it was coal tar dark and closing in on midnight when he pulled his e-car car into his driveway. The dash readout told him he had three miles of charge left on the battery. A humid breeze blew sand onto the garage floor. He grabbed a cold

Dortmunder from the refrigerator, climbed the stairs, and went to his computer.

Before leaving Samantha's home she had referred him to her assistant's email in regard to Ileay Denisovich. She had asked Colleen Reid to do a search and send the results to Derk.

"What's your connection to this guy, anyway?" Samantha had asked.

"He might be related to something I'm working on," Derk said. He was happy the complications of her own life kept her from further probing.

He opened the email from Samantha's assistant: "I found an Ileay Denisovich who changed his name to Ivan Dennis upon emigrating to America. He was, according to one theory, a relative of Ivan Denisovich and a major source of the story for Solzhenitsyn's book. (This is only an unproven theory). He was a history professor and, therefore, part of a group that was not considered loyal to the communist state during Stalin's reign. To salve Stalin's paranoia, thousands of academicians were rounded up and railroaded to Siberia or just disappeared. While in Prague, giving a lecture on Russian history, he sneaked away from his colleagues and made his way to Germany. Not long after that he sought asylum and was admitted to the United States."

She had also found an obituary in a small Michigan newspaper for someone by the name of Ivan Dennis, who had died twenty years earlier. "If you need more info, please contact me," she said.

He immediately replied, "Did Ileay Denisovich or Ivan Dennis have a son or any family in the United States?" And, just for the hell of it, he asked, "Do you know a four-letter word for insensible?"

Tired as a slug on a thousand-mile journey, he hit the sack thinking he might be the grandson of a Russian history professor. Images of characters from War and Peace roamed his mind before he fell into a deep sleep.

19

Will Perkins was at his front door after an all-night surveillance at the Port of Tampa. His team had been acting upon a tip from an informant that came up empty. He was as spent as a flat tire, but the sound of glass breaking sent his paranoia into red alert.

It was dawn, and the entry light had been broken. He drew his gun and slowly pushed open the front door. With both hands on his revolver, he crossed the living room but avoided being seen through the kitchen from the back door. He assumed an intruder had broken the glass in the back door. He held his breath and waited for trouble.

Nothing moved. He heard only silence, loud, crashing silence!

He listened for a breath or the sound of fabrics touching, a change in the path of the air conditioner, a burp, or a sigh. He heard nothing, just silence, the terrifying kind.

He doubted this was a snatch-and-run house burglar. He inhaled the longest, deepest, and quietest breath he had ever taken, knowing it could be his last.

He had spent most of the previous day trying to figure out what evidence they had against him. He guessed it was purchase orders they falsified. The chemicals were legal unless his signature was forged. The items he had ordered were legal, but in combination, they were dangerous. What he added to them was lethal.

It could not be coincidental that Doctor Morton had reported no foul play. There was foul play, people had died, and if what the Sheriff said was true, the county had been sued by the descendants of the deceased. They would have had the bodies exhumed and private analyses performed. So, why did it take so long? Why had he not heard about this before?

Then again, maybe this was about the weed he had skimmed off an old bust. He had sprayed it with a mist of Barbados Nut oil and sold it to a street dealer who sold it to the college students, probably the Hankins boy and the Crimshaw gal, who died. That was tragic, but they surely knew the dangers of illegal drugs. People had been coddling these kids for way too long. Too many States had made pot legal, even available by prescription. They didn't know what he knew. The broken hearts, snuffed dreams, and desperate families. What he had done was to boost the visibility of the danger. He was convinced it would put a dent in street drugs, and that was his job. Even so, how could they have linked that to him? The dealer, the drifter he had surreptitiously duped into being a middleman for his scheme, had left the State after the first two kids died. No one else knew. Two things were certain. First, it had something to do with drugs. Second, if the Sheriff and the dealers were working together, his life wasn't worth a plugged nickel.

He couldn't hold still much longer. His knees began to wobble, but he thought he heard a sound. Maybe what he heard came from outside. Maybe it came from next door. Maybe it was nothing. He was exhausted, edgy, and suspicious of everyone and everything. What he didn't hear was Sniffles, his dog, who normally met him at the door.

He sighed and relaxed his grip on the trigger. At the same time, the dog next door barked. Sniffles, his adopted drug search dog retiree, remained mum. Strange.

In succession, he heard a trigger set and a gun fire before the wall between him and the intruder exploded. The blast knocked him to the floor. Dazed, he heard steps coming from the kitchen. He crawled to a broken chair lying a couple of feet from him. Blood was squirting from his arm.

He saw sneakers and bulging calves before the end of a sawed-off shotgun. He rolled over, snatched one leg of the chair, and swung at the intruder's chin. When the gun hit the floor, it discharged. Will recognized the burning sensation, followed by a dampness under his left side.

He had been hit.

He got to his feet at the same time as the tanned thug, the same guy he had seen with the Sheriff at the Bay Island Country Club, arose.

"You!" Sergeant Perkins shouted and leaped for the gun laying on the floor.

As he tried to pick up the gun, the intruder grazed his arm with a blade. He was sliced again when he repeated the effort. He tried one more time, but the man in the straw hat picked up the gun and fired.

Nothing happened. The gun was empty.

Realizing he had not been shot, Will rushed the intruder, but he was so weak he fell into the man's arms. Dominic Domini let him fall to the floor. Sergeant Wilson Perkins laid on his back and made a feeble attempt to hit the intruder with his leg.

His assailant shrugged and said, "Keep swinging, Sergeant, until you bleed out."

Will watched him go into the next room. He heard the sounds of drawers being opened and closed, things being tossed about the room, and the smashing of glass. The glass in that room covered a display case containing three antique guns. One was a replica of the pistol used by John Wilkes Booth to shoot President Lincoln. They weren't loaded.

He heard the perp say, "Where the hell is it?"

Then, "We'll take this," and the sounds of computer cables being removed and his laptop being snapped shut. It was the same computer from which he sent the incriminating links to Samantha Card.

The man in the straw hat returned and put a heavy foot on Will's bleeding arm. He bent down and removed a cellphone from the Sergeant's pocket. He nodded with a cold, emotionless smirk, an expression that Will Perkins would never be able to erase from his memory.

Moments later, Will Perkins heard the back door shut, the sound of a dog bark, and another man's voice asking, "Is he dead? Did you get it? What's that?"

"That's a laptop, and this is a derringer, Dex. Now let's get out of here."

20

Before he took a sip of orange juice or picked up the morning newspaper, Derk turned on the television. An eighteen-year-old high school student was standing in front of a microphone admonishing world leaders at a conference on climate change. The street was full of demonstrators with ominous warnings.

The weather channel showed Deimos crashing into the Bahamas. It left Nassau looking like kindling dropped onto a cookie sheet. He had fond memories of the islands. On each visit, he made a point to buy a gift from one of the craftsmen at the Straw Market. Some of those entrepreneurs would never recover from this blow. He paused to consider just how fragile life can be. In a few minutes, one's entire existence can be turned upside down, and the belief that any of us are in charge of our own lives can be forever challenged as he watched the icon for Deimos spinning on the weather map, a small knot formed in his stomach. He went to each window and activated the shutters. This is going to be a bad one.

Tampa Bay was within the southern edge of the cone. He double-checked the Weather Channel app on his cell phone and took a hasty inventory of his storm readiness supplies. He was prepared, but he might have to go south if Deimos remained a Cat 3. Then he called Teach and told him he would be there in an hour and that he needed his technical skills.

"It's the Gorton case. I may be on to something," Derk said. Derk wanted to look at Gorton's invoices, and Teach knew his way around digital bookkeeping.

"Damn it, Derk, Nina is going to have a fit," said Teach.

"We'll do it later," Derk promised again and hit off on his phone.

***

It was almost noon when Derk parked across the street from a one-story CBS house just a few blocks from the football stadium on

Dale Mabry. He convinced Teach to accompany him to Will Perkins' home with another promise to install the shutters later that day. Within minutes, Samantha arrived and parked in the drive behind her brother-in-law's county-issued police cruiser. His own car was not in sight. She rang the bell, but no one answered.

"Got a key?" Derk asked.

"Trust isn't one of Will's better traits," she said. Samantha looked for signs of life through the windows, but the blinds blocked her view.

"Who's that?" Samantha said, referring to Teach, who was seated in Derk's car.

"A forensic accountant. Let's go around back," Derk lied, then signaled Teach to wait in front while they went to the rear of the house.

A Cocker Spaniel let out a shallow huff and followed them down a driveway that was bordered by a fence that separated Perkins' abode from his neighbor's home. At the end of the drive was a chain link fence with a gate that opened into the Sergeant's neglected backyard.

One frayed patio chair leaned against a single Barbados nut tree. The ground surrounding the tree was bare except for the fallen nuts. An aging water hose snaked across the lawn to a rusty water sprinkler that had been turned upside down. The wheels of a long-ago abandoned motorcycle appeared beneath a weathered army-green tarp. Its flaccid rubber tires seemed mated to the oil-stained concrete slab.

"The Sergeant is quite the landscaper," Derk said.

The screen door was broken just above the handle. It made a scraping noise when Derk shoved on it. He held it open for Samantha to enter.

"Whoa!" she said. "Broken glass."

Derk held a finger to his mouth to quiet her and pushed on the door.

The crunch under her feet was the only response when she announced herself, "Will, are you here? It's Samantha." She entered the kitchen.

"Oh, my god!" She cried out, staring at a basketball-sized hole in the kitchen wall. She turned to Derk, who had also noticed the hole in the wall, and followed his eyes to the place where the blood met the floor and then up the side of a cabinet. A glob dripped from the countertop onto the kitchen floor.

"Will!" Samantha screamed. "Will!"

Derk held out a finger to test the blood, but he knew it was fresh. "Stay here," he said and motioned for her to stay behind him.

She stayed as close to him as sap on a Maple tree. He tip-toed to the doorway and peeked into the next room. On the floor in front of them was a ragged path of blood leading to the kitchen doorway.

Samantha screamed again. Derk jumped back, caught her in the chin, and knocked her off her feet.

When he moved to help her, he stumbled over, "Oh my god!" a shotgun.

As he slipped on the blood that had been skewed upon the living room tile, he kicked the sawed-off shotgun against the tile baseboard and fell upon Samantha. He curled his body around her and waited for the blast to tear them apart.

It took only a nano-second, but it seemed longer before he realized he was still alive. The gun had not fired.

Samantha struggled to free herself from his grip and get to her feet, but the blow to her chin had disoriented her. Derk got to one knee, took her hand, and helped her get up.

"You okay?" Derk said, and she nodded.

He held up a finger and turned an ear toward the bedrooms. Each of them listened for a sound, any sound, but there was silence.

"Wait here," Derk said. This time, she stayed put.

He stuck his head into two rooms before returning to the living room.

He pointed down the hallway. "What's in there?"

"I don't know. Maybe his office," she said.

Moments later, he called out from another room, "Samantha, tell Teach to get in here."

"Did you find him?" She said as she rushed to the sound of his voice.

When she reached the doorway, Derk looked up from behind a desk. Computer cables dangled, detached from their CPU, and desk drawers were strewn about the room. Will Perkins' dog lay silent on the floor with crimson-colored streaks radiating from its head.

"He's not this sloppy," Samantha said. "Oh my god!" she gasped when she saw the dead dog.

"Tell Teach to get in here!"

Samantha left, and when she returned with Teach, Derk was sifting through the file cabinets in disarray about the room.

"There's blood in the kitchen. Holy fuck!" Teach exclaimed when he saw the dog.

"I'm calling 911," Samantha said and began to hit numbers on her cell phone. "Will's been shot."

Derk heard a voice say 911. "No," he said and tried to grab the phone from Samantha.

"What?" Samantha said and pulled away.

"Let Teach do it," Derk said.

"Why?" she said again, clutching her phone.

The voice on the phone repeated, "911, what's your emergency?"

"Trust me," he said, hoping his sincere tone would override the lame cliché he had uttered. "This man is an officer of the law." He pointed a finger at Teach. "Ask for Sergeant Perkins."

Samantha grimaced and held out the phone. Teach took it. They waited as Teach asked to speak with Sergeant Perkins.

"Mi nombre es Major Umberto from Columbia," Teach used a Spanish accent Derk had never heard him deploy.

"No," Teach whispered to Derk and Samantha.

"When will he be back?" He sounded like the bad cop in Romancing the Stone.

"I see. No necessita. Gracias," Teach said and handed it back to Samantha.

"She ragged on me for calling 911, but someone said he's on vacation," Teach said, looking at Samantha.

Samantha was shaking her head. "No, he's been shot. I'm calling back!"

"Wait!" Derk said. "Do you know your brother-in-law is not on vacation?"

"He always tells us so we can check on his place," she said.

"Always?" Derk said.

"I don't know. I'm calling 911," she said and hit call on her phone. "This is Samantha Card, Sergeant Perkins' sister-in-law. There's been a family emergency. I need to talk with him, and he's not answering his cell phone. Do you know how to contact him?"

Moments later, she hit end on her phone. Her puzzled look begged for a question, but Teach knew the answer.

"The Sheriff wouldn't approve a vacation with a hurricane coming, would he?" Teach said.

Samantha was dialing again when Derk said, "Do you believe in coincidences?"

"Even if he is on vacation, someone broke in, killed the dog, and he's missing. I'm reporting this," she said.

Derk could hear the 911 voice again as he held out his hands, palms up, and asked, "Think about it. Your brother-in-law tells you to check out a connection between the Sheriff and Sandy Gorton. Then he comes up missing. I don't..." he said.

A question mark appeared on her face.

"Believe in coincidences," Derk said.

She hit end on her phone.

***

Derk tucked a desk calendar and a manila folder full of bank statements under his arm and headed for the back door. "I'll be right back."

"You can't take those, can you?" Teach said. "Isn't this a crime scene?"

"I thought you said he was a cop," Samantha said.

"I lied," Derk said. "Here's what I see. Someone left his key elsewhere and had to break the glass to get in. In the process, he cut his hand. Samantha, here," and he pointed with the hand cradling the folders, "is a family member who allowed us entry. She hadn't heard from her brother-in-law and feared he was hurt when she found the door unlocked and spotted blood on the floor. That's rightful entry."

"So, you want me to snoop in his files?" Teach said. He was now aware of why Derk asked him to tag along.

"Affirmative, Dr. Watson," said Derk.

"You're not going to report this?" Samantha said.

"To whom?" Derk said.

She started to protest but put her hand over her mouth. She mumbled, "To the very people who may be involved. So, what are we going to do?"

"Maybe there's something in here that will help us find him," he said as he handed a thumb drive to Teach that he had found on the floor.

159

Teach grimaced. "Wholly shmolly. What about the dog?'

"Yes, that's a problem," Derk said and headed for the back door. "Hang on. I'm going to get a vial from my car for a blood sample."

He asked Samantha to join him. They stopped beside her car, and he handed her the desk calendar he had taken.

"Take a look at this and see if you recognize anyone," he said.

He took a small vial from a case in the trunk of his car. As she was backing down the driveway, he waved to stop her. She rolled down the window.

"Does he have his own car?' Derk said.

Each of them looked in the direction of the blood drops on a patch of brown grass about where an automobile was routinely parked. Samantha drooped onto the steering wheel.

"From what I've heard, your brother-in-law can take care of himself," Derk said. It was a weak attempt at consolation. For all he knew, Wilson Perkins' bones were already at the bottom of Lake Myakka, the flesh having been devoured by the largest pool of alligators in Florida, but he smiled when he added, "I'll call you later."

"Where are you going?" she said.

"Following the money, Miss Card," he said as he waved goodbye with the folder. "Be careful."

Derk scraped the blood into the vial, snapped it shut, and they left.

In the car, Derk said, "Sorry about the dog, but we've got to make another stop."

"I've got to get back. Come on, you promised," Teach said.

"Help me catch some bad guys," Derk said.

"Damn it, Derk. You love this stuff."

A glint of joy and the rise of an eyebrow was Derk's response.

"This is police business now. What are you going to do?' Teach said.

"What you always told me to do, follow the money," Derk said.

21

The thumb drive was of no use, they found when Teach plugged it into Derk's laptop. Smoke was ascending above the Port of Tampa as they approached the Gorton Farm and Garden Supply store, a few blocks from Ybor City. The police had cordoned off the area, so Derk could only see the blaze from afar. He flashed his credentials and parked his car. "You guys are quick," the officer said.

"What do you mean?" Derk said.

"If the fire reaches the warehouse, there could be big problems, right?" The officer said. He was in uniform but carried no sidearm.

"Where is it now?" Derk said.

"Main building. Offices, right?" It was more of a question than a statement.

"Right," Derk said with a side glance at Teach, which implied, "No wonder this guy is assigned to barricade duty."

"Anyone in the building?' Teach said.

"Don't know. A business has to have fire alarms, right?" The man in the uniform couldn't have been more than twenty years old. Maybe a member of a citizens' patrol, probably a wannabe cop.

"Probably," Teach said, glancing at Derk.

"Was an ambulance requested?" Derk said.

"It already left," the guard said. "Guess that means there's nobody in there, right?"

Teach rolled his eyes this time.

Derk said to Teach, "If this thing reaches the warehouse, the whole neighborhood could be toxic for years."

To the guard in uniform, Teach said, "When did the fire start?"

"Don't know, but it couldn't be long ago. I just set up the roadblock."

Derk was staring at the flames, occasionally rising above the smoke and mumbling to himself.

"What are you thinking?" Teach said.

When Derk's silent chatter stopped his eyes filled with fear. "Let's go!" He bolted for his car. After a few steps, he did a one-eighty and returned to Teach. "You want me to carry you?"

"Where?" Teach said, hurrying to catch Derk.

When Derk was behind the wheel, he said, "Buckle up. Gorton's house."

The electric car fishtailed down a side street before intersecting with the Crosstown Parkway.

"I know we're in a hurry," Teach said, "but you know, Gorton's already dead."

"Did you see the outline of dust on the sergeant's desk?" Derk said.

"They took his laptop," Teach said.

"And someone in Gorton's office said he works from home a lot," Derk said.

"Evidence," said Teach. "They're trying to destroy the evidence trail."

He called the Sheriff's office and told them to send a cruiser to Gorton's home.

Derk took the Gandy Bridge to intersect with I-275 south. Traffic on the northbound lanes was bumper to bumper. They were driving southeast, directly into the path of danger.

"Do you know a four-letter word for insensible?" Derk said.

***

As they wound through downtown St. Petersburg, Derk made a 911 call.

"This is Derk Bryan from EPED. There's about to be a fire at Sandover Gorton's house on Rt. 64. You might want to send a truck."

He hit End on the car's keyboard screen and handed his cell phone to Teach.

"Oh, no!" Teach said and turned away from Derk's outstretched hand. "They're going to call you back."

"I know," Derk said. "I'm counting upon it."

Teach relented, and Derk would have felt guilty for engaging his friend in what was borderline illegal if he could have overcome the anxiety gripping him. Each encounter with Sandy Gorton had reeked of death. He didn't expect the next one to be any different, but he had to get to the Gorton home before it, and any connection to his case was torched.

"Derk, you can't send those guys out there unarmed," Teach said as the William Tell Overture played in his hand.

Teach identified himself as Derk Bryan and repeated the question, "Is there a fire?" for Derk to hear.

"No, I mean, I don't know," Derk spoke via Bluetooth. "I'm in hot pursuit of someone suspected of arson, and I suggest you send an officer to meet me at the Gorton residence."

When asked if a fire truck was necessary, he responded, "How else would you put out a fire?"

There was so little traffic going south he hit ninety all the way down I-75. As they made the exit onto Route 64 Teach commented on the electric car's ride. "Smooth. It's like going to Disney Land but more exciting. I've got to get me one of these."

"Dead," Derk said.

"What?"

"Four-letter word for insensible, dead," said Derk.

<hr>

Smoke was visible, although they were still a couple of miles from Gorton's house. When they arrived, a fire truck and a Sheriff's deputy were in the yard. Derk pulled off the highway in front of the house.

Smoke billowed from the roof. Men in rubber suits and hard hats were aiming cannons of water at the home and the surrounding structures.

A deputy greeted them. Derk showed him his credentials. "You the guy who called this in?" the deputy said.

"Yes, someone just torched Gorton's business, and I figured this was their next target," Derk said.

"What's this have to do with the EPA?" asked the deputy.

"I'm not sure," Derk said, but his attention was focused upon the crew at the back of Gorton's house. Two men were rushing to the aid of a fireman who was carrying the limp body of a female. They helped carry her away from the heat and laid her on the lawn. One of them checked for breathing and then for a pulse. As he began CPR, an explosion blew flames sixty feet into the air.

Derk felt the shock a hundred feet away. Two firemen staggered to their feet, but one remained down. The woman, rescued moments earlier, was now smoldering. A fireman ripped off his raincoat and rolled her in it. Derk exited the car and rushed toward the victims, but he was stymied by the heat. Teach followed him at a distance until the inferno repelled him too.

The back of the house was now a shell of embers and stucco. Bodies littered the yard. Derk reached the fireman who was injured, checked for a pulse, and began CPR.

When Teach caught up with him, he said, "He's gone, Derk."

"No," Derk said and pushed him away.

After two more tries, Teach said, "Let me help," and he pulled Derk away.

Teach bent down and opened the man's frayed raincoat to find a gaping hole and a pool of blood.

Derk fell to his knees and dropped his head into his hands. When he looked up, the remains of a dead firefighter and Sandy Gorton's daughter were lying next to him. He was exhausted. He wanted to cry. At the end of the driveway, he noticed the deputy talking to a couple in a black Suburban. He thought he recognized the woman but let it pass as Teach helped him get to his feet.

"Let's get out of here," Teach said. "There's nothing more we can do."

Derk wobbled up the driveway, arm in arm, with Teach. When they reached Derk's car, Teach said, "Dead. You were right."

22

Tibbetts Foster wasn't the only one losing sleep, but it wasn't the fault of his temperamental CPAP or the diet pills he had been guffing down like snack food since Dominic Domini showed up with an entourage of muscle.

Nor were his fidgety nights due to the photos that Will Perkins took or that he hadn't heard from Dom Dom. Each was enough to unnerve a frog in an electric storm, and the latter was probably for the better. Dominic Domini didn't mind hurting people.

What had the hair on Foster's nape standing upright was the invitation he had received to play in a gay pool tournament. Since he was sixteen, he had won a lot of money playing nine-ball with amateurs and wannabe pool sharks, but this was different. This would be big stakes against people he couldn't hustle. The game was only days away, and he was on edge.

Nine-ball was played with, of course, nine balls. He got paid when he put in the three and the nine balls. If he ran the table, he won, kept the table, and played on. It was that simple, and he was damn good at it. The break was his specialty, and his strategy was also simple: spread the balls on the break to give himself scoring lanes. His mother had taught him that, as well as all the shots. Dom Dom said he could score a hundred grand in three days, but it wasn't the pool that had unleased his anxieties.

"They're easy. They think they can play pool, but they really can't," Dom Dom said. "Besides, I'll set you up."

That meant Dom Dom was going to front the entrance fee of twenty- five grand. Of course, he got a cut of the winnings.

"Why are you so sure?" Tibbetts kept asking.

"They're mostly dilettantes. They're here to have fun. You know fun, Tibbetts?" Dom Dom said.

His business partner offered confidence but with a tickler. He knew that Tibbetts had always been uncomfortable with direct gay inferences. And that's what had Tibbetts Foster so fucking nervous. The real money was in the side shows away from the tournament, and everyone there would be gayer than Boy George.

Dom Dom then offered the clincher, "You'll make your mother proud." It was a childish remark, but it was true. He wanted his mother to know that he had crawled out of the lager-scented, dirt town pool halls where she started hustling farm boys and immigrants for pocket change and beers. One night, after a high school football game, his reaction to a group of local redneck homophobes resulted in thrown rocks. One hit his mother in the eye. She died three days later.

Tibbetts winced each time he thought about it. His aversion to gays, he thought, resulted from that incident, but it was actually due to something much deeper in his psyche. It was something he had harbored for years but had been unable to act upon. He had suppressed his feelings out of deference to his mother, with whom he had never shared his inner desires. When Dom Dom showed up with his boy toys, Tibbetts knew he could no longer suppress his conflict. He was gay, and he had never been with a man.

He had stepped up his practice in anticipation of the matches. Today, he was doubly frustrated because he couldn't hit a corner pocket with a banker off three rails, a shot he used to hit blindfolded.

"Fuck, fuck, fuck," he shouted.

Each time he leaned over to set up a shot, the image of a wet, hard body brushing against his backside made him flinch. It affected him like fingernails on a chalkboard, but it also aroused him. He could make his statement at Queens Play in Orlando, but the anticipation was rattling him. Queens Play was the genius of Dominic Domini, the annual pool tournament gala for gays. There was a serious pool to be played, but it was also an orgy for wealthy men who played high-stakes pool while hundreds of pretty boys with hard bodies roamed the ballroom trolling for hookups. Dominic supplied the hard bodies, charged an entry fee, and reserved a suite of rooms for erotic trysts. His company was the major promoter and sponsor. The side games were played in private suites where every imaginable erotism was encouraged.

"No way," the Sheriff kept repeating under his breath when Dom Dom first told him it was a partners' tournament. If he didn't have a partner, he would be assigned one. If he wanted, he could swap with anyone who was willing. Swapping was common, he was told.

His hands shook like a Parkinson's patient. Before taking the next shot, he popped a Xanax. Then he topped the cue ball. The stick flew from his hands and slid off the table. The next shot side-swiped the cue ball, screamed over the rail, and broke a nearby vase.

"Holy shit!" said Doctor Morton, hopping over the ball that caromed off the wall as he entered the room with a drink in hand.

"Got any more of these, Doc?" the Sheriff said, shaking a nearly empty pill bottle.

"Ever try yoga?" Wes Morton said. His nearly permanent smirk made it difficult for Tibbetts Foster to determine if Wesley Morton was jesting or taking him seriously.

"Christ, Doc, no one is that happy all the time. You need to do something about your face."

Tibbetts knew the incessantly happy face was due to nerve damage the doctor suffered from a bicycle accident in his youth, but he didn't care. The incident, in a way Tibbetts could comprehend, had inspired Wesley Morton to become a plastic surgeon in Miami or Hollywood, but he didn't have the hands for it. He settled for medical examiner. What sidelined him was his thirst for easy cash and easier young men. The Sheriff didn't respect him, but he needed him, and he felt a little sorry for him. He knew the doctor's wife. She was a ten below the neck but a philandering bimbo above it, committed to the doctor only to the limit of his credit cards.

Tibbetts Foster couldn't handle any false mirth. He dropped another diet pill on his tongue and washed down his last Xanax with a gin and tonic.

"You're a fucking wreck," the doctor said. Wesley Morton winced as he slid his bulbous girth onto a nearby stool. "And that's not a recommended combination."

"Good thing there's a doctor in the house," the Sheriff huffed as he took aim at the cue ball.

"Deep breathing, Sheriff," Morton said. He tried to demonstrate by inhaling long and slowly but a smoker's hack caused him to cough loudly.

"So now you're my yogi," the Sheriff said, took an extended breath and fired.

The sound of his cue stick striking the cue ball dead center was followed by an explosion of balls that ricocheted from rail to rail. There was silence just before the nine-ball dropped into the leather nest in a corner pocket. The remaining eight balls were spread over the green felt like wickets on a croquet court.

"Southern fucking fairies!" shouted the Sheriff, followed by a fist pump. "Those fags don't know what they're up against."

⸻◆⸻

Doctor Wesley Morton slid off his high chair, sidled to the pool table, and picked the cue ball off the table as the Sheriff was racking for another break.

"We've got to talk," the doctor said. "Two more kids, a couple of guys in their twenties, were treated at Tampa General after they smoked some bad pot. The father of one of them convinced him to give us a sample."

"I know. We've got to stop this guy who is passing out the bad weed. It's bad for business," the Sheriff said with a serious face.

"There's more," said Morton. "The bad weed came from your Evidence Room."

"What?"

"It was from the batch Perkins and his group sprayed last Spring. Some of it had been held for evidence," Doctor Morton said.

The Sheriff, who had been as hyper as the Energizer bunny on speed, plopped into a chair with the rack still in one hand. The Xanax was beginning to kick in. He drained the beaker of gin and tonic he had been using to wash down the pills and took a deep breath.

"How the hell did it get out of there?"

"I don't know, but it had traces of Barbados Oil in it, a Jatrophin."

"A what?" said the Sheriff.

"It's a nut. Grind it up, mix it with palm oil and you can kill rats with it. That's what it's used for in Africa." The M.E. had the Sheriff's complete attention.

"You're saying someone in my department took this stuff from under our noses, filled it with rat poison, and sold it to people. What the fuck for?" said the Sheriff.

"One of the victims said he paid five bucks for a joint. He said the guy was almost giving it away," said the doctor.

"As if he wanted them to die," the Sheriff said. Suddenly, it came to him. "It's Perkins! That fucking Perkins. But why?"

The doctor nodded and said, "I don't think we can cover this up."

Will Perkins should not have taken photos at the Sheriff's home, and he shouldn't have had his attorney ask the Controller for financial records. The Controller had immediately alerted the Sheriff. Sheriff Foster realized the sergeant was no longer a reliable point man, a man of discretion, or someone who could be trusted. When he shared his concerns about his sergeant with his business partner, Dominic Domini suggested that the Sheriff give the sergeant some well-earned time off. The Sheriff then informed the desk sergeant that if anyone called for Sergeant Perkins, he was on vacation.

He had yet to hear from Dom Dom and could only share the following with the medical examiner. "We may not have to worry about that."

He went back to practicing. He had never excelled in anything in his life that hadn't involved some kind of hustle. He was anxious about the setting, but he wanted to play where there was no hustling and no dip-shit, low-class sucker games. It would be only about making the shots. Put up or shut up. He wished his mother had gotten the opportunity to play in Vegas on the big stage. He fantasized about her, actually, the two of them, escaping the small dirt town, dingy pool rooms, the dark bars, late nights, and slimy characters that filled her life. His mother came from poor southern roots, but she was a classy woman, a woman with style and her own brand of sophistication. She was the best nine-baller he had ever seen, and people respected her for that. He wanted to be that good. He wanted to succeed without the threat of his gun or his badge in the background. He wanted to come out of the shadows. He was going to play in the Queens Play tournament, and he was going to win.

With a burst of confidence, as he lined up the next shot, his cellphone rang.

***

"Your guy was fucking you, but he's gone," said Dominic Domini.

"I understand," said the Sheriff.

"We may have another problem," said Dominic Domini. "Who is Samantha Card?"

"Why?" said Sheriff Foster.

"He emailed some pictures and some invoices to her," said Dom Dom.

"What kind of pictures?" asked Tibbetts Foster.

"I guarantee it's stuff you don't want anybody to see," said Dom Dom.

"She publishes Bay Magazine. It's an entertainment weekly."

"Should I worry about her?"

"She is Sergeant Perkin's sister-in-law," said Tibbetts Foster with resignation in his voice.

"Fuck, fuck, fuck! Who else do I have to kill?" The receiver went dead.

23

As Derk Bryan and Teach McIntosh were leaving the ashes of Sandy Gorton's former life, Teach's cell phone rang.

"Yes, I know. We're on our way, sweetheart," Teach said. Turning to Derk, he whispered, "It's Nina."

"No, he hasn't forgotten," Teach said. "We're on our way. I love you." Teach hit end on his cellphone and, with panic in his voice, asked, "We are on our way, aren't we?"

Derk was conflicted. He had promised his friends to help with their shutters, and he couldn't put it off any longer, but Samantha was probably the next target. Whoever was responsible for this recent spate of slash and burn seemed willing to do anything to silence the opposition. He called to warn her.

"When they find out your brother-in-law sent those pictures to you, they're not going to be happy. Do you have a place to go?"

She said "yes" and thanked him for the heads-up. She had already told her daughter to pack her bag. She was on her way home.

"Please stay in touch," Derk said and hit end on the phone. "Nina said Deimos is heading right at us," Teach said.

"Call her back to reassure her. We are on our way," Derk said. He knew how anxious Nina became when a storm neared. It unnerved the animals.

"They possess a sense, like our smell or taste, that forewarns them of danger," she once told him. "It drives them crazy."

Violent storms could make The Sanctuary sound like a jungle of psychotics. Ironically, the hisses, barks, and screams, while menacing, also aroused his empathy. Derk had come to accept that all the creatures on the planet desire freedom as much as he does. Nina's concerns were real. Like everyone else, her animals became paranoid and aggressive when caged in the face of danger.

The Sanctuary was an old warehouse that had been converted to a halfway house for ailing, abused, and abandoned animals and birds. Other than the animals that were not native to Florida, whenever they became healthy, she let them go free. Nina rarely took in reptiles and dangerous animals, but on occasion, she could be convinced otherwise. "Okay, sure, they're all God's creatures," she would relent.

There were only a few windows in the building that required protection, not enough to hire a crew. The Sanctuary was a volunteer organization, and all of the volunteers had already left to prepare for the big blow. Derk knew that Nina was depending upon him and her husband to put up the shutters, but it was way out of his way to Passe-a-grille. When he negotiated his way to the exit for 301 North, Teach objected.

"Hey, the Sanctuary is that way," Teach said, pointing in the direction of I-275 North.

"I'm not crossing the Sunshine Skyway Bridge in this weather. Why don't you put up accordions?" Derk said.

"Plastic. That's why," Teach said.

"I get it, the plastic and petroleum connection. So why not Impact Resistant windows?"

"Is this car bad in the wind?" Derk shook his head no.

"Why do we need them when we have shutters, Nina says," Teach said.

"Of course." Derk stroked his lips with a forefinger and slowly teetered his head forward and backward.

"She's pretty fucking committed," Teach said.

Still bobbing his head while piercing his lips, Derk acquiesced, "There should be more people like her."

"Right." Teach said, mimicking Derk. "Well, let's get there as quickly as we can."

Derk thought Teach was like one of those way-laid birds his wife cared for. The devotion she had for her causes inspired anyone to be a better person. She grounded him and elevated a purpose to his life. Her uncanny wit kept him loose. They had been together over twenty years. They had become the closest thing to a family Derk had in his life since Jenny left.

It made him think about Samantha Card and her daughter. Who was looking out for them?

"As soon as Samantha finds out about the fire at Gorton's place, she'll be as nervous as a Hymenoptera at an anteater's convention," he said to Teach.

"A what, Professor?" Teach said.

"A bug, my friend," Derk said as the William Tell Overture played on his cellphone. The call came from an unknown number.

"You find Ileay Denisovich, Derek Bryan?" said the caller.

"Ivan?" Derk said. The voice was familiar but with an Oriental accent.

There were other Asian voices in the background. "I in Hong Kong. You find him?" Ivan said.

"What's with the voices?" Derk said. He had stopped trying to get Ivan to properly pronounce his name.

"Forget Ileay. Derek Bryan, you big problem," said Ivan, continuing in the Chinese tongue.

"Are you saying Ileay Denisovich is not my father?"

"I not sure. Probably not," Ivan said in a tone that lacked confidence.

"This is just a game for you," Derk said.

"No game," he whispered.

There were authoritative voices in the background shouting, "Hei ni ting xialai!"

Then Ivan's voice in rapid Chinese, "Yao zoule. Wo bei genzongle," he said. There was silence on the line. It was dead.

"That's Chinese!" exclaimed Teach. "Yes, I know, but . . ." Derk said.

Teach McIntosh grabbed the cell phone from Derk and asked Google to translate into English the exact words Ivan had spoken in Chinese. Derk knew that his friend never claimed to be a gifted songwriter, but he was rightfully proud of another extraordinary gift. He could hear an artist's song one time and play it back as if Bob Dylan, Gil Scott Heron, or Pete Seger were standing in front of you. The translation by Google over Blue Tooth through the car's speaker system was clear in spite of the heavy rains, "Got to go. I'm being followed."

The call from Ivan had the same effect as his first glance at the New York Times Sunday crossword puzzle. Panic!

Derk turned the rudder of his car into the wind to counter the rain, which pelted them in intermittent gusts from the east. The car swayed but held the road. The news from Ivan was disturbing, but Deimos was about to turn disorder into chaos.

"We've got to get those shutters up tonight," Derk said.

He punched the accelerator. The car skidded like a Disney water ride.

At the same time, his cell phone rang again.

"Someone tried to break into my house when Jamie was there!" There was absolute frenzy in Samantha's voice.

"I'll be right over," Derk said.

"No. We're on the way to Ft. Myers. I shut down the magazine and sent everyone home."

"Did you call the police?" Before she could answer, he said, "Of course not. We've got to get you some protection."

"I know somebody."

"Stay in touch and be careful," he said.

***

In a steady downpour, Derk and Teach bolted the aluminum shutters into place over the exposed windows at The Sanctuary in St. Petersburg. By the time they finished, they were as soggy as kitchen sponges. Nina loaned Derk a shirt and a pair of pants from her husband's wardrobe, thanked him profusely, and offered to prepare dinner for them. Derk told her he had to get back to Passe-a-Grille to finalize his own preparations.

It was late when he parked the electric car in his garage. He had opted for the extended-range battery, but it was almost depleted, and it would take until noon the next day to fully recharge. He doubted the power would stay on that long.

It had been daylight when he left home, and he had failed to leave a light on. The condo was not only pitch-black, it lacked the usual feeling of refuge that he counted upon to repair himself after days like this one. He turned on the kitchen light and went straight to his bedroom to be sure the accordion shutters had been cranked into place, although he had done that the previous day. He started for the bathroom but realized he had activated the shutters there, too. He couldn't slow down, and it wasn't just the storm. He was worried about Samantha. They were coming for her.

He would call the FBI. But no. What could they do? She had already left town. The State police. They were busy handling the traffic running from the Deimos. She had told him that her husband had been a cop, so maybe this was *someone she knew*. He felt helpless.

After he updated Ben Waitley in an email, he took a deep breath, a cold Heffe, and a chilled mug from the refrigerator. Then he parked himself on the living room couch.

He tried to massage the arthritis from his hands. He was seldom aware of the swelling until he stopped running around all day. The increasing physical limitations were one aspect of aging he found annoying. Someday, his body wouldn't have the energy to go all day. When that happened, he wondered, "Would the pain go on unabated?" Treating pain is how millions of people become addicted. God, he hoped that wasn't in the cards for him. He felt so tired. As he washed down a couple of Advil, he allowed the flavor of the wheat beer to linger in his mouth. This would probably be his last cold beer for a few days.

The sound of the rain hitting the building was like corn popping, and the wind howled like a wounded animal. He turned on the television for a storm update. Deimos was expected to reach Tampa Bay by noon.

24

"Where is she now?" said Dominic Domini.

"She checked into a hotel," said Dex McMullen. "Is she alone?"

"No, there's a kid with her."

"Don't let her out of your sight."

"How can I do that? I don't know what room she's in."

"I thought you went to college," Dominic said. "Anyway, I'm on my way."

"I'm in the parking lot. Should I go inside?" said Dex. "Where are you?"

"At the Marriott."

"Downtown, right?"

"No, Dom Dom. In Ft. Myers."

"What the fuck are you doing there? I thought you were in St. Pete."

"She never stopped driving," said Dex. "In a downpour, too. Why are we still chasing her? We almost got caught."

"I'll explain later," Dominic said. "Don't let her go anywhere without calling me?"

"Okay," Dex mumbled.

"You got that?" Dominic shouted. "She gets a cup of coffee I want to know about it."

"Yes, Dom Dom, I got it," said Dex, and the line went dead.

25

Tampa Bay was spared the wrath imposed upon some parts of Florida, but Deimos had taken its toll on paradise. The destruction was widespread. Storefronts facing the storm were shattered, and what never ceased to amaze Derk was the decimation of the vegetation. The glorious swath of Royal and Washingtonian palms that once lined his beach street had been stripped naked by the tempests of Deimos. The climate scientists had predicted that the hurricanes would become fiercer. This one was the strongest yet in Pass-a-grille.

The first message on his phone, after the power was restored, came from Shine: "Due to the hurricane, the Queen's Play Nine-ball Tournament had been moved back a week and relocated from Orlando to the Rock Hard Hotel in Tampa. I have arranged everything for us."

He also had a message from Samantha: "I tried to call but couldn't get through. I'm safe, but I think someone is following me. Call me as soon as you can." When he called her, it went straight to voice mail.

There were two messages from Ben Waitley. First, "I need you to go to Lake Avon. I'm sending you the file." Second, "I received your email about Samantha Card. I'll see what I can do."

Removing the debris that surrounded his condo and cleaning an inch of sand that Deimos had washed into his garage would take a week, but Ben's message said something about a golf course, a fish farm, and a dead body. Tankers are leaking oil in the Gulf, and he's going to Lake Avon to find out why a golfer ended up in some fish farmer's pond. On the other hand, it was a job, one for which he was well-equipped, and the director's description almost guaranteed something weird had gone down. Exactly his forte. It beat standing behind a pedestal six hours per day trying to make an impact upon a few twenty-year-olds who needed the course credit. As soon as the car was fully charged, the cleanup would be put on hold.

He took a glance at the file the director had sent. It contained an open case filed by an aquaculture entrepreneur near Lake Avon. The owner had accused the adjacent golf course operator of contaminating his ponds, which resulted in some fish dying. It was in one of those ponds that the body was discovered.

He immediately requested the medical report. It confirmed that the deceased tested positive for elevated levels of fertilizer, organophosphate, and Roundup, common run-offs from golf courses that were not Audubon-certified. The fish farm probably had a case against the golf course. The autopsy also revealed an indentation in the man's left temple. A blow to the head was the likely cause of death, and the blunt instrument's impression left a gouge in the shape of an eight iron. Hence, the golf course, the fish farm, and the dead body. Within the emails from Ben was a photo of the dead man, donned in loud plaid and a matching tam, who had a ninety-eight-cent practice ball clutched in one hand when he was pulled from the water.

On his way to Lake Avon, he recalled, from his golf playing days, that the higher spin rates for cheaper balls made them less controllable for those with wicked slices. At the morgue, he found, among the golfer's belongings, a receipt from a golf instructor who confirmed the curse, a wicked slice, with which Artemis Banfred had been suffering. Apparently, the two hundred dollars per hour lessons had been unable to remedy the flaw.

When he arrived on the scene, the fish farmer's hostility was blatant. In spite of knowing that stray balls would find their way into his delicately balanced ponds, he had located next to a golf course due to the affordability of the land in central Florida and its proximity to water. Central Florida was rife with small lakes. Since opening he had complained to every public official in the area. When

Derk pressed him for answers the fish farmer waxed on about the necessity of fish farms for meeting the global protein demand as the seas become over-fished and polluted. Derk's first impression was that the guy was a real prick with Trumpish arrogance who felt everyone owed him something for his foresight. Maybe they did, but it took every ounce of discretion for Derk to resist tossing the twerp into one of his own ponds.

After a walk-through of the farm, eagerly resisted by the owner whose hands smelled like rotting cod, the mystery concerning the indentation on Banfred's temple was resolved. In one of the sheds, Derk spotted an old set of Pings collecting dust. The only club missing was an eight iron.

On the way home, Derk called Ben Waitley with the news. "You won't believe this smug slug. When he was arrested, I heard him mumble, *"Cheap bastard. Should have played a Titleist."*

"What's going on with the Gorton case?" Derk said.

"I referred it to the FBI. I think they've already got somebody on it," the director said.

"You know they killed Samantha Card's brother-in-law. He was a cop," Derk said. "And the same person tried to break into her condo. Can we get her protection, Ben?" He didn't know for sure it was the same person, but that's what he told Ben Waitley.

"I said I think they're already on it," Ben said.

Derk wasn't satisfied, but what could he do? He had tried to get Samantha to sit still but she wouldn't do it. He hadn't sensed fear in her voice, but she was taking no chances. He understood. She had to protect her daughter. She told him she was going to stay with a cousin in West Palm Beach. He knew that wasn't true. She didn't trust anyone.

He hadn't heard any more from Ivan, and the Top End had yet to re-open. He had to clean his condo and he also had to prepare for a pool tournament. He hadn't lined up a pool shot in three weeks, and the pain in his joints was relentless. The change to a low inflammation diet had yet to mollify his arthritis, so he was in a shitty mood when he told Ben Waitley that he was not available for another assignment.

"I need a break. Most of the creatures on this planet are driven by self-preservation. What the fuck happened to us?" he said after telling the director he had to clean up his house and work on his pool game. "Three hurricanes, back to back to back. You can't tell me that has nothing to with man-made climate change."

"Doctor Bryan, we each know this is just the beginning of major frigging chaos on a global scale. Every man for himself," responded Ben Waitley, unusually unbureaucratic. "But what's this about pool?"

Derk was dumbfounded. He expected, at least, a modicum of defense of the current administration's environmental policy because the director worked at the pleasure of political appointees.

"I appreciate your candidness, but it doesn't really make me feel better," Derk said.

"Sorry. I didn't know you shot pool," the director said.

"It's a hobby, and I was invited to play in a nine-ball tournament," Derk said.

"What's nine-ball? Where? How long will you be unavailable this time?" The director fired the words in rapid succession.

"It's in Tampa. It's—" Derk tried to answer when Director Waitley cut him off.

"Well, let Joyce know when you'll be back," Ben Waitley said, never much for idle chit-chat. "And by the way, nice work over at Lake Avon. I think there's a case against the golf course, too."

Before Derk could ask again about protection for Samantha Card, the call had ended. The director may have preferred that he not get involved, especially with the remains of the Gorton home and business, along with Derk's patchy case scrambled by the storms. But he was involved, and Samantha Card and her daughter were at risk.

As he turned into his driveway, a blue SUV turned in behind him. Out jumped Samantha Card. She looked every which direction and then opened the back door.

"Get your stuff," he heard her say.

Jamie Card cautiously emerged from the car. Derk had lots of questions for them, but his relief was so palpable Samantha gave him a hug. Then she took her daughter by the hand.

"Come on. Let's go inside," she said.

As Derk opened the garage door with his remote, she hit her key fob twice. Her car's alarm system peeped its readiness loud enough to startle him. As he pirouetted to face Samantha, a bright yellow Hummer crept by the house. He didn't recognize the young man with the crew cut behind the wheel, but the fellow craned his neck at them as he passed. His head resembled a turret on a tank.

Once inside, Samantha searched for a window with a view of the street. It was still light outside but dark in his condo because Derk had yet to open all of the shutters. She bumped into a corner, "Ugh!" going down the hallway before Derk could turn on the lights.

"Samantha, slow down," he said. "You're safe."

She stopped for a moment. He pointed to the front door and the door that led downstairs to the garage through which they had just entered.

"Those are double-cylinder deadbolts, and I haven't rolled back the shutters yet." He had been waiting for news that the third hurricane would bypass them and take a route into the North Atlantic, as predicted.

Samantha paused as if she were contemplating her next move. Jamie hadn't moved since entering the house. She was still standing, bag in hand, in the kitchen. She had a "What next, Mother?" look on her face.

"Come on, dear," said her mother. Samantha led her daughter down the hall to one of the bedrooms. It had curtains on the windows, a plush comforter on the bed, and few if any, male influences. "Look, you've got your own TV, and there's a bathroom across the hall," Samantha said and gave her daughter a long, firm hug. "I'll be right back."

She returned to the living room and plumped down upon a straight-back leather chair. Before she could say a word, Derk said, "Are you still being followed?"

"I don't know," she said, shook her head, closed her eyes and dropped her chin. "I'm sorry, Doctor Bryan." When she looked up, she said, "I didn't know where else to go."

"You know a lot of people, and your husband was a police officer," Derk said, but Samantha interjected.

"Yes, but no one, and I mean no one, is aware of our connection. We'll be out of your hair as soon as I can, Dr. Bryan." She didn't finish the sentence. Her jaw drooped to her chest again.

Derk walked over to her and took her hands into his own. "It's Derk." She looked up at him with tired eyes, and what little make-up she had donned in the morning was showing wear. Even so, she was a stunningly strong figure.

"You look tired. I'll put your things in the bedroom. Rest up, and we'll talk when you wake," Derk said.

He showed her where he kept the towels and led her to a closet that contained some of Jenny's clothes he had yet to take to Goodwill. He wasn't sure why.

He Googled Samantha Card while she and her daughter slept. She came from a determined family with a journalistic bent. Her kind of magazine seldom received awards, but some of her headlines made it clear that she still had a thirst for hard news. He was surprised to read that she had married a cop, a lieutenant furthermore, and shocked and saddened to learn about his death. By 10 p.m., he realized they were not going to join him for dinner. He didn't see either of them again until morning.

He slept on the couch, the kind that rolled out into a bed, which put him in a melancholy mood. It was Jenny's idea to buy the sleeper sofa. She said it would be good for guests, but this was the first time anyone had ever slept on it.

He had rolled back the shutters in the front of the house before retiring. The morning sun flooded the living room with hope. The aroma of coffee brewing was in the air when Samantha emerged from the bedroom wearing a robe that had belonged to his wife. It was a little too long for her, and she had to keep from stepping on the fringe. Her daughter joined them in the kitchen shortly thereafter. She was in flannel shorts and a frumpy, matching top. She must have taken after her father because she was already taller than Samantha. Without the attitude, she seemed like a normal teenager. Each of them nodded voraciously to his offer to make breakfast. He told them to shower and dress while he filled the kitchen with the aroma of eggs and toast. It was the first time his condo had felt like a home in a long time.

As he was plating scrambled eggs and hash browns, the doorbell rang. Samantha and her daughter, now in stretch pants and tank tops, looked at Derk with leery anticipation. Derk shook his head. He was expecting no one. With the spatula in one hand and a hot plate in the other, he walked to a window with a view of the street. A black Lexus was parked nose to nose with the same yellow Hummer he had seen the day before. The driver, the same young man he had seen creep by the house yesterday, was leaning against the car with arms folded.

"Samantha," he called to her. "Come over here."

She hurried to the window. "Do you recognize him?"

"No," she said.

Jamie joined them. Derk repeated the question.

"No. Who is it?" She returned to the table. "But I think that was the same car I saw in the parking lot in Ft. Myers."

The doorbell rang again. Then, twice more in quick succession. The man in the street made a gesture with his arms in the direction of Derk's house. Then another, but this time, his hands signaled reluctance. Then, there was resignation as he walked toward the entryway of Derk's condo. If he was to join the person at his door, he would have to walk up a flight of stairs.

Two more rings.

Derk made a hurry-up motion for his guests to get going. He pointed to the door that led downstairs to the garage. "Go. Get out of here," he said.

Samantha was in a panic to locate her purse and keys.

"Hey," Derk said. He plucked the keys off a table in the living room and tossed them to her.

As they started down the stairs, he said, "When I open the front door, you make a run for it."

The ringing was replaced with heavy pounding. "Bam, bam, bam!"

On his way to the bathroom, Derk punched the garage door opener. He noticed, after the garage door had been recently serviced, which included lubrication, it was so quiet he could barely hear it open. The guys in the entryway, he hoped, wouldn't hear it either.

He ran to the bathroom, slipped off his tee shirt and his loafers, splattered some water on his face and hair, and wrapped a towel around his waist.

Two more rings, then "Bam, bam!"

He was drying his hair when he opened the door. Only the glass in the storm door separated him from a tall, muscular guy with black hair and Ray-bans, dressed completely in Tommy Bahama. Behind him was the young man in a colorful Nautica ensemble, same sunglasses.

"Sorry, I was in the shower," Derk said. "May I help you?"

Tommy Bahama opened the storm door and pointed a small gun at Derk.

Derk jumped back and tried to shut the door, but he was too late. Dominic Domini forced the door open, which knocked Derk to the floor. Dominic pointed the gun at Derk and said in a commanding voice,

"Tell Samantha Card to come out here, or I'll shoot you!"

"She's not here," Derk said.

"Miss Card, one more time, or he's a dead man."

When there was no response, Dominic motioned for Dex McMullen to enter.

"Now!" shouted Dominic. Dex did so reluctantly.

"If he moves, you know what to do," Dominic said. Then Dex stood over Derk, straddling him.

When not breaking into homes, these guys could pass for tag team wrestlers. They were huge, buff, brickhouse solid, and nattily dressed. Derk looked around for a weapon.

The Esquire model hovering above him shook his head as he frowned.

It was clear that he didn't want to be here.

Just then, the sound of squealing tires could be heard from the street below. Derk's assailants bolted for the door. Derk stuck out a leg that tripped Dominic. He stumbled into the glass storm door with a crash. He turned to fire the derringer at Derk, but the other man bumped him. The shot embedded in the laminate wood floor. Dominic kicked Derk, and before he could kick him again, the other man grabbed him and pulled him away.

"We've gotta go," Dex said.

After a few seconds of squirming, Dominic relented and rushed for the door. As he opened it, he felt the lump forming on his forehead and blood dripping down his face. He turned and, like a wounded animal, gritted his teeth. Then he bounced down the stairway.

Before Dex let the storm door close, as he was leaving, he looked at Derk and grimaced.

"Sorry, old man," Dex said.

Derk picked himself up and locked the front door. He ran to the kitchen and punched the garage door remote. From the upstairs window, he watched the two men get into separate cars and drive away. Samantha was nowhere in sight.

He breathed a sigh of relief and dialed 911.

26

Since the disappearance of Sergeant Wilson Perkins, unannounced raids on innocent civilians, as well as the ensuing lawsuits, had gone down sharply. Simultaneously, the number of people admitted to local hospitals for inhaling contaminated weed had dropped to, well, zero.

Coincidence? Samantha Card didn't think so. Her brother-in-law had gone rogue and crossed the wrong people. That included his boss, the Sheriff, and the fact that he hadn't been charged with a crime spoke to the Sheriff's complicity. After she received the incriminating emails and wallowed in the blood on Will's living room floor, she expected repercussions. The arson of her brother-in-law's house, followed by the attempted break-in of her own home, raised her paranoia level to Defcon one. With a hurricane heading her way, she moved out of her home and called the FBI.

"Get those ashes. Check the dental records and see for yourself. I guarantee you it's not him," Samantha told Special Agent Madeline Millar, the agent to whom the call was referred after three transfers.

Samantha had read the official announcement from the Sheriff's Department:

"After returning from a vacation, Sergeant Wilson Perkins surprised a burglar who shot him and then burned down his house. As a decorated officer for over twenty years, the department and our community will dearly miss his effort and dedication. The Sheriff, and the entire department, extends its sympathy for the loss to his family."

"That's was lie," she said. "No one from the Sheriff's Office has said "Boo" to me, and the fire occurred after the alleged robbery and shooting occurred. I know that because Doctor Bryan and I were in his home and witnessed the hole in the wall. There was blood all over the cabinets," she told Agent Millar.

It had been reported that the remains of the body recovered from Will Perkins' home more resembled a scorched capybara than an actual human being. In spite of this Doctor Wesley Morton, Chief Medical Examiner, had confirmed that the DNA from the ashes was none other than Wilson Anthony Perkins.

"The M.E. certified that the deceased was Sergeant Perkins, and frankly, it's a local matter," responded Agent Millar, none too eager to engage with a reporter from an entertainment rag.

"The perp came back and burned down his house. You don't find that odd?" Samantha Card said. "Somebody brought Will's body back into the house, or it's someone else."

"I agree. That is odd, in fact, improbable. I'll look into it and get back to you," said Special Agent Madeline Millar. A search of missing person reports filed with local police departments turned up a male about the same age and physical description as Wilson Perkins, but she hesitated to call Samantha Card. She had more pressing matters.

Over the past six months, she had been investigating Dominic Domini for interstate sex crimes. When she inquired as to whether the Sheriff's Office could provide any information about Dominic Domini, she was informed that there were no pending investigations involving such a person.

Agent Millar knew that Mr. Domini, among others, had supported the Sheriff's re-election campaign, and she was aware that they were well known to each other. She assigned Agent Mence Caldwell to shadow Mister Domini. Agent Caldwell subsequently reported that the suspect and the Sheriff had met at a private club north of Tampa several times and that Dominic had also been in the vicinity of the Perkins' home on the day of the fire. It wasn't until she had been given a heads up by the director of the EPA's regional office and driven by the Gorton house on the day it was torched that she had a tail placed on Samantha Card. None of this did she share with the reporter from Bay Magazine.

"And you should check out Doc Morton. I'm going to send you some interesting pictures of the doctor and the Sheriff," Samantha told Agent Millar.

Agent Millar's lack of enthusiasm was so disheartening that Samantha left Ft. Myers and headed for a Red Roof Inn in Brandon. On the way, she decided to stop at Doctor Bryan's house. It was a long shot, but the only person who was remotely aware that Dr. Bryan and she knew each other was her assistant, Connie Reid. Jamie would be safe there. She had intended to stay only long enough to determine that no one was following her and to find a place where her daughter would be safe. Like many of her recent ideas, this one hadn't gone as planned.

***

As Samantha blew across the bridge from Pass-a-grille to St. Pete, she reached for her cell phone.

"Damn!" she said. "Damn, damn, damn." She left it at Derk's house.

"What is it, Mom?" Jamie said. She was turned in her seat and watching through the rear window for the guys who were chasing them.

"Do you have your phone?" Samantha said.

"Yes, Mom. Why?" Jamie said. Except while she was sleeping and showering, it had seldom left her palm.

"Do you remember where we used to get your Halloween costumes?"

"No, Mom, but is this the time to think about Halloween?" She turned around again to look for anyone following them.

"Alias or Aliases or something like that, wasn't it?" Samantha said. "Maybe, I don't know."

"Look it up and call them."

193

When her daughter resisted, continuing to watch for the men chasing men, Samantha said, "Now, Jamie."

As the road curved so that their route could not be seen from the elevated bridge behind them, Samantha took the first side street. She drove to the end of the block, turned the corner, and did a one-eighty. She parked so that they could see the cars passing on the street into St. Petersburg.

"It's ringing, Mom."

Samantha took the phone and listened to the recorded message. The store would be open at ten. It was now eight-thirty. They waited.

After thirty minutes, Jamie said, "I think we lost them, Mom. I'm hungry."

Having ditched the guys following them, Samantha drove back into Pass-a-grille and took the beach road north to Clearwater Beach. From there, she took the Causeway into Tampa. She passed her office but didn't go in. She used the GPS on Jamie's phone to guide them to the costume store. They were waiting in the parking lot when the owner came to unlock the door.

27

"Are you alright?" Samantha Card asked. She called Derk from the parking lot of the costume store.

"Yes, what about you?" Derk said. "I'm good."

Her voice was much calmer than he expected. "Where are you?"

"I'm safe," she said without detail, "but I left my phone at your place."

"I noticed," he said.

"I'm sorry. I brought them right to your door."

"I'm okay, but I'm worried about you. Those guys are carnivores," he said.

"I'll be okay. I know somebody. Gotta go," she said.

"Samantha. Samantha?" he said, but no one was there.

After buying a couple of wigs and some clothes from the costume shop, she headed for the motel in Brandon. Before checking in, she bought a newspaper, some toiletries, and a couple of frozen dinners from a convenience store.

As soon as they settled in the motel, Jamie said, "Mom, I left my meds at Dr. Bryan's house."

28

What annoyed Dominic Domini more than anything was "Namby-pambies" - squishy sentimentalists. Their mawkishness affected their decision-making. Unfortunately, when it came to the most consequential matters, Dom Dom had surrounded himself with a bunch of pretty boys with little appetites for the grimy stuff. He had to do the hard work himself.

His old friend, Tibbetts Foster, was that kind of guy. Very smart, very clever. Hell, he had figured out how to get a law degree without ever entering a classroom. Then he hood-winked enough people to get elected Sheriff. And turning the forfeiture laws into free enterprise, that was sheer genius. But he didn't have the balls to make the difficult personnel decisions. Nor was he a good judge of character. He thought he was, but he wasn't. Probably because he was sexually confused.

"When are you ever going to appreciate what the world has provided for you?" Dominic had told him. He had been standing in front of a mirror for five minutes trying to comb a lock of his black hair into place.

Dominic Domini could have a different partner every night if he so desired, and he often desired. Dominic pegged Tibbetts as gay the first time he met him, but Tibbetts Foster had always denied his sexuality. Dom Dom knew that his partner relied upon him to do the dirty work, and he seldom asked any questions.

He ran his business from an office in Delaware, and he lived on the Jersey shore, but his partnership with the Sheriff provided for a winter home in Florida with all the accouterments of resort living. From there, he could travel to Key West to recruit men for his porn sites and extra-curricular activities. The cash flow, as Tibbetts referred to it, was stunning. It was a dream job.

Normally, Dominic looked forward to his Florida trips, but cleaning up Tibbett's recent mess had driven him into an irritable frenzy. It was less than a week to the Queen's Play Nine-ball Tournament, his favorite annual event, and now, in the aftermath of the worst storm he had ever seen, he was traipsing through the debris of west Florida in pursuit of a rogue reporter. As far as he could tell from the emails sent by the late Sergeant Wilson Perkins to Samantha Card, she was the only other person in possession of anything that could link him or his partner to their lucrative scheme.

Dominic slammed his fist on the steering wheel. "Where the fuck did she go?"

He had pulled off the road a block short of the intersection with U.S. 19 north.

Dex McMullen didn't realize that Dom Dom was stopping and hit the brakes too late. The Hummer thumped the back bumper of Dom Dom's car. The whiplash to Dominic's neck would negate six weeks of Rolfing. He got out of the car, steaming mad.

"You fucking, dumb fucking muscle head. Pay some fucking attention to what's going on!" Dominic shouted at Dex as he rolled down the window of the Hummer.

Dex tried to apologize but Dominic was having none of it. "Did you see her?" said Dominic, waving his hands in the air. Dex shook his head.

"She couldn't just disappear," said Dominic.

"She probably turned off, and we didn't see her," Dex said.

"Duh," said Dominic. He stepped away from the Hummer and looked in both directions. "What the fuck was that back there?"

Dex had a sad puppy look on his face.

"You effete wimp," he said. As he backed away, he waived a dismissive gesture at Dex. "Didn't I tell you to get rid of this tank?"

There was no question that the Hummer was as noticeable as a stripper at a Rays baseball game, but that was of little consequence this morning. Derk's call to 911 had been directed to the local police, half of whom were home mending fences, post-Deimos, and half were on a "sick out." The latter was the result of a small but vocal group of the road patrol that had been demanding legislation to ban assault weapons. They said they were tired of going to school shootings. None of this mattered to Dominic Domini, but the thirty minutes it took for the cops to show up at Derk's door meant that Dominic and his lover were able to reach the next county without any obstruction.

29

The pain in Derk's tailbone caused by Dominic Domini's forceful entry had mostly subsided, but he didn't like all the painkillers he had to pop to overcome it. It was for situations like this that some of his colleagues suggested he get a concealed weapons permit. He refused to do it.

The cops reported that the yellow Hummer, rented by a man from New Jersey, had been returned. Derk identified the man from his driver's license photo. His name was Dexter McMullen. The other man's identity remained unknown.

He told them about Samantha and asked if he could send a copy of Dexter's photo to her. They wanted to contact her, but he still had her cell phone. He suggested they contact her through her magazine. He tried to contact her through her daughter's cell phone, but he could only leave messages.

He hadn't heard any more from Ivan, and his saliva swabs hadn't linked him to anyone named Dennis or Denisovich. Nor had he heard from Shine since she made his reservation at the hotel for the nine-ball tournament. CBDelites, the company that Shine purportedly repped, was footing the bill for the entire weekend. Whomever she is, and whatever her real name is, she had some nice expense accounts. He was looking forward to room service, expensive wine, and the prospect of Shine's embrace.

Eris, the last of Greek-named hurricanes, was smashing the north-Atlantic shores, but sunny skies had returned to west Florida. It was late afternoon, and there wasn't a cloud in the sky when he pulled into the entrance of The Rock Hard Hotel. A valet nudged between the protestors milling in front of the entrance to the lobby. They carried signs that read: "My Body, My Choice!" and "The New Bill of Rights." Among them were reporters and journalists with press badges. He spotted one from People Magazine and another from the

Marijuana Business Journal. He wondered what had brought together such a disparate bunch.

He thought he recognized a petite black woman with dreads wearing a Rays ball cap, but he was sidetracked by the valet requesting the keys to this car. When he looked for her again, she was gone. The uniformed attendant began to apologize for the congestion, but Derk was distracted by one of the attendants parking a yellow Hummer. No, it couldn't be, he thought.

"Some dude is making an announcement about a Constitutional Amendment," the parking lot attendant said.

"What amendment?" Derk asked the desk clerk when the two men ahead of him finished checking in. They embraced and departed hand in hand. Each was carrying a leather bag exactly the size of Derk's pool cue case.

"Ask that man," the desk clerk pointed to a photo of the Reverend Peter Wirth. His picture was on a large poster next to the roster of events that the hotel was hosting for the weekend.

"You must be here for the pool tournament," said the desk clerk, a way too chipper and over-dressed lad in his mid-twenties. He was eyeing Derk's leather case.

"Sure. What about him?" He steered toward the picture of the Reverend as he handed his identification to the clerk.

"I don't think so," said the desk clerk with hesitation, clearly not used to Professor Bryan's sense of humor.

While the clerk completed the check-in, Derk scoured the lobby. Along with two men in police uniforms with cowboy hats and sidearms, he spotted two young men in Hawaiian shirts. They were engaged in a whimsical discussion with a couple of older guys with graying temples and casual business attire. Each one carried a leather pool case on a strap over his shoulder. Occasionally, one of the younger men would lean into one of the older guys and hook his little finger onto the man's hand. How sweet! That's when he realized the dilemma he was facing. Half of the people here were as gay as Fruit Punch, and his partner was a stunning blonde female. An elderly black man with a salt and pepper goatee announced, "He's about to make his announcement," and directed a crowd, gathered in the lobby, to the conference room.

Derk gave the bellboy twenty bucks to take his bags to the room and then followed the throng into a large conference room off the main lobby. The sign over the entrance read Lucky You room. He quickly retraced his steps and recovered the case containing his cue stick.

In passing the Calendar of Events posted in the lobby, he noticed a welcome sign for The National Association of Sheriffs. A photo of Tibbetts Foster was displayed on the poster. The Sheriff would be assessing the "Current Status of Forfeiture Laws." Derk couldn't help but think about Emma Young's predicament. He sidled his way into the crowded room where the Reverend Peter Wirth was already addressing the audience.

"An ethical society grants freedom of choice as long as others are not harmed by his or her actions. In such a society we aspire to reduce the incidence of conflict while assuring maximum freedom of choice. In that society, we don't blame a plant for a man's ills. What a person puts into his or her own body should be his choice, just as it should be his or her choice to marry whom he or she desires. It should also be his, excuse me, her choice as to when to give birth. And, there is no greater freedom, that is an inalienable human right, than the choice of where, when, and how to die. Once granted, under The New Bill of Rights, each and every person here across this nation will possess the most basic of all human rights, the control of one's own body."

A raucous cheer arose from the crowd. Those with signs stabbed the sky and stomped the floor. A soft chant evolved into a mantra:

"My body, my choice. My body, my choice!" Cameras flashed, and cellphones, overheads, snapped photos.

The Reverend continued, "Some have said that we cannot allow recreational drugs on the marketplace. My friends, you should be aware by now that prescription drugs kill more people each year than illicit drugs. It is time to let people have more benign and safer remedies without the threat of incarceration, which, by the way, is costing us an abhorrent fortune."

More chants. "My body, my choice. My body, my choice."

Peter Wirth's tone was firm but fatherly. The crowd was a mix of young and elderly people. It was hot and sticky. Some in the crowd turned their signs into cooling fans.

"There are those that argue that we shouldn't legalize something that can cause us harm. Let me tell you about a substance that comes from all-natural ingredients, is inexpensive, widely available, and can create great euphoria. It is also the catalyst for so much aggressive behavior, broken homes, uprooted families, lost wages, battered careers, financial catastrophes, and tens of thousands of deaths each year. Most of us would say *absolutely not* to that kind of substance. *It should not be legal.* Now, what if I told you that this powerful chemical could be cooked up cheaply in any basement in any home in America, which makes it impossible to stop? Knowing this, would you cast a vote to make beer illegal again?"

This time the roar from the supporters was louder than the home crowd after a goal in the Ice Palace. The stomping continued in conjunction with the mantra: "My body, my choice. My body, my choice." A couple of folks chanted, "Wirth for President."

To his throng of supporters, neither Lou Gehrig, Martin Luther King, nor Moses could have been more inspiring.

"Of course not!" he said. "And why? Because even though you and I may not be tenured economists, we know what happens when the supply of something people really want is constrained."

His longtime ally, Amos, shouted, "Black markets, my brother!"

"That's right, my brothers and sisters. Not only do the black markets flourish, the corruption of our police and our public officials skyrockets. The murder rate during this Drug War has been the highest since Prohibition, and it hasn't stopped anything. The result of this hypocrisy is cynicism. We are losing our respect for authority and our need to act in cooperation with law enforcement. My friends, we are in an adversarial position with our own government and the overall spiritual energy on the Planet. We can, and we must do something about it. And I make this promise to you. We are not going to stop until every State endorses The New Bill of Rights, however long it takes."

When the Reverend turned to the subject of death with dignity, Derk slithered his way to the exit. That subject was too close to home. Outside the conference room, as he passed the poster of Sheriff Foster, it occurred to him that the confirmation of Peter Wirth's "New Bill of Rights" would make the current drug laws passe, but who didn't want to have control over his or her own body?

He wanted to get to his room and relax prior to the introductory event that evening in the Winner's ballroom. He hoped that Shine, his playing partner, would be joining him soon and take his mind off the guys who were chasing Samantha. And he wanted to find a table to practice. He hadn't been at his best when they first met.

30

Derk fetched the key from the desk clerk and took the elevator to the eighth floor. On the way up, he realized he had responded impulsively when he agreed to participate in this tournament. He was a scientist and a criminologist, trained to observe details and methodically turn clues into evidence. When Shine asked him to be her partner, he said yes without asking for a single detail about the tournament. He hadn't reviewed a flyer, researched it on the Internet, or asked anyone else about it. A gay pool tournament. It would be a first for him. Stickman must have known about this when he invited Derk to be his partner. He had no idea Stickman went both ways or why he thought Derk might be gender flexible. Although he was supportive of the LGBT culture, he had no idea he might be radiating gay pheromones.

It didn't matter. Nothing else mattered more than the tingle he felt that surged through him like a sexual serum. Except for some residual swelling in his left hand, he felt twenty years younger as he entered his room.

His first thought, upon hearing the sound of the shower, was that Shine must have checked in when he was at the Reverend's press conference. She probably wanted to surprise him. His heart began beating like a Ginger Baker drum.

Only one small suitcase was visible in the room. No woman travels this light but he overlooked it as he stripped off his clothes. When he got to his skivvies, he noticed in succession a man's suit jacket tossed over the back of a chair, a pair of burgundy brogues, and a revolver on the bedside table. Before he could say, "Holy Moly, wrong room!" a man came out of the bathroom with only the towel he was using to dry himself.

Derk danced around, trying to recover his clothes.

"I'm so sorry. Wrong room, but this is the key they gave me." He reached for his pocket but he had on no pants. "I'll get out of here right away."

In contrast to Derk's panic, the gentleman casually finished drying his hair and held out his hand.

"Special Agent Mence Caldwell. You must be Dr. Bryan."

The stranger's mood was too upbeat, and his resemblance to Adonis was embarrassing. Early thirties, curly hair and hard as porcelain, it was difficult not to stare at him.

Disrobed and disarmed, Derk walked to the door, opened it a crack, and looked at the number on the door: 816.

"Eight sixteen?" he said to the man.

Mence Caldwell nodded. "Agent Milarkey will join us later. We have to attend an event in the main ballroom at twenty hundred hours."

"Agent who?" Derk said.

"Sorry, that's what we call her. It's actually Millar, Madeline Millar, sir. I mean, Doctor."

He took a shirt from the closet and held it up in front of him as he fancied his reflection in the mirror. "I'll be your partner tonight. Does this look okay?" He oscillated between roles - federal agent and transvestite impersonator.

"Shine's a federal agent?" Derk said as he pulled up his trousers. "Who?"

"Miss Millar," Derk said.

"Oh, yea. As long as I've been here," Caldwell said as he held up a tie against the shirt." "What do you think?"

Mence Caldwell was clearly gay, and he was suggesting that he was going to be Derk's partner in the Queen's Play pool tournament.

"What the hell is going on, and would you cover that thing up?" Derk said, averting his attention away from what must be one of the

FBI's prized dicks. Mostly dressed, Derk picked up his bag to leave. Before leaving, he said, "Why am I really here?"

"Sir, Doctor Bryan, wait," said Caldwell. With one leg in his trousers, he punched a button on his cell phone and said, "He's here." He handed the phone to Derk.

"Scratch! How are you?" The female voice was familiar.

"What the hell is going on, Agent Millar? Why am I here?" Derk said.

"It's okay, Scratch. I'll be there tomorrow."

"But I won't," said Derk.

"I'm sorry, sweetie. I'll explain everything tomorrow." She sounded sincere, but she was too much of a chameleon to be trusted again.

"That's not enough and what's pretty boy doing here?" he said.

"Oh, he's harmless. Affirmative action, you know," she said.

"Really, he's built like a road-grader, and he has a gun. You lied to me. I'm out of here."

"Don't go, Derk. Please," she said. "Give me one good reason."

"You are familiar with Sandover Gorton?" she said.

31

To avoid detection, she enrolled Jamie in a charter school and relocated every other day. Without her Jazzercize classes, because the hurricane had taken the roof off the center's studio, the stress piled upon her in layers.

She dropped by a local Vitamin Shop and picked up a thirty-day supply of RediCalm.

Adding stress to a bipolar child is like dropping napalm onto a bonfire. Trying to explain her theory of Uncle Will's disappearance to Jamie served only to exacerbate Jamie's affliction. Without her meds, Jamie's moods swung more than an Adele album. As a result of the frequent moves, fast food, and constant reprovals for texting her friends, Jamie became so exasperated she threatened to hurt herself again. Samantha responded by taking away her cell phone and placing restrictions on her access to social media, but she was afraid to leave her daughter unsupervised. Every moment she was away from her, Samantha worried that Jamie would do something crazy or expose their whereabouts. They stayed in their motel room as much as they could. If she had to venture out, she wore a disguise.

To the Reverend Peter Wirth's press conference, she donned long dreads and a black tee emblazoned with a green marijuana leaf she discovered when combing through a clothes bin at a Goodwill Store. To her benefit, no one seemed to recognize her. She noticed Derk Bryan enter the hotel, but she said nothing. She would have liked to see him again, but she didn't want to blow her cover.

Using a newly acquired cell phone, she streamed texts and photos of the people and the event to Colleen Reid. The ramifications of the Constitutional Amendment the Reverend had proposed would revamp the political landscape. Even though the changes may not mute the debate over drugs, abortion, and end-of-life measures, who wouldn't be in favor of having control over one's own body? It would embolden the anti-vaxxers, but it was political genius. She was amazed that no one had thought about it before now.

As she was leaving the press conference, someone who looked exactly like Tibbetts Foster entered the hotel carrying a long black leather case, the kind used to store a pool cue. The poster in the lobby advertised the Sheriff as a speaker at the National Sheriff's Conference, but this guy was there to shoot some pool at none other than the Queen's Play Nine-ball Tournament. She snapped a couple of photos and called Colleen Reid with the scoop.

"One more thing," she said, "Could you please pick up Jamie for the weekend?"

Then she reserved a room close to the Rock Hard Hotel.

32

Tibbetts Foster was engulfed by a giant, flaming shit-ball. His department had been in the news for its violent, no-knock drug raids followed by wrongful death lawsuits and budget-breaking settlements. Then, the Sheriff's Drug Czar was murdered. And "Out to Lunch!" was the headline in the Times about the Sheriff's leadership during Deimos.

While this was happening the Times ran a picture of the Medical Examiner that added kindling to an already incendiary divorce case. In the photo, the doctor was bare-naked and face down on an examination table while a young stud, with a woody, straddled him, doing push-ups in and out of the place where the sun don't shine. In the background was a campaign poster for Sheriff Foster.

The Sheriff was walking a tightrope over his support of Wesley Morton. Tibbetts knew that the doctor had been enticed by, and gradually relented to, access to the young men in heat Dominic Domini had made available. The doctor wasn't a crook by heart, and his divorce was going to be costly. He felt bad for the guy.

All of this should have been of primary concern to someone running for re-election. It was not. Nor was the anticipation of playing in a big-time pool tournament with the backing of his unpredictable partner, who had overly zealous expectations of him. He also had to make a speech, for which he was completely unprepared, in front of a national convention of his peers the next day. All of that paled next to his primary concern.

Tibbetts Foster was going to have sex with a man. He recalled when someone brushed against him while passing in the men's room earlier that day. The extended apology. The eye-contact. The touchy-feely-ness of it. These interactions were always accompanied by contradictions. He would never allow this to occur in his lawman world, but he liked it. He couldn't recall the last time he had been with a woman, but he told himself it was a physical thing, Low-T, according to the television ads. Below the surface, he knew different. He felt different.

He was the head law enforcement officer in the county, a man of power and influence, and he was dripping with anticipation. His hands were heavy. He was chugging gin and tonics and pacing back and forth while his pulse reached tachycardia levels. Dom Dom had promised he would be paired with someone, but what if the guy wasn't his type? What is his type? Who would make the first move? He was more nervous than a chicken in a den of coyotes.

Dom Dom was expecting him to participate in this evening's money games with the Queen's Play Nine-ball Tournament to commence the following day. In his current state of mind, he couldn't shoot a game of Bumper Pool.

Wes Morton had told him to breathe and even gave him a relaxation tape that he trashed as soon as the doctor left his office. He closed his eyes, shook his head and shoulders, and inhaled like a vacuum cleaner. After a gigantic sigh, he popped a Xanax. At the same time there was a knock at his door.

33

Anger was Derk's reaction. Shine had lied to him. Followed by "Holy Moly, I slept with an FBI agent!" Succeeded by "What the devil does the FBI have to do with Sandy Gorton?"

Standing in front of him was FBI Special Agent Mence Caldwell half dressed, with an expression that could not be mistaken for anything other than, "Are we good here?"

"No, we're not good here," Derk said. "I've been misled by a federal agent who has undisclosed information on a case I've been working on."

Agent Caldwell threw up both hands in a gesture of surrender, which allowed his pants to fall to his knees. "No, no," he said.

"Jesus, kid," Derk said and looked away. "Put that thing away." Derk had his bag in one hand and the door knob in the other.

"Yes, yes, sir. I mean, no. Don't leave. Sir, Doctor Bryan, the FBI doesn't expect anything from you other than your professional assistance," Caldwell said.

"Professional assistance?" Derk said.

"Apparently, Agent Millar didn't apprise you of our mission," Caldwell said.

"Mission?" Derk laughed. "She picked me up in a bar, got me drunk, and fucked my brains out. Missionary and every other way. Is that what you're talking about?"

As soon as he said it, he realized that their tryst was the best thing that had happened to him since the two adventurous women he met at a Mensa club networking event not long after Jenny's death. In addition to high IQs, they were hot and ready, but it was too soon for a *menage a trois*.

Before leaving, he needed an answer to one question. "What does this charade have to do with Sandy Gorton?" Derk said.

The question mark on young Caldwell's face answered before he let out, "Who?"

Derk opened the door and left. After three steps, he returned, walked in, and dropped his bag onto the bed. He leaned the leather case holding his Meucci cue stick against the bedside table and picked up the house phone.

As he hit the button for the Front Desk, he said, "I'm staying, but you're getting another room."

34

"I want to be your partner," blurted out the young man with the worried face. He was wearing gym shorts, sandals, and a tank tee. His arms were full of clothes. He was trying not to stain his Tommy Bahama silk shirt with the beads of sweat that dripped from his brow. The perspiration, which glistened on his chest like water on a crystal, was the residual from a workout in the hotel's exercise room.

"What are you talking about?" said Tibbetts Foster. "I can't do this anymore."

"Can't do what?' said Tibbetts as he resisted Dex McMullen's attempt to slide by him.

"Any of it," said Dex, "or him." He glanced repeatedly up and down the hallway.

When Tibbetts Foster craned his neck through the hotel room door, Dex edged past him into the room.

"Close the door," urged Dex. He looked for a place to put his clothes. After losing Samantha's Card, Dex returned the Hummer to the rental agency and took Dominic to his hotel room at the Rock Hard Hotel. Dominic told him to take his car and wait for Samantha's return outside her home. He was instructed to call Dom Dom the moment she showed up. When Dex returned to the hotel the next day, Dom Dom became furious. First, because Dex had been rousted by the police for falling asleep in the car and second, for falling asleep in the car. "You moron, you probably missed her," he assailed Dex. Then he wanted to have sex with him. Dex stomped out and headed for the hotel's gym.

Dex McMullen had been blessed with the body of Adonis. He could have been a male model, but he had the decision-making tools of an army ant. The steroids he once gulped down like breath mints swelled his muscles, along with his proclivity for spontaneous rage and a ravenous appetite for OTC acne creams. Before the 'roids,' he

213

had been handsome, coy, and often demurring but sexually confused. That lasted until Dominic Domini introduced him to the world of the high-priced male escort. Before long, he had become a prized stud in Dom Dom's stable of dim, docile, pretty boys. Dom Dom had weened College, as he referred to him, of the PEDs, and along the way, he became a lover and an accomplice to Dominic's sinister pleasures and crimes.

Tibbetts Foster knew that Dex McMullen was as gay as a Key West parade, and he assumed that he and Dom Dom had more than a business relationship. But, *Sweet Caligula*, he was so damn cute. Tibbetts Foster knew right then that this boy was going to be the one.

Dex paced back and forth while his white linen dress pants, shirt, and shoes draped from his arms. He started to say something, but each time, the words came out like mulch.

"Well, boy, spit it out," Tibbetts said in a comforting Mississippi drawl. "It's a sin, Sheriff. I can't do it anymore," Dex surprised Tibbetts with a true southern Georgia accent. All two hundred pounds of drooling *studness* drooped as he collapsed into a large Victorian chair. He was forlorn, almost teary-eyed.

Tibbetts was used to being around men who faked emotion, especially remorse. It was standard M.O. for thugs who beat up defenseless women and grieving dads who left loaded guns accessible to their children. But this young man reeked of vulnerability.

Tibbetts walked over, kneeled down, and put an arm around the kid's shoulders. Dex nestled against him like a puppy to its mother. Tibbetts stroked the kid's blonde hair and said in a soft voice, "Tell me about it."

An hour later, Tibbetts Foster knew all he needed to know about his first male lover. Dex had nice clothes, a little money in the bank, and his own car, but he couldn't escape the feeling that he was committing a sin. Although he didn't have a religious fast twitch fiber in his body, he had grown up in a neighborhood of southern Baptists. Tibbetts knew these people. In fact, when he was eleven, a fire and brimstone preacher had moved next door to his mother. As a neighborly gesture, she dragged Tibbetts to the church once a year, usually on Easter or Christmas Eve, to hear the pastor rail against '*homosetuals.*' According to the preacher, Tibbetts and Dexter, and every other boy like them, were going *straight to hell* if they didn't mend their woeful ways.

Tibbetts held him and assured him, "Everything will be all right."

35

"Quieres que vaya a buscarlo," said Peluche. It was Spanish for, "You want I go get him."

Peluche was also Spanish for teddy as in teddy bear, oso del peluche. His given name was Fernando de los Oso. He was the Latino star in Dom Dom's international entourage of male models available for hire. He had black hair, high cheekbones, and a chiseled torso that he combined with a soft-spoken demeanor to stimulate men of a certain persuasion to drool in his presence.

The two men were in Dom Dom's private suite preparing for the evening's sidebar of high-stakes nine-ball. He had been anticipating the arrival of his old friend to join him. The game he had set up for Tibbetts Foster could net him a cool hundred Gs. Moreso, he expected this would be the night that Tibby got his cherry popped. Along with a selection of champagne, aphrodisiacs, and flavored vapes came a flirtatious group of hard-bodied male waiters in skin-tight, black-and-white formal wear. The buy-in for the game was twenty-five grand, and each player was guaranteed a hook-up.

Dom Dom was fuming as he walked away from Peluche. He took a draw of some Pure Joy from his vape. It was a new strain of cannabis that one of his legal grow operations had developed. He turned and exhaled a cumulus cloud into the room.

"Hola jefa, no fume agui," said Peluche.

"English, God dammit! How many times do I have to tell you?" said Dom Dom. "I know there's no smoking in here. That's why I had you bring up the HEPAs." He pointed to the knee-high air filters placed in each corner of the room.

"Lo siento. I mean, sorry, Boss," Peluche said.

Dom Dom continued pacing while he took another drag on the vape.

A mushroom-shaped shroud rose above him and then evaporated. "He's got religion," Peluche said.

"To hell he does," said Dom Dom. "Unless he's been fucking the Pope, there's not a pious bone in his body."

Peluche laughed. "You should do stand up, Boss." He called every male *boss* as a way of expressing fealty to them. It was learned behavior and good for business. Dom Dom's clients were not only men of means; they expected their escorts to behave obsequiously.

"He has to come back," said Peluche. "For he's clothes." He pointed to a closet with a pair of slacks and a matching jacket.

"You don't know that," said Dom Dom.

"For the keys to he's car," added Peluche. "He's mind is confused."

Dom Dom stumbled to the dish on the table where College always tossed his keys upon entering the room. They were gone.

"Fuck, fuck, fuck!" said Dom Dom. He rubbed his fingers together quickly as he paced, a habit brought on by stress. "People don't walk away from me. I walk away from them."

"Si, Boss. He will be back," Peluche's assurance was draped with patronage. "He doesn't have a car. He returned the Hummer as you told him." As Dom Dom darted about the room, his Machiavellian mind went to work. He sat down and took another hit from the vape. The blue exhaust left a hint of Jasmine in the air.

"This is seriously good shit," Dom Dom said.

Peluche coughed. He didn't smoke, and he was a vegetarian. He said, "Hey Boss, you know the smoke, it's not good for my skin. Soft skin is worth hundreds more."

"You watch too much American TV. Secondhand smoke is just burro barf," said Dom Dom. These self-imposed limitations, according to Dom Dom, were curbing Peluche's appeal to his sophisticated steak and cigar-loving clientele. Nevertheless, a hopeful buzz had returned to Dom Dom's face.

"What?" Peluche said.

"You are right. He will be back," said Dom Dom. He rubbed his fingers together again. "For he's money," he said, imitating Peluche.

***

Dominic Domini was smart enough to have organized several rewarding enterprises, even if they did operate on the fringes, but he was otherwise lazy. He found the use of bribery, extortion, and fraud to be less intellectually demanding than adhering to principles. And he found intimidation both effective and expedient. What he had observed about powerful people was that only the weak played by the rules. Successful men did what the unsuccessful were unwilling to do. For Dominic Domini, that included arson and the use of whatever weapon was handy.

He prided himself on being more than an average judge of character. He vetted every candidate for his internet brothel, and he looked for weaknesses he could exploit. After he developed a young man's trust, clothed him in linen and silk, and provided him with an expense account, he demanded and almost always got loyalty.

It was different with Dex McMullen. He had developed an affection for him. He had rewarded Dex with the title of Chief of Security. Then he put his name on an investment account so he would think he had a major financial stake in Dom Dom's affairs. In actuality, the investments were stock in companies associated with Dom Dom's cannabis ventures. They weren't much now but might be when the federal prohibition of marijuana ended. This was the first time Dom Dom had taken Dex to Florida and the first time he had exposed him to the grittier aspects of his affairs.

So, it came as a *gigantulous fucking surprise* when Dom Dom checked Dex's investment account to find that he had sold every share and swept the money from the account, all forty-seven thousand, three hundred and forty dollars.

"That back-stabbing little prick!" Dom Dom slammed down the top of his laptop and swatted the Tiffany on the desk. Peluche had to duck to avoid the lamp that splintered a mirror behind the bed.

36

Dexter McMullen's religious affliction lasted as long as it took Tibbetts Foster to seduce him. With Dex cantilevered over a red Natuzzi leather sofa, the Sheriff used a double dose Viagra hard-on and the prospect of immunity from prosecution to relieve him of his guilt.

Dex had been an unwitting participant in multiple criminal offenses committed by his former lover, but "That was nothing like what Dom Dom did to the owner of that garden shop and that policeman," he whimpered.

"He burned down their homes, too. He didn't have to do that," Dex confessed.

While Tibbetts cradled him in his arms, he coaxed him to "Release your pain, son."

The guilt that Dex carried from his childhood was exceeded by his fear of incarceration. That fear turned to paranoia when the Sheriff told him, "As a first-time offender, given your age, judges seldom authorize lethal injection." Then, he whispered, "But people died."

Dex shook like a baby with chills as the Sheriff assured him that he could protect him while he undressed him.

"Can you really do that?" Dex asked.

"I'm the Sheriff. I can do anything. You've never been safer," Tibbetts Foster said as he gently aroused the young man to a state of readiness.

Tibbetts Foster was amazed that it never occurred to Dex that the person with whom his former lover was complicit in multiple felonies couldn't provide him with anything other than a ticket to butt-fuck city. Nor was he aware how soon this would become apparent.

***

While Tibbetts Foster was lusting in Dex McMullen's young, buff body, he missed a life-altering text.

It came from the security camera at his country club home. The alarm had been tripped, which signified an attempted break-in. Had he been paying attention, he would have seen the video that showed a tall man dressed in police-issue boots and a flak vest, with a heavily bandaged arm wielding a wrecking bar. Under a ballcap that prevented full facial recognition was a rabid appearing male banging upon triple-layered, impact-resistant, sliding glass patio doors until one cracked. As the man exited the home, the video revealed the distended, furry body of a black Chow floating in the pool. As he looked up directly into the security camera that was capturing his movements, the Sheriff would have easily made out the words, "You killed my dog."

While all of this was going on, Tibbetts Foster missed the opening introduction for the Queen's Play Nine-ball Tournament as well as the open bar and high stakes pool games in Dominic Domini's twenty-five hundred dollar per night suite.

37

As soon as Mence Caldwell collected his suit, polished brogues, and revolver and left the room, Derk made the call from the hotel phone.

He had memorized the number when Agent Caldwell handed him his cell phone to talk to her.

"Special Agent Millar," she answered. She seemed hurried.

"Either you tell me what's going on, or I'm out of here," Derk said. "And by the way, what do you know about Sandy Gorton?"

"Slow down, Professor. Is Agent Caldwell there?" she said.

"He got another room, SPECIAL AGENT MILLAR." There was no mistaking the sarcasm in his voice.

She responded, "I know you're working on a case related to his death, and I may be able to help you, but I can't talk with you about it now."

There was another voice in the background. "Will that be all, Agent Millar?"

"Yes. Thank you, Judge," she said.

He heard a door shut and someone say, "Did you get it?"

"Madeline, Madeline!" Derk said.

In as sincere a tone as Derk had heard her speak, she said, "Derk, my dear, I need you to hang in there for one more night. Please. It's really important to me. I'll be there tomorrow. I promise."

She knew about the Gorton case because Director Waitley had informed the FBI a week ago. She was interested only because the video forwarded to her by Samantha Card showed someone resembling Dominic Domini trying to break into her home. Domini had been linked to the Sheriff in the information forwarded to her by Samantha Card. She had also been informed that the case had been closed.

She knew more about Derk Bryan. She knew he was a tireless investigator who was willing, when necessary, to color outside the lines, not unlike herself. This she had heard from a fellow agent who had worked a case with Doctor Bryan the previous year. Bryan had nailed a suspect by posing as a handicapped janitor who discovered that chemicals were being illegally dumped by a shell company owned by the company Derk was investigating.

Madeline Millar had used creative schemes in the past, and the limits to propriety in solving cases were probably more imaginative than most agents possessed, but she had never seduced a guy to help her with a case.

She had gone to the Top End to observe Doctor Bryan in action because she was looking for someone who could shoot pool without embarrassing himself. She wanted him to participate in a ruse to get close to Dominic Domini. She had been investigating his organization for running an interstate sex-for-hire enterprise, and she thought he was pimping for underage boys. She had probably gone too far, but she liked him.

Domini was seldom seen in public with the exception of the annual Queen's Play tournament. He always hit the first shot to open the "Queer Ball Bash," as Agent Millar referred to it. When she received a video clip from Samantha Card's cell phone of him trying to break into her condominium, she asked the local P.D. to obtain a warrant for the arrest of Dominic Domini, one of the men in the video. She wanted it served the next day at the opening of the tournament. She was in the process of rounding up agents and coordinating with the local police.

"Why?" he said. "Why should I?"

"Because I owe you, and I want to make it up to you. And I like the way you handle your," she paused for emphasis, "stick."

"You know what kind of tournament this is?" Derk said. "I do."

"And you're expecting me to play with Caldwell?"

"No, with me. I'll talk with Caldwell."

"You do that."

38

The reception on the night before the commencement of the Queen's Play Nine-ball Tournament was held in a large banquet room called the Players Celebration Room. It featured a medieval bar with a wooden sign overhead that read Players Retreat. The grog, as well as the wine, was being served in iron-strapped wooden mugs. A huge buffet was served by a bevy of young male waiters dressed like a Renaissance ballet troupe. Their tights were so taut Derk was afraid of slipping on the drool left by the early arrivals.

In the informational pack, given to Derk at the door, was a name tag in the shape and color of a pool table. In the background were the images of two people holding pool sticks and toasting each other. At the top of the card was the tournament moniker: Queen's Play. Centered in the middle of the pool table was the player's name and Room Number. Derk immediately scribbled over his name and room number and wrote *Straight Shooter*.

He felt like a target. He had already been approached in the lobby by a bellboy in a skin-tight outfit, offering him a room service upgrade. He had partied with friends at gay clubs. They were fun, spontaneous, and energized by wine and dance. Also, a lot of libidinous throbbing. He had no issues with the throbbing, but he wasn't gay.

He reluctantly looked for Agent Caldwell. He didn't really want to hang out with the guy. Caldwell was too damned happy. Doubling up, though, might take some eyes off him. Caldwell had yet to arrive.

He thought he recognized a couple of faces, most likely guys he knew from the Top End, but he couldn't recall a name. Not remembering names had become an issue. His self-designated prognosis he attributed to a condition he called Early Onset Decrepitude. He was happy he did not see Stickman in attendance. He would have had a difficult time explaining why he was there.

The aroma of barbeque wafted through the room. Two men behind a large grille were turning strips of tender beef and poultry. He perused the buffet, looking to avoid anything shaped like a Phallus or that could be interpreted as an aphrodisiac. That left out the Jell-o-filled salad, with shredded carrots in the shape of Greek gods in great detail, including their genitals. He settled on the broiled haddock with a lemon dill sauce, canned green beans, and a baked yam. In spite of the miles he put on his bicycle, his doctor recommended that he reduce the carbs.

He took a seat at a table with two black fellows from New York. He knew that because they had written their cities on their name tags. They were in room 716, just below Derk's room. One wore chiffon and bobby socks, and the other sported a Zoot suit. The one in the woman's clothing giggled each time the Zoot suit put his hand under her/his skirt.

Derk asked one of the Chippendales in tights to bring him a Costco-size gin and tonic. He hoped to dull the disappointment he felt. It looked as if he had become a pawn in an FBI sting, and he didn't like it. He didn't like it when someone else was in charge, but he had promised Shine he would wait until she showed up. He convinced himself he might learn something about the Gorton case, or he might spend the day and the night with Shine, Agent Millar, or whomever she is. Either of those was a good thing.

A group of minstrels in period costumes played the Dances from Terpsichore while men gayly pranced around the room with each other. The haddock was unexpectedly satisfying, and the Juniper-infused gin and tonic worked its magic.

On large overhead screens, movies that featured pool games were showing. One featured the classy Jackie Gleason playing **The Hustler**, an old black and white, with lessons for an aspiring pool shark. In this case, the brash rookie was played by a young Paul Newman as Fast Eddie Felson. Derk had seen this film and the later version in which Newman reprised the role, playing a weathered and more cynical Felson, in **The Color of Money.** In the more recent film, the young shark was played by Tom Cruise. He had seen that movie with Jenny. She adored Newman. This film was side by side with **The Hustler.**

On another wall there were scenes from **The Shooting Gallery** with Ving Rhames and Freddie Prinze, Jr. as Jericho Hudson. Lots of action and heavy-handedness drummed out the exquisite display of billiards. It was too violent for his taste.

On another wall, the **Baltimore Bullet** was beaming with cameos of mythical players such as Willie Mosconi, Steve Mizerak, and Lou Butera. He hadn't seen it but decided he would order it when he got home.

Oohs and aahs permeated the room when the trick shots for the filming of **Pool Hall Junkies** were projected onto the main screen. This was followed by raucous applause when Jennifer Barretta buried shot after shot in **Nine Ball**, the first full-length film utilizing real professionals. He was surprised to discover so many movies in which pool was the focal point as well as the appreciation that those in attendance had for the game.

It reminded him of the other reason he came to the Rock Hard for the weekend. He loved to shoot pool. Burying difficult shots into pockets off multiple rails confirmed that his physical skills were still intact. He was now looking forward to the competition, and he wanted to practice. A couple of men in tuxedos, one in his twenties and the other over fifty arose from the front table and welcomed the participants and the sponsors. The winner of last year's tournament was awarded a plaque and a new stick with an embossed leather sheaf. He asked someone to come up and draw a name from a box of entries for a new pool cue. One of the two Queens sitting next to Derk shrieked when her/his name was announced. "Oooee! I won.

Jermaine, I won," he squeaked and then kissed Jermaine on the cheek.

After all of the door prizes were awarded, someone took the microphone and explained the rules for the matches. "If you have any questions, they're in your packet."

Derk located them. Matches would begin tomorrow at one sharp in the Grand Ballroom. It would be double elimination, with the winners in one bracket and the losers shuffled to another. This format would allow each team to lose and still arise again. The winning team would be the last team standing.

After a few housekeeping announcements, there was a brief Q&A. When all the concerns were addressed, he closed the formal part of the evening with, "Hey, girls, don't party too hard. Good luck, and see you tomorrow."

With that, the informal part of the evening commenced. Some went hand in hand with private suites that featured big-money games and more. Others paired up, drank, and danced the night away. Derk headed to the Grand Ballroom for some practice. He flashed his name tag and was provided with a shopping bag full of vendor gifts, coupons, and multi-colored condoms, including a card from a local HIV clinic.

There must have been thirty pool tables aligned down the center of the Ballroom and divided into two equal rows. The walls were adorned with oversized pictures of the biggest names in the history of billiards. A few booths, reserved by equipment suppliers, were being given final touches. Chairs and tables were scattered in group settings for those in between games. A cash bar was set up at one end of the room.

White-clothed tables were lined up for check-in and administrative personnel. Behind those tables, a massive digital scoreboard was positioned to display the winners of each match. He was relieved to see the name M. Millar next to his. He resisted the urge to call Shine and thank her.

He borrowed a pool cue from one of the vendors and hit a few shots to get a feel for the plush blue felt that would be the gridiron for the weekend's games. As he practiced, he kept an eye on the other players. They were competent, but he'd seen better pool shot at the Top End on a slow night. With his gin and tonic-infused confidence boosted, he went to the lobby to get a copy of the Times for its crossword puzzle and then returned to his room. He took an Ibuprofen for his arthritis, slipped into bed, and fell asleep searching for an eleven-letter word for transitory.

39

Then Samantha discovered the link between Tibbetts Foster and Global; she had Colleen Reid dig up everything she could on Global.

The company claimed to be an international distributor, but Samantha's assistant deduced was it was primarily a shell company. A shell company's primary purpose is to launder money, often to hide illegal cash flows.

Samantha emailed what she had uncovered to a veteran reporter at the Times. He called her immediately. She then asked D'Thomas LaFontaine to meet her at the Rock Hard Hotel fifteen minutes before the Sheriff's scheduled address. She breathed a sigh of relief when he agreed.

There were two reasons she wanted to team up with D-Tom, as he was known during his college football days. LaFontaine was an ACL injury away from becoming a first-round NFL draftee. First, he was a respected reporter from a big city newspaper who was better prepared to withstand the blitz of verbal and legal assaults that the twice-elected Sheriff would surely throw at them. Second, Samantha needed a bodyguard, and D-Tom was a six-foot-five black man with the strength of a linebacker and the agility of a "Dancing with the Stars" contestant.

She was planning to interview the Sheriff who was making a morning address to a national conference. She had a couple of theories about the Sheriff's involvement in her brother-in-law's death, but she decided to open her questioning with a single query: *"Do you think that funneling public funds to a private company, in which you and your campaign contributor are partners, is a conflict of interest?"*

She told D-Tom, upon his arrival, that he might be a better choice to ask that question than a diminutive black female reporter from a weekly entertainment magazine. He reluctantly agreed because, after covering the Willie and Esther Hixon case, he thought the Sheriff's policies were detrimental to the African-American community, and he should be replaced.

She huddled at the back of the room with LaFontaine as the body of graying men in uniforms took their seats after grazing the breakfast buffet. The dearth of non-whites in the room suggested to her that the unequal application of justice in the country would continue unabated. In spite of her preparations, things didn't go as planned.

When Tibbetts Foster approached the podium, smug and glowing, it was too much for Samantha Card to coddle. As the Sheriff began to welcome his counterparts from every State in the Union, a petite, middle-aged black woman approached from the back of the room and blurted out, "Whose body did you put in the morgue?"

As Samantha slipped between tables on her way to confront the Sheriff, she answered her own question, loud enough for everyone in the room to hear, "It's not Wilson Anthony Perkins. Is it?"

She stopped in the middle of the room, surrounded by a hundred men with guns, and announced, "Sheriff Tibbetts, tell us your position with Global, LLC, the company you've been funneling public funds to?"

The giddiness that had accompanied the Sheriff since he awakened next to Dex McMullen had disappeared. He scanned the room for help.

"Sergeant Perkins found out, and you killed him," she said.

She was a tiny thing, brandished no weapons, and sported an official press name tag. Even so, she was emboldened because no one rose to stop her. When she was a few feet from the podium, where Sheriff Tibbetts Foster stood, mouth agape, she turned to the lawmen in attendance and said, "Don't believe a thing this man says. He killed a cop!"

As a uniformed officer approached her from each entrance of the conference room, she said, "How do you explain this?" She held up a copy of the invoice her brother-in-law said was a forgery.

As the local cops corralled her, she handed one of them a picture of the Sheriff with the ME and two naked men in the background.

With every eye riveted upon her, she said, "Arrest him. He's a fraud and a faggot."

40

He slept on eight hundred counts, Egyptian percale, but Derk still awakened early. The gin and tonic had aggravated his arthritis. A little too stiff to hit the hotel exercise room, he shuffled into the shower before going to breakfast. As he was drying his hair, the phone rang. "Derk, I just sent you a Tox Report," said Joyce.

"Really? It's Saturday," Derk said.

"It's about Gorton," she said. "You're still on that, aren't you?"

"Yes," she had his attention.

"Thought you were on vacation."

"Ben called me in. It's been sitting here for a week," she said.

"I wondered what happened to that," he said.

Due to the fire at Gorton's home and business, followed by a major storm, no one was around to answer the call from the impound to arrange for the disposition of the Gorton company van. When someone contacted Derk about it, he had the van towed to a lab for a second look.

"We had a temp here. Things got backed up," Joyce said. The frustration in her voice was obvious.

"I'll look at it now. Thanks," Derk said.

He slipped on a tee shirt, chinos, and a pair of sneakers and went downstairs to the hotel communications center. In his email was the report showing traces of two chemicals that were in the van but not included in the ME's report. They were discovered on the steering wheel.

"What did Sandy 'Wink' Gorton and Sergeant Wilson Perkins have in common?" he wondered, and only one thing came to mind: Doctor Wesley Morton. The ME had signed each of their death certificates.

He called Joyce back, gave her the names of the pesticides, and said, "Find out who distributes these and call me back."

Ten minutes later, in the middle of a bowl of cinnamon-covered oatmeal with nuts and raisins, his cell phone played the William Tell Overture. Someone at the next table sang aloud, "Dum da dum, da dum dum dum."

"Sorry," Derk said and stepped out of the restaurant for privacy.

"Global," Joyce said, and Derk finished with "LLC."

"Global was the last known distributor. You know them?" she said.

"Maybe," he said, recalling the name that Samantha Card had uncovered. "Do you have a list of their partners or officers?"

"Hold on." Moments later, she came back. "I'll read them to you."

When she named Dominic Domini and Tibbetts Foster, he said, "Thank you, Doctor Watson!"

"What is it?"

"Joyce, you're the best."

"So, what's the connection?"

"Those formulas are restricted," he said.

"As in banned," she said.

"As in not even allowed into the country," Derk said.

"So how did they get here?"

"I think I know the answer to that, but why?" he said.

"What are you going to do now?" she said.

"Shoot some pool," he said and hit End on his phone.

41

It was now clear why he had been allured and then entreated to participate in the Queen's Play Nine-ball Tournament. The FBI was investigating Dominic Domini. Somehow, Dominic Domini, Sheriff Tibbetts Foster, and the medical examiner were mixed up in the death of Sandover Gorton and probably the disappearance of Samantha's brother-in-law. He wondered if Domini was one of the large bodies chasing Samantha Card. He didn't know what they were up to, but the voice in his head said, "Follow the money."

What was discovered on Gorton's steering wheel was a combination of chemicals that can enter the body via contact with the skin. After coming into direct contact with those poisons, Gorton would have had just enough time to make it to the bridge at Lake Manatee. Sandover Gorton was murdered.

In defense of Doc Morton, he probably wouldn't have found these toxins if he were not looking for them. When mixed together, they are colorless and more lethal than when separated. They could have come from the plastic containers strewn upon Gorton's lawn that aroused Derk's suspicion on his first visit to the Gorton home.

He finished the oatmeal, poured a tall glass of orange juice, and grabbed a couple of bananas before returning to his room.

On the way through the lobby, he heard a familiar voice shouting in the banquet room. Moments later, a lithe, frenzied black woman was being escorted from the room by two police officers. Venom spewed from her lips as they coerced her through the front door. They stood guard at the door until she was off the property.

By the time he reached his floor, his cell phone was ringing.

"I had no idea you had such a colorful vocabulary," he said to Samantha Card.

"I knew that was you. What are you doing there?"

"I'm playing pool. You, it seems, are making the news, not just reporting it," he said.

"He killed him, Dr. Bryan. I know he did. He and that Domini guy who's been after me," she said.

"I know. Where are you now?" he said.

"How do you know?" she said.

"They killed Sandy Gorton. You know, the case I was working on?"

"Him, too," she said.

"They poisoned Gorton and burned down his home and his business trying to cover something up," Derk added. "Do you know what that might be?"

"That's why they killed Will. He must have known what it was," she said.

"Probably."

"Maybe it had to do with the purchase orders that had his name on them, but he said he didn't sign them," she said.

"P.O.s for what?" Derk asked.

"Chemicals. Orders from a company connected to Domini," said Samantha. "They have a history together."

"I'd like to see those P.O.s," he said.

"I'll forward them to you," she said. "I think they're funneling money to an overseas company."

Follow the money, thought Derk. "So, tell me about Domini."

"He financed the Sheriff's campaign, and he runs gay porn sites," she said.

"Speaking of the Sheriff," Derk said. "He's here making a speech."

"I know. I lost it. I called him a murderer in front of every other Sheriff in the country," she said.

"Where are you?"

"Across the street in the coffee shop." "And your daughter?"

"She's safe."

"I'll come right over," he said.

"No. I got myself a bodyguard. Say hello to D'Thomas LaFontaine."

"Hello, I've heard good things about you, Doctor Bryan. I'd like to do a story on you sometime," Derk heard a deep voice.

"I'm not the story. She is. Can you keep her out of sight?" Derk said.

"I think so," he said.

"They want to kill her," Derk said.

"I'll be all right," she was back on the line.

"Oh my god! I just frightened you to death. I'm so sorry. I didn't mean to," he said, but she interrupted him.

"What are you doing?" she said.

Given the gravity of the situation, he hesitated to tell her the truth, but he was committed. "I'm going to shoot some pool," Derk said.

42

He was about to call Special Agent Madeline Millar when there was a knock at his door. Simultaneously, his cell phone rang again.

Derk opened the door and said "Hello" to the caller at the same time. A guy with long black hair and sideburns stood in front of him. He had on dark jeans, a black leather vest, and charcoal-tinted Aviator sunglasses. With the black hat and pool cue, except for the small black purse on a long silver chain that draped one shoulder, he looked like Johnny Cash in The Baron and the Kid. Except for one thing.

"What?" said Derk, looking at Madeline Millar in drag.

"Derk, it's Teach," said the caller.

Distracted by the call, he allowed Madeline Millar to pass him, emitting her seductive pheromones as she entered. Mence Caldwell shadowed her but kept his distance from Derk.

"It's Teach. You've got to see this."

"No damn way," Derk said to Special Agent Millar.

"Bad time?" said Teach.

"Sorry," said Derk.

"I'm sending it to you now. You're my inspiration," Teach said.

"What?" Derk said, staring at Madeline in the Johnny Cash get-up, but Teach was gone.

Madeline Millar stood in the middle of Derk's hotel room and lined up an air ball with her pool cue. Caldwell moved to one side.

"Who are you?" Derk said.

Agent Millar, pool cue cradled in her hands, said with enthusiasm, "Scratch, you ready to shoot some pool?"

Before she walked through the door he had a bevy of questions for her, the most important concerned Dominic Domini. What did she know about him? Did they have anything on him? Was there a connection between Sandy Gorton and him? Now, the woman with whom he had been wanting to share every breath in his body stood in front of him as a female FBI agent dressed like a country singer. Only one question emerged.

"You really think this is going to work?"

She stepped closer while maintaining a guy-to-guy distance and, with the seriousness of a gall bladder surgeon, said to him, "There's something I need to tell you." Then she added with a wink, "Then, let's have some fun." She paced while Mence Caldwell plopped down on the couch.

Derk remained standing, arms folded. She revealed the essentials of her investigation of Dominic Domini and her plan to pinch him for pimping underage boys. She left out the part about Agent Caldwell securing an invitation to one of Domini's private games and the backup plan to have Domini arrested for attempted burglary.

Derk reiterated Samantha's account of the connection between Domini and the Sheriff.

"They killed Sandy Gorton and burned down his house. Probably a cop, and now they're after Samantha Card," he told her. "She needs protection."

"We would if we could find her," Millar said.

"I don't think she wants to be found," he said with a deadpan expression.

"Well, I've got this place covered," she said. When Derk acquiesced, she added, "So let's go practice and have a little lunch before this Queer Ball Bash begins," she said.

Agent Caldwell frowned. She seemed ready to recognize the insult, but instead, shook her head and said, "Agent Caldwell will remain close if we need him. Right?" It was an order, not a question.

There was only one reason he decided to go along with her plan. It was her Johnny Cash impersonation. He had always trusted the

Man in Black. After he showered and dressed, they headed for the Grand Ballroom.

"Wait a minute," Derk said, recalling that Teach McIntosh had sent him something to review.

He opened his cell phone to the video his friend had forwarded. Teach was standing in front of an all-electric SUV and panning one arm over the new automobile. "Check out my new ride, all-electric, and you were my inspiration, Derk Bryan."

Teach began singing as the FBI agents huddled close to the cell phone.

The voice resembled Bob Dylan: "I used to think that I was cool driving around on fossil fuel. 'Til I discovered that all I was doing was driving down the road to ruin."

"Catchy tune. Who is he?" Madeline said.

"Friend of mine," Derk said.

"Sounds more like Dylan than James Taylor," she said.

"I'm impressed, Agent Millar, that you would know the difference."

43

When Derk entered the Grand Ballroom with Agent Millar, other than an occasional rise of the brow, little interest was paid to them. On any other day, everyone in the room would have been staring at the woman dressed in black impersonating Johnny Cash as the Baron, but this was the Queens's Play Nine-ball Tournament. Pool was almost secondary to the potpourri of fashions.

Standing out were the two queens from Queens with whom Derk shared a table the previous evening. Each of them was born with one X and one Y chromosome, but the hormone replacement treatments affected them differently. One was donned in an oversized egg-white Halston number, and the other in over-the-knee red leather Pinky Boots, black leggings, and a white tee embossed with a red, green, and yellow abstract. His hair was jet black and looked like the back end of a mallard in flight. He coifed it with a 1950s red linen Gatsby chapeau.

Derk's outfit demanded no extra attention. He looked good and he felt comfortable in his blue pin-striped Oxford shirt and Lucky Brand stretch jeans, designed to accommodate waistline changes due to any indulgence he permitted himself. He was far from making any fashion statement, and side by side, he and Johnny were just another gay couple.

By half past noon, most of the participants had gathered with their cue sticks in hand. Each team consisted of two males, with the exception of the Derk and the Baron, who would alternate turns. The first team to win ten games at each table would be declared the winner and advance to the winners' bracket. Losers went into the losers' brackets, only to re-immerge with the winners on the second day. Win or lose the champagne, and the party was to go on unabated.

Derk had been a spectator at a pool tournament only once. The atmosphere at most tournaments is serene and polite, not unlike a busy library. Occasional but muted applause was not improper. At Queen's Play, the air was abuzz with energy. Traditional pool players required a quietude not unlike that of golfers before their swings. Here, they ached with "Aaahs" on misses and cheered with "You go, *girl*" for the successes. With a pool cue in one hand and a Moet in the other, people were having fun.

The constant in the room was the sound of balls being struck, caroms off the walls of felt-covered tables, and ivory orbs dropping into leather pockets. It was the sound of pool and source of comfort for Derk. His adrenaline began to flow. He was ready to shoot some pool.

The tables were set in long rows across from each other and close enough for a badly scratched ball to land on the next closest table or in someone's drink. The fact that it didn't occur even once during the warm-ups suggested he may have underestimated the talent in the room.

Prior to the official commencement of the tournament, segments of the best billiards' films were again projected onto the walls of the great hall as they had been last night. *We Are the Champions* filled the hall. In a strange way, it was inspiring, not unlike the feeling he got in the pit of his stomach on the Fourth of July when the local radio station simulcasted Queen's iconic masterpiece with the fireworks.

It was an almost corny Chevrolet and apple pie kind of moment. Agent Millar, who was exchanging nonverbal messages with Mence Caldwell three tables to their right, seemed unmoved. Nevertheless, if she hadn't looked like *"The Man in Black,"* he would have taken her into his arms right there and kissed her like Rhett took Scarlett.

The music stopped just before one o'clock, and the room quieted. Surveying the room, he spotted Stickman who seemed more than surprised at his presence. Other than Stickman, he saw only four familiar faces in the room, and three of them had a permit to carry a concealed weapon.

One of those he recognized was Dex McMullen, playing at a table a few rows from him. Oh my god, he wanted to alert Agent Millar, but she and Caldwell already had a bead on him. He probably had one stashed in his sock or strapped onto his leg. Surely, Agent Millar carried something under her waistband, and there was Sheriff Tibbetts Foster, dressed in a slightly baggy, white linen leisure suit. He certainly had one stuffed inside his coat pocket. Inspiration faded as the prospect of being caught in the crossfire seemed imminent. The FBI wasn't really there to shoot pool. After an explanation of the rules, the public announcer introduced Dominic Domini. It was tradition for him to make the first break to commence the tournament.

"That's the guy. That's him!" he whispered aloud to Agent Millar.

She held Derk's arm firmly and nodded her affirmation. Then she exchanged glances with Agent Caldwell and his playing partner.

Domini's eyes were bloodshot, and his jaw seemed out of place. A bandage covered part of his forehead. He managed a mechanical smile and lip-synced *"Thank you"* a couple of times as the attendees applauded. He was obviously a familiar figure to them.

Derk noticed his disposition turn from sour to surly when Domini, lining up the shot for the break, caught Tibbetts Foster patting Dex McMullen on the backside. In the middle of his backstroke, four people entered the room, one after another.

The first was a middle-aged white man with one arm in a sling. He was in a frenzied state, steadied only by the Percocet taken to ease the pain in his arm and the buzz from some Skunk he had pilfered from the evidence room several weeks ago.

The second was one of Dom Dom's boy toys who was serving as security for the event. "Sir, you have to have a pass to get in," he kept entreating the intruder to stop, but it was to no avail.

Sergeant Wilson Perkins turned and held up a police I.D. without breaking stride. He was heading straight for Sheriff Tibbetts Foster.

The third was a petite black woman sporting press credentials, accompanied by a large black man with a camera. She was shouting, "Will, stop, Will!"

Dominic Domini was no better than average at billiards, but he was strong enough to slip his stick under the cue ball. He launched it, like a short pitch shot, over two tables where it struck Tibbetts Foster, distracted by the interlopers, in the balls, his own private set. He went down like a wounded hyena, wincing and whining.

As Sergeant Wilson Perkins weaved his way between pool tables toward the fallen Sheriff, he grabbed a pool cue from someone and broke it over the corner of a pool table. It splintered and hit another guest, who dropped to the floor, clutching his side. People were now ducking and fleeing the rampaging lawman.

Samantha Card kept shouting, "Will, don't. Will!"

As Perkins was about to hit the Sheriff with the broken pool cue, Samantha screamed, "It's you!"

She was looking at Dominic Domini. He was holding a small Deringer, the same one he had pilfered from the Sergeant before leaving him for dead. The same gun he misfired on Derk.

"Will, he's got a gun," she shouted.

"You!" Sergeant Perkins yelled, looking at Domini. The gun went off. Then another.

Panic prevailed. Most dropped to the floor. Some ran for the exits. Still standing were Derk Bryan, Madeline Millar, and Mence Caldwell.

As soon as Agent Millar, who had been focused upon Domini since he entered the room, watched him take the Derringer from his pocket, she drew the revolver she had hidden in her vest. When he raised it above his waist, she fired one fatal shot.

When the commotion began, Derk was behind a pool table opposite Sheriff Foster, staring at the man who tried to kill him in his own home, Dominic Domini. He froze when Domini pulled out the weapon. When Sergeant Perkins yelled at Domini, Derk looked back toward him. The Sheriff had gotten to his feet, pulled a nine-millimeter handgun from behind his back, and aimed it at Perkins. Derk adjusted his aim and drove the ball in a straight line into the Sheriff's midsection. When it hit him, the gun went off and the bullet grazed the sergeant. Perkins turned toward the Sheriff and rammed the jagged end of the pool cue repeatedly into his torso. He didn't stop until Agent Caldwell took him down with his service revolver.

After the gunshots, the local police, there to serve the arrest warrant for Dominic Domini, burst through every entrance into the Grand Ballroom, forcing back the crowd that was exiting.

Left in the room were a bunch of frightened partiers, each with a pool cue that could be construed as a weapon, and three FBI agents, each with his or her gun drawn. The Grand Ballroom became eerily silent while the aroma of gunfire wafted in the air.

"FBI! FBI!"" shouted Agent Millar. She held up one hand with her badge for the approaching officers to see. Her gun, in the other hand, was dropped to her side.

M. Sloan, the detective in charge, motioned his officers to stand down. "Agent Millar?" he said, looking at Johnny Cash.

"Detective Sloan," she responded.

He walked over to her and said in a low growl, "This was supposed to be service of a simple arrest warrant, Special Agent Millar, and now I'm going to miss the Hurricanes' game. What the fuck happened here?" Before she responded he gave orders that no one was allowed to leave the room.

Derk had rushed to comfort Samantha Card, who was kneeling over her brother-in-law's lifeless body. Only a few feet away was Dexter McMullen, repelling at the sight of his dead lover, the Sheriff.

When their eyes met, Dex tightened. The grip on his pool cue hardened. He looked as if he wanted to strike somebody, anybody.

When his eyes met Derk, Derk slowly shook his head and said firmly, "It's over," and when he repeated it, Dex dropped the pool cue and cried.

The questioning of witnesses went on throughout the afternoon while the crime scene crew did its job. Few in attendance seemed to know those involved other than Dominic Domini, and from the conversations that Derk overheard, there were various opinions about who was responsible for what had transpired and why it had happened.

Although a full report would follow, Special Agent Madeline Millar provided a brief statement to Detective Sloan. "Special Agent Caldwell and I were here, under-cover, as part of an investigation of a suspect thought to be engaging in inter-state prostitution. When the suspect, Dominic Domini, pulled a gun, I pulled my service revolver and shot him. Agent Caldwell did the same when Sergeant Perkins attacked the Sheriff." She stated that, before today, she hadn't met nor did she know Sergeant Wilson Perkins other than she thought he was dead.

It would be weeks before Derk would read in Bay Magazine the article about the wide-ranging scheme by Dominic Domini, the medical examiner, the controller, and the Sheriff to exploit the drug forfeiture laws for personal gain. This would be exposed in a series of articles for which Samantha Card would be nominated for a Pulitzer.

Derk was disheartened by the entire event. The nine ball that hit

Tibbetts Foster was the only shot he got off all weekend. He hadn't gotten the answers to the questions about Sandy Gorton, but he figured the primary characters were all dead. And his fire for Shine, aka Madeline Millar, had been extinguished by deception and gunfire. He had to let that go.

By late afternoon, he had told the police what he knew, and he was released. As he was departing, Madeline Millar offered a hollow apology and said she wished they would have met under different circumstances. When she asked if he would like to meet with her for drinks at another time, he said he would think about it.

His attempt to console Samantha Card was received with an invitation for an interview the next day. She had a story to write, and Derk Bryan would be part of it. He liked her, but she was the most intense woman he had ever met.

He thought about Agnes Wiley's explanation for not wanting to pursue any further relationship with him. He had to admit that an investigator's life was constantly in flux. The day turned out to be an extension of the case on which he had been working, and he was fortunate he hadn't been in the line of fire. He missed his wife. Jenny understood the relationship of his work to his life and she tolerated the risks.

Right now, he sought calmness, solitude, and peace. He looked forward to a hot shower in hope that it would wash away the disappointment he was feeling.

As he was leaving, he overheard the two queens from Queens provide their unique perspective on what had happened that day.

"The younger man, wasn't he cute," they looked at each other and winked. "Well, he'd been eyeing the other guy, the big one with the badge, and everybody knew he a lawman *cuz his pitcher* was on the sign in the lobby," said the man in knee-high, red Pinky Boots and hands that painted the air as he spoke.

"Oh, he liked to cream his panties the first time he set eyes on the Sheriff," said his partner dressed in the Halston, but he was interrupted.

"Yes, sweetcakes, that's been established," he said and turned to the detective. "Ain't that right, officer?"

"It's Detective," said Sloan.

"Yes, it is," he said and turned back to his main squeeze in the Halston. "Cuz it said that on the poster."

"He is right. Excuse me. Ain't he something? Smart and cute," he said and pulled Pinky Boots closer to him. "But what I was trying to tell you was that boy almost dropped to his knees the first time he watched that tall, dreamy man in the Minnesota Fats suit chalk his cue. It was almost embarrassing."

"So, what she is trying to tell you is that it was just plain jealousy that started the whole thing," chimed in his partner. "That's why he shot that boy."

"My goodness, that badge man was messing with this boy, and he was already some other queen's toy. A girl knows you can't do that shit, or there's gonna be trouble."

44

Derk sat on his patio sipping a cup of tea while he watched a couple of gulls soar above the shoreline in search of breakfast. A well-weathered man in swim trunks walked the beach, culling the debris that had come in with the morning tide. He stooped, picked up a shell, examined it, and tossed it away. A young couple, jogging in the sand, stopped and reversed course, probably heading back to their hotel. From this vantage point, life seemed simple.

It wasn't. He was an anthropologist by education. That meant he had a knowledge of the brevity and the fragility of life. On his bookshelf, he had a set of fossilized trilobites that were nine hundred million years old. At one time, they covered the ocean's floors. They have been gone for a long time. Someday, not long from now, he would be long gone, too. After two or three generations, unless a building was named after him or he discovered the cure for cancer, no one would remember him.

No one would remember Derk Bryan, protector of the Planet Earth. Nor will they recall Derk Bryan, the teacher; Derk Bryan, the widower; Derk Bryan, child of a missing man; and certainly not Derk Bryan, owner of a wounded heart.

He was acutely aware that Earth is four and one half billion years old, and that people have been on the planet only two and one half million of those years. Not only have the trilobites vanished, but more than ninety-nine percent of all the creatures that have ever inhabited the Earth are no longer here.

Lately, his life had been consumed by loss. His normally optimistic outlook had been replaced with doubt. His doubts were not only for his future but for the future of mankind.

He had been pondering a conversation he recently had with one of his colleagues at the university, a mathematician, who had tried to cheer him up. "Why are you so damned worried about things?"

Professor Aragon said. "You're not going to be around for the demise of humanity, and if you think that attitude is cavalier, the odds of winning the Irish Sweepstakes are astronomically better than our chances of survival on this planet."

That was so depressing he booked a flight to Cancun. He had been to thirty-seven countries, and even though this was a tourist trap, he'd never been there. The ruins of Tulum were nearby, an advanced culture that had completely disappeared if he wanted to explore them, but he wasn't looking for answers.

He wanted to stop thinking for a while. He wanted to fish offshore for the big ones. He wanted to drink cervezas with the locals and listen to Spanish guitars. He wanted to walk barefoot in the sand and let the tide ripple over his toes as Jenny and he once did. He wanted to forget, and he wanted to believe. What he needed to believe was that life was good and that he would love again.

His trip to Mexico accomplished some of what vacations are supposed to do. He came back relaxed.

On the airplane, he pondered his future. Maybe he would travel more. He hadn't been to the Outback or Vancouver or the DMZ. He heard it had become a wildlife sanctuary and a testimony to what man could accomplish, even as a result of conflict.

He had been developing a plan with his condominium board to place solar panels on the roofs of all of the condos. The cost would be added to their monthly HOA fees. He wanted to see that plan come to fruition. He wanted to learn a new language, French, say. He wondered if he could roll the Rs. He wanted to finish reading Hamlet. Actually, he wanted to start reading Hamlet.

He had always wanted to ride the Appalachian Trail on his bicycle, but he wasn't sure that his knees would allow it. He really needed to find a nutritional and exercise regimen to combat his arthritis. That could help a lot of people.

During a recent conversation with Samantha Card, she encouraged him to write a book. She told him she would feature him in her magazine: *Meet the Indiana Jones of the 21st Century.* He laughed when she suggested it. But now, he thought, "Why not?" He had much to do.

He dropped his bags in the bedroom and adjusted the thermostat. In the kitchen, he opened a bottle of Grolsch and sat down to sort the mail. On the kitchen table was an old crossword puzzle he had been working on for weeks. On it lay a blank envelope, unopened. He didn't recall placing it there. His eyes darted about the room in search of anything else out of place.

The envelope was thick and filled with paper. When he opened it, he noticed that the five-letter word for *trespass* had been filled in on the puzzle with the word *wrong.* It wasn't his handwriting. Another word in the puzzle, *dead*, had been circled. He hadn't done that either.

He stood up, looked around, and listened carefully. He heard nothing. He went to each room, but no one was there. Nothing seemed to be missing or out of place.

Back in the kitchen, he opened the envelope. Inside were fifty-one-hundred dollar bills and a note: *"Sorry, I couldn't find your father."*

"Ivan," he thought. He jumped to his feet and looked around his condo again, expecting to see the enigma sitting on his couch with his legs crossed and sipping a glass of vodka. How did he get in? Ivan really was a snoop. At first, the news about his real father was depressing, leaving that hollow, carved-out feeling in his stomach. He was about to collapse into a living room chair when a photo on a Parson's table caught his attention. It was a picture of Charlie Bryan with his arms around his mother and him.

The look on Charlie's face was pride. In the same photo, Derk was smiling, and his mother seemed more than happy. She seemed content.

He picked up the picture, walked back into the kitchen, and sat down, holding the photo in one hand while probing the minds behind the smiling faces. Charlie Bryan had been a good father. It was time for him to appreciate that.

He spread the money across the table. Five grand in crisp green bills.

This is good.

In the mail was also a small package that contained his new six-panel cycling shorts. He rubbed his knees and extended each leg without pain. He opened and closed his hands quickly. He felt no stiffness. "Mmm," he murmured. Things were actually looking up.

He poured the rest of the beer down the drain and changed into his new shorts. He would ride to Frenchy's Café for a grouper sandwich. While there, he might think about penning that novel Samantha had encouraged him to write. When he got back, he would call someone about upgrading his home security system. There was much to do.

About The Author

G. Spencer Myers' specialty is the eco-political thriller, featuring Dr. Derk Bryan, college professor, obsessive environmentalist and intrepid EPA investigator who works only on cases involving environmental chaos and dead bodies. His blogs feature controversial issues from an ecological point of view.

His first book, <u>Pest</u>, featured a race against the clock to save his former lover from a fraudulent pesticide manufacturer and an ex-wrestler turned body guard with anger management issues. In <u>Dead Wrong</u> he exposes the link between a toxic spill, police corruption and a Johnny Cash look alike. His memoir, <u>A Letter to My Grandson</u>, inspired the 1st Palm Beach County Short Story Contest entitled, "In Search of Integrity."

WE ARE PLAYING ROULETTE WITH YOUR FUTURE is an update of A Letter to My Grandson calling upon all grandchildren to heed the challenge of global warming.

In <u>The Girl with the Red Nails</u>, the antagonist is Pendleton Danswirth III, but the real villain is plastics. Since its completion the EPA has chosen to regulate so called forever chemicals in drinking water. His recent article on sustainable cruising has appeared in newspapers throughout Florida under The Invading Seas series. A long-time environmentalist, he was the first person in the U.S. to put solar panels on a multi-family home listed on the National Register of Historic Places.

Mr. Myers is a graduate of the University of Michigan, holds an MBA from Bowling Green State University and is Certified by the American College of Sports Medicine.

He is a native of Michigan but lives in Boynton Beach, FL where he is still in pursuit of par. Contact him at <u>Author@GSpencerMyers.com</u>.